Prideful & Persuaded

A Jane Austen Crossover Romance

Bethany Delleman

Cover Portrait by Edmund Blair Leighton, Yes or No

bethanydellemanwriter.com

Copyright 2021
All rights reserved

ISBN: 9798787079401

The characters and events portrayed in this book are fictitious. Any similarity to real persons, living or dead, is coincidental and not intended by the author.

No part of this book may be reproduced, or stored in a retrieval system, or transmitted in any form or by any means, electronic, mechanical, photocopying, recording, or otherwise, without express written permission of the publisher.

With gratitude to:
Gina for proofreading and providing valuable feedback,
Amelia Marie Logan for brainstorming, proofreading, and being my biggest fangirl,
to my mom, for trying Jane Austen just for me,
and to all my friends and family who have endured me talking about this novel.

Preface

This story is meant as an homage to Jane Austen's collected works, and therefore frequently uses either direct quotes or paraphrased lines from her seven completed novels and Juvenilia. If they are embedded in the text, they will not be explicitly quoted, but I am sure the devoted reader of Austen will recognize them! The story may be mine, but the genius I attribute entirely to Jane Austen. In proper respect to her art, each chapter will also begin with a relevant quote from one of her six novels.

For the purposes of this story, every Jane Austen book happened about two years ago. Two years ago, Caroline Bingley (***Pride and Prejudice***) lost Mr. Darcy to Elizabeth Bennet, Sir Walter (***Persuasion***) was duped by his cousin Mr. Elliot, Elizabeth Elliot (***Persuasion***) was rejected by the same man, Captain Frederick Tilney (***Northanger Abbey***, now promoted to Major) broke up an engagement in Bath, Tom Bertram (***Mansfield Park***) recovered after a near mortal illness, and Nancy's sister Lucy Steele (***Sense and Sensibility***) got married. I am using Nancy, which seems to be Anne Steele's nickname, to avoid confusion with Mrs. Anne Wentworth, Sir Walter's second daughter. (It's almost like Jane Austen was trying to avoid future crossovers, she re-uses so many first names!)

You must excuse me for not being able to include a character from Emma, alas, Jane Austen herself is the one at fault. She married off every person so well, so happily, that I could not separate them. Just read the book again, there is no one left. And I know what you're thinking, what about Miss Bates? Well she moved to Enscombe after her mother's death and is very happily settled with Jane, Frank, and their new baby. She had no inclination to go to Bath.

List of Principal Characters

Caroline Bingley: sister to Charles Bingley (now married to Jane Bennet) and Mrs. Louisa Hurst. Parents deceased. Was trying to attract the attention of Mr. Darcy, who married Elizabeth Bennet instead.

Sir Walter Elliot: baronet; father of Elizabeth Elliot, Mrs. Anne Wentworth, and Mrs. Mary Musgrove. Wife deceased. Was forced to move to Bath because he was deeply in debt. A reconciliation with his cousin and heir, Mr. Elliot, turned out to be a ruse designed to keep him from remarrying.

Elizabeth Elliot: unmarried daughter of Sir Walter, largely due to wanting to marry her cousin, Mr. Elliot, the heir to the baronetcy and Kellynch Hall. Was also betrayed by her companion, Mrs. Clay, who was trying to seduce her father and then ran off with Mr. Elliot.

Major Frederick Tilney: formerly Captain Tilney. Eldest son of General Tilney of Northanger Abbey and elder brother to Eleanor (now a viscountess) and Henry (now married to Catherine Morland). He trifled with the engaged Isabella Thorpe resulting in the end of her engagement to Catherine's brother.

Nancy (Anne) Steele: sister to Lucy Ferrars (married to Robert Ferrars). Nancy was a constant companion to her younger, smarter sister. Lucy stole Nancy's money to elope with Robert, leaving her stranded in London.

Tom Bertram: heir to a baronetcy and eldest brother to Edmund (now married to Fanny Price), Mrs. Julia Yates, and the disgraced and divorced Maria Rushworth. Tom's indulgence and gambling resulted in the loss of half of Edmund's inheritance. After a near fatal illness, he has reformed.

1
Caroline

They (Caroline and Louisa) were in fact very fine ladies; not deficient in good humour when they were pleased, nor in the power of being agreeable where they chose it; but proud and conceited. They were rather handsome, had been educated in one of the first private seminaries in town, had a fortune of twenty thousand pounds, were in the habit of spending more than they ought, and of associating with people of rank; and were therefore in every respect entitled to think well of themselves, and meanly of others. **Pride and Prejudice Ch 4**

It must be a universal truth that the children of others are detestable and make their parents insufferable. Caroline Bingley had been dwelling on this thought for the last few weeks. Her sister, Louisa Hurst, had finally made good on the promise of her marriage and produced a healthy baby boy. Even with a proper nursery-maid, Louisa was far too besotted by her offspring to pay much attention to her sister. Caroline could leave town and return to her brother's estate in Derbyshire, but she knew that there would be no improvement in society. Caroline's last stay had been as horrid as her current situation: dear little Jane was everything.

Mr. Hurst was not very taken with his child. He maintained the common, but unfatherly opinion among his sex, of all infants being alike. Caroline could almost believe that he had been indifferent to the idea of a son at all! His level of attachment to his child little mattered; he had always been poor company. Mr. Hurst at least provided some service in making his own sister, Mrs. Fraser, accompany Caroline to parties and balls, which Louisa no longer wished to do. That was all she could thank him for now.

London had lost most of its charm to Caroline, there was no one who compared to Darcy among the ranks of idle heir-apparents and dashing gentlemen. Her choices seemed narrow. The men she had once considered were married and most of her female friends were as well. Of those she liked from school, only one had yet to achieve matrimony and that was on account of a drastic change in family circumstances. No one else with all of Caroline's charm and fortune remained.

"Four-and-twenty," Caroline muttered to herself as she watched her sister dote upon her son. Louisa's face was no longer quite so lovely, there was a growing number of lines across it. Caroline was five years younger than her sister; how much longer would it take for her to find her own establishment? She quickly reproached herself, she had been too idle! Since the disappointment of Darcy, she had not applied herself as she could. A woman of worth like Caroline needed only to fix on her number of thousands a year (within reason) and there can be no doubt of their coming.

The post arrived and Caroline was pleased to see a letter from a dear friend, Mrs. Susan Taylor, who she knew from school. Susan had married at just eighteen to an older man of good fortune, only for him to die, leaving her a generous jointure and no children. Susan had no interest in entering the married state again; she kept a small house in town and took part in whatever pleasures she chose. However, Susan had been in the country for some months. Her sister had recently delivered a child and begged for Susan's assistance. Caroline opened the letter eagerly.

Dearest Caroline,

I am exhausted here in Surrey, I have never spent my time with people so dull and company so restricted! My sister, once a source of so many pleasant conversations and ideas, is entirely consumed by her baby. I have never seen such a change in a woman. She speaks of nothing but her Edward. She thinks of nothing but the babe's health. I have had no enjoyment these last weeks and I am in need of change.

I have a grand scheme to spend some of the next season in Bath with you as my companion. I have secured accommodation for two months, though, if we should tire of the society there will be no cause to stay so long. Please tell me you will come; I will be wretched without you! I am determined to have you engaged to a handsome gentleman by the time we quit Bath.

Yours ever etc. Susan Taylor

Caroline could not have been more pleased with the idea of removing to Bath. There was no pleasure elsewhere, not with all her sisters turned into mothers. She was beginning to think matrimony a duty, she only wanted a gentleman of fortune, maybe a title, but most certainly an eldest son. Caroline was sure she deserved everything she wished for, she was handsome, well-educated, and clever; and she did not have a fortune of twenty thousand pounds for nothing!

2
Sir Walter

Vanity was the beginning and the end of Sir Walter Elliot's character; vanity of person and of situation. He had been remarkably handsome in his youth; and, at fifty-four, was still a very fine man. Few women could think more of their personal appearance than he did, nor could the valet of any new made lord be more delighted with the place he held in society. He considered the blessing of beauty as inferior only to the blessing of a baronetcy; and the Sir Walter Elliot, who united these gifts, was the constant object of his warmest respect and devotion. **Persuasion Ch 1**

Sir Walter Elliot, most properly of Kellynch Hall, but currently residing at Camden Place in Bath, was a troubled man. The book which had for his entire life of fifty-six years been his greatest comfort, the Baronetage, had become a constant source of displeasure. It had begun around the time of his second daughter's engagement to the very proper Captain Frederick Wentworth, which had naturally resulted in an addition to the book. The event had at first been very pleasing to him but what followed had caused consternation. Mr. William Walter Elliot, his cousin, who had been the heir presumptive since the sad day of Lady Elliot's death, had scorned his recent attachment to the family and Sir Walter's dear daughter Elizabeth. Mr. Elliot had moved to London, and refused all further association with the family. Soon afterwards, Mrs. Clay, Elizabeth's companion, had been discovered living under his protection.

His wound had only deepened when his daughter Anne, seeing his distress, had unfolded the entirety of Mr. Elliot's character to him. He was to learn that his
own cousin despised him and his beloved Elizabeth, that
he had only renewed the family connection to ensure his eventual inheritance of the baronetcy, and that Mrs. Clay had been working with Mr. Elliot for some unknown amount of time.

It did not suit Sir Walter's vanity to be thus thrown off by a man who ought to be a dear family connection. His pride was wounded, his daughter Elizabeth insulted, and to gaze upon the name of so improper an heir now brought nothing but anger. The book was put away for the first time, in a drawer where perhaps its influence on Sir Walter would diminish, but it was not to be. He found himself searching it out again and again, turning to his own page and glaring at the line: heir presumptive Mr. William Walter Elliot.

Sir Walter could not break the entail which settled Kellynch Hall and the title of baronet on Mr. Elliot and nor did he truly wish to, for to see any other man with less claim through blood in his place would be almost as much of an affront to his sensibilities. However, one option had always lain before him, one which pride and vanity had for many years prevented: Sir Walter could remarry. He fancied that he had not done so for the benefit of his dear daughters for these many long years. The reasoning had changed however: he worried now for Elizabeth's fate. Suddenly recalling that she was one-and-thirty and that she would not have a kind relation in Mr. Elliot to care for her at Kellynch when Sir Walter, God forbid he think of it, was to die; he found himself spurred into action. Therefore, he was quite resolved, he
ought to marry and Elizabeth ought to marry and as
quickly as they could.

He was determined to marry high, to a woman with fortune, title, character, education, pedigree, beauty, and youth. Fortunately for his chances, he happened to mention his scheme to Lady Russell on her yearly pilgrimage to Bath. Lady Russell recruited Mr. Shepherd, his agent and lawyer, and they visited Camden Place with a united purpose to cajole and reason Sir Walter into slightly lower expectations.

"I presume to observe, Sir Walter," Mr. Shepherd began, "That you, as Sir Walter Elliot of Kellynch Hall, offer so distinguished a pedigree, such a long line of noble sirs and ladies, that you might not require a wife of such distinguished heritage. Indeed, as long as she is the daughter of a gentleman, even if he is only a squire, she must become your equal through marriage. How can a woman who has entered into an alliance with yourself not become all that society would expect from her?"

"You must also remember that my dear friend, the late Lady Elliot, was the daughter of a mere squire" Lady Russell added mildly, "She was a credit to your family, you must agree that she was in every way the lady that Kellynch deserved."

Sir Walter could say nothing to the contrary, for the late Lady Elliot had indeed been an excellent woman and a credit to the Elliot name. She had descended from an ancient family. Sir Walter had grown more prideful with age, he recalled now that he had thought little of her rank when he had made the offer of marriage. He had been deeply in love and she had been beautiful, nothing else had seemed to matter.

"The late Lady Elliot was of excellent character, beauty, and education. Her family was beyond reproach," he agreed.

"A lady of such recommendations can certainly be found, I must take leave to say," Mr. Shepherd continued, "You must consider that other great houses often find themselves in your particular situation. A woman of twenty thousand pounds or more has as much to recommend her as the daughter of a viscount who has retrenched."

Sir Walter agreed after some hesitation. He had in fact made an offer to the daughter of a viscount, not two years ago. It had been summarily refused.

"My friend," Lady Russell continued, "Am I not also a lady brought to higher respectability by her husband? Have you not considered myself as a respectable acquaintance?"

Sir Walter was forced to speak on the merits of Lady Russell, for he did value her friendship and her attention towards his daughters. Lady Russell could not have chosen a better line of attack, for Sir Walter heard his own voice recall her many commendable attributes and there was no voice he believed more than his own. Lady Russell had long wished for Sir Walter to marry and secure the future of the family in better hands. It had been impossible, however, to mention such a plan when Sir Walter still held out hope for an alliance between his daughter and Mr. Elliot.

Mr. Shepherd continued in his praise of the idea with zeal, "Consider also, Sir Walter, that with a proper dowry, and the right negotiation of the marriage articles, you might return to Kellynch the day of your wedding, perhaps even upon your engagement. You must be growing tired with the society in Bath and your return to

Kellynch, with your current expenses, cannot occur for several more years."

"You will want a woman with experience managing a household," Lady Russell offered, "For you are so used to have Elizabeth and she knows you well. Find a woman who has been doing the service for her father or brother, one very much like Elizabeth. Do not look too young, you know as well as I that a woman past eighteen still has many years in which to produce a son."

"Yes, this is true," Sir Walter said. He believed they were correct. It would not be a great evil to find a wife who was slightly more advanced in years, though surely not above five-and-twenty! Sir Walter was not entirely honest with himself when it came to his age, but he knew he remained handsome. The six mirrors installed in his dressing room could not all lie. Thus was Sir Walter persuaded to set his sights rationally. He was determined to find himself a wife: she only needed to be beautiful, well-educated, and worth at least twenty thousand pounds.

Lady Russell promised to give aid to her friend: to look about the town and find a few suitable ladies. Sir Walter, much as he worried about her diminishing looks, could not refuse her help. He had had nothing to do with matrimony for far too long. Anne's marriage had happened without his help or hindrance. Lady Russell was a woman and must know what she was about.

Elizabeth was present for this discussion and surprised when suddenly she was subjected to the plan as well.

"Dear Elizabeth, I would rather wish that nothing could take you from my home or protection, but the actions of your cousin have given me great cause for alarm. Your personal fortune will be comfortable, but not enough to maintain you in the style of living that you are accustomed and entitled to. I wish therefore, for you to join me in my pursuit, and find a suitable gentleman to marry," said Sir Walter.

Elizabeth did not appear at all persuaded. Sir Walter turned to the others.

Lady Russell was silent for some time. Mr. Shepherd seemed sure that Elizabeth might secure any man in the kingdom, but Lady Russell was far less sanguine. Elizabeth had less to recommend her than her father: her fortune was not small, that must be a temptation, but her manners were proud, her beauty ephemeral, and her mind uninformed. She had not youth or character, and at one-and-thirty, while not so very old, would be hardly proper for a young man wishing for a wealth of progeny. Lady Russell searched for the words to express what she felt without offending.

"Elizabeth, you must consider your own tastes," she finally said, "You have for so long lived with your father; a man of a certain age and manner. You will not want a young puppy! It must be disgusting to you to have to educate your husband as well as your children. No, you must want a man more established in life, who knows himself already. It can be no great evil besides, if he is a widower, for you must imagine he will be in great need of your services. A widowed man knows the true value of a woman who can keep his house."

Mr. Shepherd was happy to follow where Lady Russell had led, "I must observe that young men, the greatest portion of them, never understand what a necessity a proper wife is to their domestic comfort. They are happy to live in dirt and disarray without any thought to their dreadful circumstances. Lady Russell speaks wisely, a man who has known the comforts of a well-run home is desperate to return to them; quite determined to settle

again." They all thought this was rational argument enough and left Elizabeth to understand their wisdom.

3
Elizabeth Elliot

Thirteen years had seen her (Elizabeth) mistress of Kellynch Hall, presiding and directing with a self-possession and decision which could never have given the idea of her being younger than she was. For thirteen years had she been doing the honours, and laying down the domestic law at home, and leading the way to the chaise and four... she had the consciousness of being nine-and-twenty to give her some regrets and some apprehensions; she was fully satisfied of being still quite as handsome as ever, but she felt her approach to the years of danger, and would have rejoiced to be certain of being properly solicited by baronet-blood within the next twelvemonth or two. **Persuasion Ch 1**

Elizabeth returned to her own room, after that mortifying discussion, angry at her father. She had only imagined one man to be worthy of her hand, her cousin Mr. Elliot. Her double disappointment on that front had been a near mortal blow to her wish for marriage. She knew, however, that her own fortune in the five percents it would hardly be enough to live on, even in Bath. Elizabeth did not attend to Lady Russell or her sister Anne, who had spoken on the same topic months ago, but she was willing to consider it for her father. She doubted however, that any suitable gentleman could truly be found.

She paced her room irritably; she wanted to return to Kellynch with her father! The plan of economy had been working, they were hardly two years away from discharging their debts. Kellynch had always been Elizabeth's home and while she had often wished to marry, she abhorred any diminishment to her importance.

Elizabeth accepted that in one thing Lady Russell was right, she would not want to marry a young man still waiting for his inheritance; she deserved to command a great house. She deserved to command one, very specific great house. She loved herself and her home enough that her most ardent wish was that she would never have to change her name.

Begrudgingly, Elizabeth listed the appropriate men who were at this time in Bath. She could not find a single prospect. There were a few second sons of varying ranks, but they could not depend on inheriting anything. She recalled there was one widowed baronet in town, five years older than her father, but he was, in Elizabeth's opinion, uncommonly plain. She must merit a man as handsome as herself.

No, the more she thought of it, the more impossible her marriage seemed. As much as she had some envy of her sisters, Anne and Mary, who were both well married, she considered both of their husbands inadequate for *her* current position in life. Unless she met someone very handsome, very rich, and titled, she would not deign to marry Maybe Mr. Elliot would tire of Mrs. Clay and finally do what he ought? Was that too much to hope for?

4
Tom Bertram

There was comfort also in Tom, who gradually regained his health, without regaining the thoughtlessness and selfishness of his previous habits. He was the better for ever for his illness. He had suffered, and he had learned to think: two advantages that he had never known before. **Mansfield Park Ch 48**

Tom Bertram was supposed to be in Bath. His parents were hoping that taking the waters would help continue his improvement. Nearly two years after his injury and illness, he still was not quite the healthy young man he had been. He was also, to everyone's boundless happiness, far less frivolous and irresponsible than before. Tom did feel the weight of family duty, he wanted to be a better son to his father; to be worthy of his eventual inheritance. Would his progress all be naught in his father's eyes? Had the horse not slipped, had he not indulged for what he swore was the last time- but it was too late.

He wanted to blame Yates, yes, it was that damned Yates who had invited him to town, under the pretence of seeing his sister. Julia was as she had ever been, more interested in fashion than family. Yates was the indulgent dandy he had always known, taking the best lodgings in town without a thought for the cost. They would be heavily in debt before long, Tom was sure. Yet, he was already in debt- but it was Yates' fault! Yates had thought nothing of a little trip to the races, Yates did not care if he lost some money, he was sure he would win it back tomorrow.

Tom could not return home, not with the amount he had lost. He would not bring pain to his father and Edmund again. Edmund, who was perfectly happy and settled now with little Fanny. Tom had already ruined Edmund's inheritance once, he would not put the family in such danger again. Edmund, who had been so diligent in Tom's care during the illness, when he would have been the greatest benefactor if Tom had died. It was a sobering thought, one that he ought to have had before he bet such a foolish amount.

His parents rose in his mind. There was enough turmoil in the house without Tom adding to it. Aunt Norris' departure, while welcome, had exposed just how very little his mother, Lady Bertram, was able to do. Suddenly supplies were left unordered, servants unpaid, and clothes in disrepair. Fanny and Susan tried to keep up with the demands of the household, but Susan was still inexperienced and Fanny had her own house to manage now. Perhaps Tom should return home, admit to his debts, and try and put the house back in order.

No, Tom decided, he would proceed to Bath. If he could find an acceptable woman to be his wife, she could set everything right. His lodgings were already paid for two months, that must be enough time. He would do what any single man did in hard financial times, he would find a woman of fortune to marry. It had to be quick, but he would not settle for anything less than twenty thousand pounds.

5
Nancy Steele

Nothing escaped her (Nancy Steele's) minute observation and general curiosity; she saw every thing, and asked every thing; was never easy till she knew the price of every part of Marianne's dress; could have guessed the number of her gowns altogether with better judgment than Marianne herself, and was not without hopes of finding out before they parted, how much her washing cost per week, and how much she had every year to spend upon herself. The impertinence of these kind of scrutinies, moreover, was generally concluded with a compliment… for after undergoing an examination into the value and make of her gown, the colour of her shoes, and the arrangement of her hair, she was almost sure of being told that upon "her word she looked vastly smart, and she dared to say she would make a great many conquests." **Sense and Sensibility Ch 36**

No one who had ever seen Nancy Steele in her life would have supposed her born to be a heroine. Her situation in life, her silliness, her poor manners, her own person and disposition, were all equally against her. The only small claim that she had was that she was an orphan, but this must not have been enough to make her interesting. She never could learn or understand anything before she was taught; and sometimes not even then. She was often inattentive and had trouble understanding what was required of her. However, not everything was against Nancy's character, she was rather caring, eager to please, and loyal to those who showed her kindness.

Nancy was in her small chamber at Camden Place, arranging her clothes. She checked to make sure there was not a tear in her best muslin (eight shillings per yard), ensured that the new stitching was straight on her second best frock (five shillings per yard), and wondered if she ought to discard her worst gown (seven shillings per yard, but two years old) or tear it up for rags. She needed to maintain appearances! She had met Miss Elliot during a visit to Bath and spoken so ardently of their being cousins, as Lucy had taught her, that Miss Elliot had decided to welcome her to their home at Camden Place. She had been living with them, as Miss

Elliot's friend and companion, for nearly two years now. Miss Elliot had never attempted to verify Nancy's claim of kinship, which was all the better since Nancy was fairly certain that no such connection existed.

The future had once looked very bright for Nancy. Her younger sister had married and she was invited to their home, after a small debacle involving some stolen money. She watched Lucy, with all her clever words, reclaim her husband's favour with his mother. Nancy imagined that she could forever claim a home with Lucy, but it was not to be. She could not live in the same house as a man who despised her. Mr. Robert Ferrars, when he found himself alone with Nancy, would take out an overly fine toothpick case and say things to her that confirmed every fear she had within her own heart. To him, she was everything ugly, vulgar, and old. She had only stayed for two months.

Nancy missed her sister terribly. Why had Lucy not married Edward? They might have been less wealthy, but Edward was far more kind than his brother. Nancy tried not to dwell on the past, at least she had managed
to talk her way into a new home. Lucy had taught her
well. Yet, despite not really liking the Elliots, Nancy had been too unsure of her own skill to make another attempt; she also suspected that Miss Elliot might be more than uncommonly stupid.

She had resided at Camden Place for some time, but she knew it was not a home. There was no permanency here. Miss Elliot had for some time spoken about finding Nancy a husband; had talked of improving her manners and making her acceptable to a gentleman of a few hundred a year. Nothing had come of it; she had never seemed interested in following through on her promise. Nancy had overheard Sir Walter's intentions for Miss Elliot. She doubted that once married Miss Elliot would need her. Nancy was going to have to find a husband of her own.

Nancy did not have very high expectations for matrimony, she was, after all, one-and-thirty and only had a thousand pounds to her name. The bulk of her income was always spent on her wardrobe; Lucy always said that no one would invite them in if they wore rags. She did not know who would marry an older woman with little fortune who was always saying the wrong thing, but she had to try. He only needed to treat her better than Robert Ferrars, would that be so hard to find? If only she had any idea how to do it!

6
Major Frederick Tilney

Captain Tilney, was expected almost every hour, she was at no loss for the name of a very fashionable-looking, handsome young man, whom she had never seen before, and who now evidently belonged to their party. She looked at him with great admiration, and even supposed it possible that some people might think him handsomer than his brother, though, in her eyes, his air was more assuming, and his countenance less prepossessing. **Northanger Abbey Ch 16**

Major Frederick Tilney, handsome, clever, and rich, with a large future inheritance and a frivolous disposition, thought he united some of the best blessings of existence. However, circumstances had arisen to put all of this in danger. Somehow, General Tilney had learned about his affair with Isabella Thorpe, and the General was livid. Frederick was hardly welcome at home; his father expected certain principles to be followed. An assignation with a servant or lady of certain character would have gone unmentioned, but for him to have seduced a girl from the gentility... Frederick had tried to defend himself, was the lady not playing a dangerous game herself? Had he not saved poor Catherine's brother from a very imprudent match? He had not done anything that she herself had not invited!

His first thought was to discover who had been the source of the report. It seemed that the general gossip about Isabella and her possible child did not include himself, so the whole story was not widely known. Someone must have told the General directly. The most likely suspects were all obviously innocent. His brother, Henry, avoided the subject whenever possible, the pious preacher. Catherine, his wife, had very few words for Frederick at all. She must still be hurt for her brother, who had been engaged to Isabella. This might have made her a prime suspect, but it could not be her as she was not friendly with the General. While General Tilney had come to accept Catherine as Henry's choice; it was not the choice he would have made for his second son and everyone understood that. Frederick's sister, the new viscountess, was likewise excused, she was far away and happy.

That left the Thorpes themselves; he would not put it past them. Isabella's reputation was already ruined, her second sister had been lucky enough to marry an attorney, but Isabella herself and the youngest remained unmarried. Frederick would not put it past John Thorpe to talk, he was always talking and saying nothing at the same time. If he could prove it was Thorpe something might be done (be it only revenge), but Frederick had been in the company of some indiscreet friends of his own during that trip to Bath. It was impossible to know.

Frederick had eventually realized that the original source of the report was immaterial: the damage was done. As much as he might desire revenge, it would not heal the breach between him and his father. General Tilney demanded that he marry, to secure the future and safeguard the family honour. Frederick almost laughed when he thought of it, he knew many a man with a worse reputation than himself, despite being married for years! Yet, why not marry? Even his father had seemed happier when Frederick's mother was alive, though Frederick wondered if his father had ever been truly happy. He seemed like the man who would inherit a kingdom and then look over his fellow monarch's shoulder to compare their wealth.

The truth, as little as Frederick wished to admit it, was that if he did not follow his father's will, he might lose his fortune. Northanger Abbey and its great wealth was not entailed. Without the favour of his father, Frederick might have nothing at all. His brother Henry's marriage had been frightening enough, his brother had nearly been cut off from everything! Frederick had already been deprived of the indulgence and idleness of a normal eldest son; forced to accept the mortification of a career. He would not lose now what he had worked so hard to obtain!

Frederick finally made his mind up: he would go to Bath to find a wife. It had worked so well for Henry, after all. He only needed a woman who was intelligent, no, that might not do. Beautiful for certain, but maybe just educated *enough* to keep a house. Intelligent... enough. Enough that she might not object to or even notice a few... indiscretions. Definitely young. She would need to be passably rich for his father to accept her at all. The perfect woman might be hard to find.

7
Sir Walter

(Lady Russell) was of strict integrity herself, with a delicate sense of honour; but she was as desirous of saving Sir Walter's feelings, as solicitous for the credit of the family, as aristocratic in her ideas of what was due to them, as anybody of sense and honesty could well be. She was a benevolent, charitable, good woman, and capable of strong attachments, most correct in her conduct, strict in her notions of decorum, and with manners that were held a standard of good-breeding. She had a cultivated mind, and was, generally speaking, rational and consistent; but she had prejudices on the side of ancestry; she had a value for rank and consequence, which blinded her a little to the faults of those who possessed them.
Persuasion Ch 2

Now that Sir Walter had determined that marrying was the most prosperous plan for both him and his eldest daughter, there was the matter of how he might announce his intentions to general society. It must be an important piece of news that he was searching among his peers for an attachment, but he did not wish to appear improper or, most importantly, desperate. Sir Walter had been long enough in Bath for it to be decided that he was not in the business of looking for a wife; his presence was sought by his friends and acquaintances for other reasons. Those who might have aspired to tempt him into matrimony had all, by this time, given up their fruitless ambitions.

Sir Walter supposed that it was the right thing to attend a ball. He would have preferred a private one, but it would be several weeks until the next one that he knew of and now that he had made up his mind he meant to act immediately. Where among his distinguished friends
was a woman unattached, handsome, and wealthy to be
found? It was a pity that his honourable cousin, Miss Carteret, had not taken him up on the offer. For today, he would condescend to seek his fortune at the Pump Room.

Sir Walter set out, Elizabeth on his arm, with every intention of finding one or two young women and perhaps asking to be introduced to them. However, his sanguine hopes were soon overthrown. It was possibly too early or the wrong season but Sir Walter could not glimpse a woman who he wished to look at for longer than a moment. They were each and every one of them plain or worse! He could see nothing better for Elizabeth among the men. Sir Walter was soon talking to his daughter in hushed tones, judging the face and dress of each person they came upon and remarking, with great surprise, that the room could hold such a motley assortment of unattractive people.

"Do look there, Elizabeth, have you ever seen such cheap lace? That hem has been mended so many times I can hardly believe she dares to wear it. You would have passed that gown on months ago or had it torn for rags!"

"I believe there is a stain on the sleeve, they must be quite poor. I'm shocked they were even admitted," Elizabeth replied, perhaps not remembering that the walk had been very dirty and the lady might have only gotten some on her arm during her journey.

"There is a man there, not very plain," Sir Walter motioned only slightly with his head.

"You cannot be serious, Father," Elizabeth protested, "he must still have his milk teeth! Remember that I am looking for a gentleman, not a child."

"Indeed." Sir Walter glanced again about the room. He had counted twenty women at least, some quite younger than he wished, who appeared to be unattached. Of those, six were underdressed, twelve were intolerably plain, and the two remaining, he looked upon them again as they passed. The first seemed acceptably handsome, but her hat was not the latest style, it must be six months old at least, and she had a slight tan. No doubt her face was heading towards a very wretched condition. The second was pretty, but Sir Walter admitted gravely that she could not be more than sixteen and the advice so firmly pressed upon him by Lady Russell and Mr. Shepherd was remembered. She was dismissed from his thoughts and Sir Walter turned to Elizabeth again to learn of the men.

"I must confess father; I find fault with every face and coat before me! I have never seen such poor representations of gentility in my life. There are not even two worth being admired." If Elizabeth ever took time to assess her own feelings, she might be found that after her disappointments with Mr. Elliot, she began to find fault with every prospective man, but she was not given to such reflection. Her father only agreed with every flaw she perceived and she was able to maintain the illusion that it was the men, and not herself, who had failed.

"Father, I must protest this plan in general, where am I to find, among these meagre offerings, a man who can truly deserve an Elliot?"

"It will be difficult, I am sure, but think of all the distinguished men of our acquaintance, there must be one or two among them that you esteem?"

"Hardly a one that I would truly consider for a husband. I must suppose that all the best of them are already married. I cannot think that a man with status and wealth spends much time at all looking for a wife. A suitable woman appears as soon as he wants one."

"Ah but my task will be as difficult, dear daughter. Men of property might be thin on the ground, but artful women are common. I cannot let myself attend to any woman without a handsome fortune."

It must now be stated that the two Elliots walking the room that morning had so little idea of what they were about that an observer *might* have even been moved to pity. The pity must have been brief, for their sentiments were repulsive. They were both of them too far from their days of intentions, too long had all thoughts of matrimony been banished. Elizabeth had for far too long considered Mr. Elliot, her father's heir, the only option. Sir Walter had only considered women out of his reach. It was at this moment that Lady Russell arrived and stopped their fruitless judgement of the crowd.

"You, Sir Walter, must be judicious. You cannot judge a woman's fortune by looking at her hem! Tomorrow night there is a ball and I will attend with you. Once we determine which ladies are worth your attention, you may proceed."

Sir Walter, observing that his old friend's hem was also in some disrepair despite her generous jointure, was again forced to submit to her wisdom. There were always new people in Bath, Lady Russell knew better their incomes and heritage. To the ball they would go.

8
Caroline

The season was full, the room crowded, and the two ladies squeezed in as well as they could. **Northanger Abbey Ch 2**

Caroline and Susan entered the ball with some trepidation. There was a crowd at the entrance and each attempt to move within revealed an ever-increasing crush of humanity: of fine dresses, high feathers, and handsome coats. Each of the women had many acquaintances in Bath but they were both unable to find a soul they knew. They made their way, carefully as to avoid damage to their gowns, to where the couples were dancing. The set had already begun and after looking about and perceiving not a person of their acquaintance, Caroline suggested they sit and wait for someone to appear. Susan was happy to settle into a seat. She loved to dance but the heat in the room made that delightful activity less appealing.

Caroline luckily found two seats empty and they quickly claimed them, lest another tired person should steal them away. Caroline opened her fan and tried to make use of it, but the air was stale and did her no service. She gazed at the crowd, hoping to see anyone she knew. She heard voices behind her speaking in earnest and found herself (though she knew she should not) attending to them.

"That lady, in the sprigged muslin, she is Miss Morton, the only daughter of Lord Morton, and with at least the fortune you desire, I am sure. I have heard her talked of as a beauty," said a lady.

"A beauty? I cannot say I agree, but every woman I have heard of is called a beauty and accomplished. Truth must be continually mortified! What of the lady to her left? She is striking," the man replied.

"You must not attend to her, she is Miss Isabella Thorpe, and from what I have heard, she spent a curious few months in the country and returned somewhat different than before. Besides, she has almost nothing."

"The only two women you have found appropriate thus far are uncommonly ugly and have no sense of fashion."

Caroline turned gracefully to the side, away from Susan, that she might glance at the couple. The woman was older, though certainly not any more than the gentleman she spoke to. She wore a well-made dress but it was not of the current style. The man was not young, but his looks had hardly suffered from the years. Caroline could not help but admit that he was handsome, his hair was full and black, his face not weathered or tired and his form pleasing. He was very finely dressed, with more embroidery in gold thread than Caroline had ever seen on a man, and he had an air of gentility.

"Has no other family managed to unite beauty and wealth?" grumbled the man.

"Has a family ever managed such a distinction?" the lady replied, with a strong hint of irony. Caroline caught herself from laughing. By now Susan, who had been looking intently around the room, had caught sight of some friends and motioning to Caroline, rose to meet them. Caroline saw no choice but to stand and walk towards the small party.

Susan made the introductions, Major Tilney of Northanger Abbey and his friend Lieutenant Wallis. "I was not certain you would be in Bath," Susan said as the formalities finished.

"I have leave of my regiment," Major Tilney replied, "It is always a pleasure to see you Mrs. Taylor, your husband was a dear friend."

"You have been dancing?"

"Oh yes, but with no one; no one I recall," Major Tilney smiled. Caroline looked for a moment at the other dancers and saw the beautiful woman, Isabella Thorpe if she recalled, look at Major Tilney and blanch, but perhaps it was the light for as quickly as Miss Thorpe appeared, she was gone, taken by the dance. The Major soon offered his hand to Caroline and she readily accepted. Mrs. Taylor and Lieutenant Wallis followed them into the set. Caroline caught sight, once or twice, of the older gentleman behind her, still in earnest conversation with his friend.

"Do you know that gentleman?" she asked her partner, "Mrs. Taylor said you were often in Bath."

"Yes, my regiment is stationed nearby," he replied, "His name is Sir Walter Elliot, he has been residing in Bath these last three years I believe. He has a daughter living with him as well."

"They have remained so long?"

"It is not generally spoken of, but his country seat, Kellynch Hall, is let to a tenant from the navy. There is some talk of debts."

"So he means to marry well," Caroline said, though more to herself than her partner. What luck!

"Marry? I have never heard of such a thing. He has never given any sign of it."

Caroline blushed and was ashamed to have spoken of what she should not have rightly known, "I only thought- if he is unattached."

"I have met Sir Walter several times in the card rooms, he has never spoken of a search of any kind. He has become something of an institution in Bath. His parties are well attended events."

"You must think very poorly of me, to believe any single man in financial distress must turn their thoughts to matrimony."

"I think you the exact picture of a woman, A lady's imagination is very rapid; it jumps from finding a single man to admiration, from admiration to love, from love to matrimony, in a moment."

Caroline laughed, "What can I say to that reprimand? It is because I have been distracted, I ought not speak of another man when I am engaged to dance with you. Accept my apologies."

"It is only what I expect, songs and proverbs, all talk of woman's fickleness. Whom among your sex does not secure a partner and then cast their eye around for one more promising?"

"I will not allow books to prove anything in a ballroom; it is not them that I look to if I wish to understand a person's character. Please allow me to prove the constancy of my sex, if only for half an hour."

"I shall depend upon it."

They were next to go up the set and the conversation was cut short. Caroline glanced again at Sir Walter and saw his eyes fixed on her for a moment. She luckily turned away as he looked at her. What might the lady have said of her? Perhaps more importantly, what might Sir Walter have thought? She had not heard so frank a discussion of a woman's physical merits in all her life, at least not in public.

When the two dances were over and Caroline's promise of attention kept, she could see that Sir Walter remained. His eyes were still fixed on the dancers. Major Tilney excused himself to seek another friend. Caroline knew there would be only two dances left before tea, Caroline turned to Susan, "Are you acquainted with Sir Walter?"

"Of course, anyone in Bath knows of him."

"Enough to introduce me?"

"Whatever for? Well, if you are determined. I am intimate with Lady Russell and that will certainly serve."

Susan moved towards the two friends, who rose to greet her, "Sir Walter, Lady Russell, my friend Miss Bingley."

"Miss Bingley," said he, formally.

"Miss Bingley. It is a pleasure to see you again, Mrs. Taylor," Lady Russell smiled, "You have been away from Bath too long."

"It has been an age Lady Russell, ten ages at least! I have missed you terribly. You are in your usual quarters? I have only just arrived and have not yet brought my card."

"Yes, on Rivers Street I will expect your visit tomorrow morning. Please bring your friend."

Sir Walter, who had judiciously left the women to their conversation, now directed his attention to Caroline, "Have you been to Bath before, Miss Bingley."

"Yes, but it was at least four years ago. My brother is more partial to Scarborough."

"You are then from the north?"

"Yes, though my brother now resides at Woodhaven estate in Derbyshire and I have a sister in London. I divide my time between them."

"How long have you been in Bath?"

Caroline started, but he must not have been attending to them before, "We arrived yesterday."

"Oh," he seemed at a loss for anything else to say. She could not have graced the Pump Room, the theatre, or concert in so short a time. Another set of formalities arose, "Was the journey pleasant?"

"The weather and roads were very fine, there was no trouble at all."

"It has been very fair."

Caroline only smiled, while she searched for the next civil thing to say, Lady Russell, who had continued speaking to Susan, now turned to Sir Walter, "My friend assures me that Miss Bingley requires a partner."

There was some sort of look between Lady Russell and Sir Walter before he offered his hand. Caroline was happily led away from her friend, who after an expressive look to Caroline, was content to remain with Lady Russell.

Caroline could see that Sir Walter was uncomfortable and he made no attempt to speak. Caroline took it upon herself to begin and she boldly led with a subject she would never have tried with another man, "I do not recall Bath being so devoid of beauty when I last came, I hardly see a handsome face in ten."

Sir Walter replied instantly, "You are entirely correct, the number of plain women is far out of proportion! The handsome ones are few among them," he paused, and then added, "The men though are far worse."

"Do not feel you must be so severe on your own sex; I was not affronted. I had never noticed before how lacking Bath was in the physical merits of its visitors."

"I can only speak what I observe, one would think the women here are starved for sight of a proper gentleman," said Sir Walter.

"I have been uncommonly lucky then," Caroline observed, her confidence not failing her. Her mind was moving quickly, if she was the first to know of Sir Walter's intentions, she had a great opportunity to make herself his object. Major Tilney was younger and certainly more handsome, but she had met men like him before: they lived for pleasure and rarely settled. If their allowance was generous enough there was nothing to persuade them to marry. After the disaster of Mr. Darcy, Caroline was not inclined to wait again. Besides, the Major had not yet come into his inheritance, Sir Walter, whatever the state of his debts, certainly had.

"It is I, who have been fortunate," Sir Walter replied gallantly. Caroline could only smile. She was delighted to find her partner graceful and lively, despite his apparent age. As the dances ended, she was escorted to the tea table by Sir Walter where they joined

Lady Russell and Susan. They were fortunate to have a group leave as they approached, for the ball was still full and several others stood waiting for a place.

Caroline knew very little about Sir Walter, but the art of flattery was her domain and Major Tilney had given her quite enough to begin, "I understand you are of Kellynch Hall? That is in Somersetshire?"

"Yes, but my daughter and I have resided in Bath for some time now."

Caroline carefully avoided what must be a source of displeasure, if not shame, "I have seen so little beyond Bath, can you tell me of the area? A man such as yourself must come from an extraordinary estate."

Caroline had chosen prudently and Sir Walter was soon speaking of his grounds and the sights beyond with enthusiasm. Caroline was a skilled conversationalist and she showed exactly the interest, knowledge, and pleasure required. Sir Walter seemed much more at ease than he had been when they had first met, though Caroline still saw him, once or twice, look to Lady Russell as if he needed assurance.

Susan and Lady Russell were chiefly ignoring the friends they had arrived with and were focused on renewing their intimacy. Lady Russell extended them invitations to a private concert happening in a few days and Susan accepted on behalf of Caroline, after ensuring that the Elliots would be in attendance. Susan had every intention of being Caroline's faithful assistant.

As the music began again, the group began to part so the younger women could find new partners, but Caroline was pleased enough with her evening and anxious to be out of the heat. Turning to her friend, she said in a tone she knew the others might hear, "I have been dancing with the only handsome man in the room, the others are tolerable but not enough to tempt me."

With that Caroline and Susan left, waiting until they were out of sight and hidden by the swarm of people before they both burst into laughter.

9
Elizabeth Elliot

I see you smile and look cunning, but, upon my honour, I never bribed a physician in my life. **Mansfield Park Ch 45**

Elizabeth was having an entirely different experience. She had decided to attend with her informal companion, Nancy. Elizabeth had met Nancy shortly after her previous friend, Mrs. Clay, had abandoned her to follow Mr. Elliot to London. She always wished for some sort of lady in the house, Anne, Elizabeth's sister, might have served, but she was unavailable. Married and gone with her husband, Captain Wentworth. Nancy had found Elizabeth in the Pump Room, made known her claim of family, and been cordially invited, after only a few days, to join Elizabeth at Camden Place. With the exception of a few visits to her sister, Mrs. Ferrars, Nancy had remained in Elizabeth's company since then. She was a lady of fashion, little fortune, and little sense. Elizabeth did not mind, Nancy admired her and to hear daily of her own superiority was all Elizabeth desired in a friend.

Elizabeth could not have chosen a better companion if she wished to recommend her own merits. While Nancy was plain and worn, Elizabeth remained beautiful and blooming -even at one-and-thirty-; Nancy was kind but uneducated and often vulgar; Elizabeth hid her vapid mind well behind her education. While Nancy could only dress well on her small inheritance, Elizabeth was wealthy. Yet even with her best dress, ornaments, and hair, Elizabeth felt acutely nervous. It had still not been long enough to heal the wound of Mr. Elliot.

"I cannot settle for less than a baronet," Elizabeth said at last to her friend, as they surveyed the crowded ballroom, "If I settle for a squire, I will be no better than Mary; I could not abide it. Lady Russell does not judge rightly, thinking I must settle for less. I have not been available to approach recently; my potential in prospects is unknown at present."

"There is hardly a woman more lovely than yourself," Nancy pleasantly responded, "I had rather hoped you would wear that blue gown; it suits you perfectly. Was it ten shillings a yard? Any beau would be pleased to have your attentions."

"Nancy, I have told you not to say 'beau' enough times for you to remember! No matter, there are so many new faces. My knowledge of the other baronets is adequate, but their sons- would I settle for a son?"

"I suppose if his father is quite old and likely to die."

"Nancy, you must not say it like that," Elizabeth whispered. She had taken on Nancy almost entirely for the company, but if asked, she would say that she wished to improve her. It had been a project of some time, for Nancy was not terribly intelligent. Elizabeth liked to think that her vulgarity had been polished and her manners improved. Elizabeth's stated goal, to find Nancy a suitable husband, had not resulted in anything. She wanted Nancy for herself.

"Yes, let me try again: if his inheritance is not so far off, what is the danger?"

"Very astute. Several of the heirs however, I only know by name. This is not the proper place; we must read the list tomorrow in the rooms. Or wait for a card. My father always reads the cards, why did I not read them before we departed?"

Elizabeth was lucky that so many men in attendance were new to Bath, those who had seen her before, in her long stay, knew well enough not to approach. She had always turned them down before and without any regard for their feelings. Several men did ask to be introduced to her, the master of ceremonies was not needed given the length of Elizabeth's residence in the area and their ever-growing circle, but she turned each of them down. No man, save for one, had the right family name, and he was revealed to be a second son. Nancy, Elizabeth knew, would have loved to dance, but she remembered her place and did not ask.

When tea was ready, Elizabeth tried to find any place to sit with little success; she could not even find her father. She might have seen him, but his back was turned to her and not recognizing the woman he spoke to, she looked elsewhere. Disappointed and frustrated, Elizabeth ordered the carriage.

"It is a foolish endeavour," Elizabeth declared as she left the assembly, "I cannot understand why my father wishes me to marry at all."

"You must know," Nancy said quietly, "That he will find someone soon enough, and she will take your place."

"No woman can take my place in my father's affections!"

"No, perhaps not, but she will by rights take your place in his house."

This was true enough. Lady Russell had said it several times to Elizabeth, but she had not bothered to hear. Lady Elliot, her mother, had been gone long enough that Elizabeth quite forgot what her father had been like before, when he was married. In essentials, he was always the same, but his vanity and extravagance had been tempered and he had truly loved his wife. Elizabeth had kept her father's house and confidence for so long she forgot what a more proper arrangement should be. Yes, she must diminish, she would be second to Lady Elliot and now she could never be Lady Elliot herself. Her vile cousin had taken that from her forever!

10
Caroline

He was nowhere to be met with; every search for him was equally unsuccessful, in morning lounges or evening assemblies; neither at the Upper nor Lower Rooms, at dressed or undressed balls, was he perceivable; nor among the walkers, the horsemen, or the curricle-drivers of the morning. His name was not in the pump-room book, and curiosity could do no more. He must be gone from Bath.
Northanger Abbey Ch 5

    Caroline Bingley was very pleased by her progress the previous evening and had every intention of carrying out plans the next day to meet Sir Walter again.
    "Shall we proceed to the Pump Room?" she asked Susan.
    "Sir Walter is rarely at the Pump Room; he prefers to visit at the homes of his friends."
    "We have Lady Russell's card."
    "Yes, but I do not think they will visit there, Lady Russell is in a less fashionable building. The Elliots are more likely to entertain her than visit."
    "Shall we leave a card then?"
    "We may, though I hear they always have a large pile."
    Caroline could only hope that her particular card would attract some notice. Therefore, it was resolved that they would leave a card at the Elliot house at Camden Place and visit Lady Russell afterwards. The day was mild and the ladies set out on foot; Susan kept a carriage but she hired her horses. They were also lodging on Rivers Street and Lady Russell was only a few minutes away. Susan had been hoping to see her friend frequently. They had met several times in Bath and Lady Russell had been a great comfort to Susan the year of her husband's death. He had taken the waters for some time to no good effect.
    The card was deposited but Lady Russell, who greeted Caroline with interest, had curious news. Sir Walter was no longer in Bath. There had been an express post in the morning and Sir Walter had set out as soon as his carriage could be prepared. Lady Russell did not know what to think of it. Caroline was crestfallen, had another

lady heard of Sir Walter's desire to be married? She tried to put the news out of her mind, it had only been the work of a single evening! She had not invested much effort if it all came to naught. She was not entirely sure why Sir Walter leaving town was affecting her so strongly.

After the visit, they went to the Pump Room and Susan could hardly walk a few steps without spying a new friend she wished to speak to. A woman of respectable fortune and good manners, who spends the chief of her time in London or Bath must be a friend to all and Susan was attentive to everyone. She remembered every name, every child, the title of each great house and its county. She recalled who had been sick and asked after them with such genuine concern that every person was flattered by her attention. Caroline was known to some and was introduced to others. By the end of an hour there were promises for visits for the next three weeks and invitations to balls, plays, and concerts besides. There would be entertainment enough, and Caroline was sure, as many young eligible men as her friend could gather.

"I would never encourage any woman to enter the married state, you know, if they can help it. I held my husband in high esteem, but I have not regretted for a moment my present situation. I will not be persuaded to marry again, unless I am to fall deeply in love. I have met enough of the world to be fairly certain I am safe from that fate," Susan said.

"You cannot be entirely serious," Caroline replied, "Would you not prefer a more settled establishment?"

"If I was married, I would not have time to secure you, my dear friend, a husband," Susan smiled, "And besides, I am a childless widow. Men are always interested in producing children. I cannot be trusted."

"You know that is not sound, there are plenty of men looking to remarry with an established flock of children," Caroline laughed.

"That sounds horrid, if I wish to spend time with children, I will visit my nephew. Now, here is a fine prospect."

They were approaching the entrance and Caroline saw that Major Tilney, Lieutenant Wallis, and a few of his friends were entering. Susan pulled Caroline towards them, clearly, she had determined that Major Tilney was worth Caroline's attention. Caroline nearly blushed, her first encounter with him was hardly notable, she had spent too long asking about Sir Walter. Had she not seen anything in Major Tilney? Upon further reflection, she noticed he had very fine dark eyes.

"Miss Bingley," he began, "I am surprised we have never met here before, if you are an intimate friend of Mrs. Taylor. It seems Mrs. Taylor and I are forever finding each other here in Bath."

"I have been living with my brother in Derbyshire. The last time I was here must have been nearly four years ago and during the winter season."

"We must have missed each other by only a few days, I was in Bath for a short time that year."

"Was it a memorable visit?"

"Hardly, they almost never are, but there is distraction enough if one wishes to pursue it."

"The distractions I most enjoy are not those I must pursue," Caroline replied.

He laughed, "I daresay men must have their pursuits and sport, we cannot properly enjoy our leisure without effort."

"Now I must defend my pursuit of a choice fabric I suppose, or a particularly smart hat, but I will not endeavour to do so. I am in Bath to be idle and merry. There is pleasure enough without any effort on my part," Caroline replied.

"How tired you must be of leisure."

"I have only been in Bath a single day!"

"But you must have been idle long before. What could a woman of means without a husband or children have for employment?"

"Nothing I am sure, only to buy dresses, trim hats, net purses, cover screens, and paint tables. You of course might not consider any of those employment, for they promote only beauty and have no function."

"Art recommends itself; we men have eyes and beauty gives us torment enough."

This comment seemed pointed and Caroline wondered what he meant by it. She remembered the beautiful woman at the ball, Miss Thorpe. Had Miss Thorpe brought him torment? It was more likely that he had brought ruin to her. Caroline wished to dismiss the thought entirely: this was nothing but the way of rich young men. Yet she was wary, there was a mark of inconstancy in his manner.

Caroline had not bothered to speak to Susan about Major Tilney, she knew him enough by reputation. That he was to inherit a vast estate she was well aware, his sister was a viscountess, and his father was a general. She could not recall anything particularly glaring in his past conduct or anything to excite the gossips of London. Not that it would matter, rich young men never seemed to suffer from their misdeeds for long.

The conversation continued but Caroline only attended enough to respond where she was required. Major Tilney spoke of nothing and Caroline answered likewise. They parted, after a few turns of the room, with little feeling of being agreeable on Caroline's side, much to her surprise.

11
Caroline

"You have only knowledge enough of the language to translate at sight these inverted, transposed, curtailed Italian lines, into clear, comprehensible, elegant English. You need not say anything more of your ignorance. Here is complete proof." **Persuasion Ch 20**

Two further days passed without any word from Sir Walter. There was speculation in Bath on the nature of his departure, as he and Elizabeth had only been gone from Camden Place during announced visits to his married daughters. That he should be gone, without a word, and leave his daughter Elizabeth behind was unheard of. Caroline listened with interest. She wished to know why he had gone; perhaps the society in Bath did not prove conducive to his new interest in marriage. She wondered that it mattered to herself at all, but she was anxious to see him again.

This was the day of the concert that Lady Russell had invited them to and Caroline was anxious to meet Miss Elliot again. From what she had heard around the city, Miss Elliot must know what her father was doing. Caroline had learned that she went almost everywhere with a Miss Steele, a woman of little beauty, mean intelligence, and pleasing flattery. Caroline fancied that Miss Elliot might appreciate more stimulating conversation.

Caroline was going to be wrong.

Lady Russell, Miss Elliot, and Miss Steele arrived together in Lady Russell's carriage but they came somewhat later than Caroline and Susan. While they were waiting in the octagon room, Susan whispered to her friend, "Do you see that man? With the red working on his waistcoat?"

"He has sand-coloured hair and a fair complexion?"

"Yes, that is Mr. Thomas Bertram, the heir to Mansfield Park. I have not seen him in society for nearly two years; what luck! He suffered a terrible accident and had a long recovery. I am told the second son nearly ascended."

"He looks fairly well now, perhaps slightly worn from the ordeal."

"I am surprised to see him here at all, there is talk he has reformed."

"Reformed? What did he seek reformation from?"

"Why the usual sins: reckless spending, betting on horses; I must say I never heard about women but one rarely does unless they are very indiscreet."

"The usual sins indeed."

"I cannot believe your fortune, Caroline, Mr. Bertram and Major Tilney! Bath plays host to two men, either of whom, I would greatly desire to see you marry. You must admit, they are almost as handsome as Mr. Darcy."

Caroline gave her friend a disapproving look, "Mr. Darcy had many recommendations beyond appearance. I cannot hope to find another man like him."

"Of course, I doubt there are ten such men in England with such handsome incomes, fastidious principles, and prudent families. I can hardly imagine how this Miss Eliza from nowhere managed to ensnare him."

"I assure you, my friend, as much as I am not an admirer of Mrs. Darcy, her actions were entirely proper. It was he who pursued her. She was unaccountably prejudiced against him!"

"For your sake, Caroline, I wished to believe ill of her. I have heard nothing against her, but it would have been my sincerest wish to see you in her place."

"You are a true friend! Now, of Mr. Bertram, do you know anything more of his situation?"

Their conversation was cut short by the arrival of Lady Russell. All the proper introductions were made and the group of women proceeded to their seats, Caroline carefully placed herself to Miss Elliot's left as Miss Steele took her right. Susan and Lady Russell settled at Caroline's other side. Miss Steele was whispering to Miss Elliot.

"I do not know Italian; can you explain it to me?"

"Nancy, you must appreciate it without knowing the words, I do not wish to translate."

"Please excuse me," Caroline interjected, "May I explain it to you, Miss Steele? My Italian should be sufficient." Caroline was careful to direct the offer to Miss Steele, but Miss Elliot looked insulted by the possible insinuation all the same.

"If you would, please," Miss Steele replied happily, not perceiving her friend's discomfort, "But first, where did you get the fabric for your gown?"

Miss Elliot shot Miss Steele an angry look but it was ignored, Caroline sputtered, "I cannot recall, I purchased it in London nearly six months ago."

"A shame you have forgotten, it is a fine muslin," lamented Miss Steele, "but please, continue."

Caroline translated the first act with ease and distress. Miss Elliot hardly seemed impressed and Caroline quickly guessed that Italian had not formed a part of her education or that she was old enough to have forgotten it. This had been a poor attempt of friendship on her part. Miss Steele, however, was perfectly happy to flatter and fawn over Caroline's abilities.

"Now that you are quite done, I wish to hear the singers," Miss Elliot said coldly, "There is an emotion in the song that translation never achieves."

Caroline made no reply. There was nothing else to be done, the concert was beginning. Miss Elliot listened with apparent great attention, Miss Steele, even with knowledge of what was being sung, fidgeted enough to seem indifferent, though she was prudent enough to at least fix her eyes upon the stage to give the appearance of attending.

The intermission brought new disappointment, Caroline tried several topics and failed each time. Miss Elliot was taciturn and nearly rude. Caroline thought that Miss Elliot might be determined to dislike her. She was not entirely sure why, unless Miss Elliot had found some fault in her rank. Caroline was not used to being dismissed.

"You seem to so enjoy the concert," Caroline observed finally, "You must have astute taste."

"If I do, it is natural taste." Miss Elliot replied curtly.

"Natural taste is the purest kind; one must not be influenced too much by the whims of the masters and critics."

Miss Elliot merely bowed in response and turned pointedly back to Miss Steele.

"You are by far the most handsome woman in the room," Miss Steele said obligingly, "I daresay that over-trimmed lady in the back thinks she is the most lovely but to me, she is nothing but tawdry."

"Yes, I know her, Mrs. Elton, an upstart if I ever saw one. Her father was a tradesman in Bristol. She presumes herself among peers but her husband is nothing but a vicar of small property. They do not know their place."

"The chief of her income must pay for those baubles, though, the gown cannot be more than five shillings a yard. Not a true Indian muslin if I have anything to say about it."

"Horrid couple. I had hoped they were gone back to Surrey. Let them parade their pathetic garments there."

Caroline was then called upon by Miss Steele to explain the Italian again, which she did kindly while wishing to be away from the pair of them. Caroline could not call herself a saint, she was as apt to mock an over-trimmed dress as the next lady of fortune, but the genuine disgust she saw from Miss Elliot made her wary to even attempt a greater intimacy. Miss Elliot was speaking indiscreetly enough that others must have heard! She meant to elevate herself by the public diminishment of others. Caroline could not see it without feeling it was shameful. If she were to mock Mrs. Elton (she certainly would) she would do it within the closed company of dear friends.

The concert resumed and Caroline could only wish to depart. Miss Elliot was not what she had hoped. It was no wonder now that she attached herself to women far beneath herself, she only wished to magnify her own standing. Caroline had no desire to be a sycophant to a woman with less education and manner than herself! Hopefully, intimacy with the daughter would not be required to win the father, if he indeed could still be won. Mr. Bertram was forgotten in her ire.

When the concert ended, Miss Elliot took some time to speak to the wealthiest and highest among the crowd. Miss Steele followed, much like a puppy, and only spoke when her friend seemed to allow it. Caroline's distaste for the scene grew. Miss Elliot stayed for some time talking to Mr. Bertram, who did not seem pleased to renew the acquaintance. It hardly seemed a wonder that Miss Elliot, despite her rank and fortune, remained unmarried.

Lady Russell was as kind as ever and a promise was soon extracted to join her at the theatre. Absently, she mentioned that Sir Walter might have returned by that time, but then she made her goodbyes and Caroline was not able to inquire further.

Caroline's foul mood did not last very long. Once she and Susan were home, she was quite ready to privately and properly mock Mrs Elton, Miss Steele, and especially Miss Elliot. She had a great deal to say and her witticisms on Elizabeth's "natural taste" flowed long.

12
Sir Walter

"I have done very little besides sending away some of the large looking-glasses from my dressing-room, which was your father's. A very good man, and very much the gentleman I am sure: but I should think, Miss Elliot," (looking with serious reflection), "I should think he must be rather a dressy man for his time of life. Such a number of looking-glasses! oh Lord! there was no getting away from one's self." **Persuasion Ch 13**

Sir Walter was at Kellynch Hall. A fierce and sudden storm had violently toppled a tree directly into his dressing room. Admiral and Mrs. Croft had thought it best to send for him to oversee the repairs. He had found the Crofts in a very forward state, having already assembled the workmen required, but he felt obligated as the owner to remain and ensure the work was completed properly. If he was fortunate, he would return to Bath before the week was out. The greatest relief was that nearly all his looking glasses had already been removed and stored, safe from damage. Though why Admiral Croft had decided to remove them was quite beyond Sir Walter's comprehension. After all, the Admiral had somehow escaped most of the ravages to his visage suffered by a seagoing man.

The week in relative seclusion had been strange for Sir Walter, as he found his thoughts often turning to the woman he had met at the ball: Miss Bingley. It seemed foolish to hope to see her again. He had not even asked Lady Russell how long her stay would be in Bath or where she came from. Lady Russell had been quick, saying only that the woman was acceptable for his interests. He must hope that her stay would be the traditional six weeks.

What Miss Bingley herself had said was repeated often in Sir Walter's mind. She had spoken exactly as he liked. The idea that he was the most handsome in the room was what Sir Walter thought himself, though if he had been asked to reply he would have been falsely modest. That she would leave the ball, rather than court the attention of other men, pleased him greatly.

She was certainly lovely enough to fit his expectations for a wife. He could recall her exactly. She had deep auburn hair, which was a more than acceptable alternative to black, at least it was not orange or sandy coloured. Her skin was very fair; she must take proper precautions when out of doors! She had been rather light of figure, with very graceful air and well-styled hair about her cap. She must have a very elegant French maid. Her dress had been light blue, which accented her natural colouring, and had been decorated with silver thread. Her face was uncommonly pretty and her eyes a bright light blue. She certainly had beauty and fortune together, though he knew not how large a fortune.

The chief of the work was completed within seven days and Sir Walter was eager to be away. He paid the final respects to his tenants and made with all haste towards Bath. He had formed a plan, there was no need to make himself known as seeking a wife if he had already found one. He would pursue Miss Bingley, after all, what woman in the kingdom would refuse him? (Sir Walter liked to forget the ones who had.)

13
Caroline

His wife was not always out of humour, nor his (Willoughby's) home always uncomfortable; and in his breed of horses and dogs, and in sporting of every kind, he found no inconsiderable degree of domestic felicity. **Sense and Sensibility Ch 50**

Caroline was surprised to receive an invitation to play cards at Camden Place by Miss Elliot, given her cold reception at the concert, but she was eager to go. Susan sent her excuses to whatever engagement they had planned for the night; they were nearly a week now in Bath and there were ever more people inviting Susan and Caroline to something. They were certainly never left to be idle.

Major Tilney and Mr. Bertram were both in attendance. Caroline observed Miss Elliot greet each of them with particular attention, but to Caroline's credit, both sat with her, leaving the hostess to Lady Russell, Miss Steele, and Lieutenant Wallis. Caroline soon observed that each of them seemed to be focused on herself.

"Major Tilney, you must tell me about your horse, it is a prodigious animal, I am told," she began at the topic most likely to please men in general. Major Tilney was only too happy to oblige and soon both he and Mr. Bertram were deeply engrossed in the topic, turning to her for praise as they described their horses, carriages, and eventually, their various dogs. Caroline naturally only cared if a horse might convey her home without much trouble, but she could feign interest in anything. Unfortunately, Caroline had chosen too well and the conversation was suddenly getting a little too warm. Mr. Bertram was defending his choice at the recent races and Major Tilney was mocking him for his imprudence.

"That horse nearly went lame before the first turn! You ought to have seen it was never a prime specimen," Major Tilney declared.

"Mr. Willoughby does not breed poor quality horses; you must at least agree to that!"

"Agree? I would not for a thousand pounds. His last two offerings have been pitiful."

"I have never heard of a horse of his sold for less than fifty pounds. Tell me otherwise."

"He breeds calm mares for women and thinks that gives him the skill for races! He's a d--- fool and anyone can see it. If I was purchasing a horse for my sister, I would go to him directly. But I would not trust him to produce a hunter for the world!"

Caroline was becoming alarmed and was pleased to see the tea things brought out. She stood and approached the table. The two men remembered their place and the room returned to a gentle calm. Caroline took her tea and was content to settle back into her seat. She hoped the quiet would last, but it was not to be.

"I just saw the play *Lover's Vows* performed last evening; did you see it?" Caroline asked.

Mr. Bertram was quick to reply, "It is perhaps an older play now but I have always loved it. I am only sorry I was not able to accompany you, for I would greatly enjoy seeing it again."

"*Lover's Vows*? What a silly play. It is all daft and over-dramatic. I would much rather see a work of Shakespeare. One cannot have enough of the Bard," Major Tilney interjected.

Both now looked at Caroline and she looked to her friend Susan, who was gazing at her tea and trying not to laugh. Caroline understood, with some pride, that they were competing for her recognition and were now waiting for her choice between them.

"I too," she said carefully, "am always delighted to see a work of Shakespeare, but a modern play can make for a very enjoyable evening. I have seen *Lover's Vows* before and I was pleased to see it offered again."

Major Tilney and Mr. Bertram looked at Caroline, unable to derive any victory in her response. She had agreed with both of them and neither.

Mr. Bertram started again, "I have been remiss, I daresay you would not want to see that play again, but I have not reviewed the others being offered. Is there anything else you wished to see?"

"We have been invited to see *A Midsummer's Night Dream* tomorrow evening," Caroline replied cordially.

"Mr. Bertram can have no interest in that," Major Tilney interjected, "He only wishes to see modern works."

Mr. Bertram glared at Major Tilney; looking back at Caroline he said, "I have already secured a box for that evening's performance, perhaps you might join me, and Mrs. Taylor of course." Mr. Bertram was lying, but he knew he could secure a box in time.

There was not time for Caroline to reply, Major Tilney was already speaking to her.

"You must not go tomorrow night, Miss Bingley, I have it on good authority that the understudy will be playing Lysander. You would be better to go the next evening. I have a box with some of my friends."

"I must, I am afraid, maintain my prior engagement. I was aware of the understudy for Lysander, but Mrs. Taylor has assured me that he is the better player."

Susan had other plans, looking coyly at her friend she added, "I am sure my friends would not be at all put out if we were to share Mr. Bertram's box. They only had seats for us in the gallery. We shall pay them a visit in the morning and make our excuses."

Caroline was prepared to correct her friend, but Miss. Elliot, who had approached the table, was the next to speak.

"My father is to return tomorrow and we will attend as well. I am told this Lysander is quite superior."

"My enjoyment will be all the greater for your presence," Caroline said sweetly. Mr. Bertram seemed very pleased, Major Tilney looked sour, and Susan was observing everything with undisguised glee, which she quickly hid by opening her fan.

Major Tilney however, was not yet to be outdone, "Miss Bingley, you will be gracing the Lower rooms with your presence at the next ball?"

"Yes, I believe I shall."

"I would be honoured if you would accept my entreaty for the first two dances?"

Caroline accepted pleasantly and, having given each man a small victory, found that the rest of the evening proceeded with relative calm. Her spirits were so high that even Miss Elliot's cross looks and hinting comments about trade could not disturb her.

14
Sir Walter

She had not waited her arrival to look out for a suitable match for her: she had fixed on Tom Bertram; the eldest son of a baronet was not too good for a girl of twenty thousand pounds, with all the elegance and accomplishments which Mrs. Grant foresaw in her- **Mansfield Park Ch 4**

Sir Walter called on Lady Russell as soon as he returned to Bath. He did not come entirely directly, his personal vanity prevented that, however, he had only spent a single hour dressing and washing instead of two which must give credit to his haste. He was sure he was only hardly acceptable in public! Lady Russell was surprised to receive him but seeing his level of agitation she was quick to offer him a chair and a glass of wine.

"You must tell me more about Miss Bingley" Sir Walter said, "I do not wish it advertised that I am searching for a wife. I have fixed on her."

Lady Russell looked at him for a moment and replied, "You may have competition."

"From whom? Who could possibly be in Bath with equal claims to myself?"

"Mr. Thomas Bertram of Mansfield Park and Major Frederick Tilney of Northanger Abbey."

"Mr. Bertram will be a baronet, I suppose, but his father is healthy, and I hear their family has not made prudent investments." Lady Russell held any reply to this observation. "And Major Tilney!" he laughed, "A rich family to be sure, but untitled, and he has a profession! Would a lady of fortune wish to be an officer's wife?"

"They are both handsome men," Lady Russell was kind enough not to add "young".

"Mr. Bertram is pale, his hair is blond, and he is thin, his illness has nearly worn him away to nothing. Major Tilney I concede, but I have recommendations above his."

Lady Russell decided not to press the point. She could have made clear that currently, unlike Sir Walter, neither man's father or estate were in debt. They were also each at least twenty years younger than him. She instead answered his first question, "Miss Caroline Bingley, here with my dear friend Mrs. Taylor, is an heiress from the north. Her brother is settled at a reasonable estate in Derbyshire, her older sister, Mrs. Hurst, lives in town and is well-established in society. The only objection is that the family fortune was made in trade."

Sir Walter was displeased. He had imagined a woman of higher birth; he had thought Lady Russell better understood his intentions. "That is an objection indeed," he observed.

"I would not trouble yourself with the trade, it was a respectable line. Mr. Bingley, her brother, is very gentleman-like. He is, I am told, intimate friends with the Darcys of Pemberley."

"A fine family to be sure," he said reluctantly, though he was quick to remember that Mr. Darcy was the nephew of an earl. Connections to an earl could never be despised.

"Yes, and the connection is strong, they have both married sisters from the same family: daughters of a country squire in Hertfordshire. I would not dwell on Miss Bingley's origins; she went to one of the best seminaries in London and moves in the proper circles. What you really need is her fortune and that is more than sufficient. She has twenty thousand pounds."

"Then there is nothing to impede my suit, I am told by Elizabeth that we are to see her tonight at the theatre."

Lady Russell thought to herself, "Nothing, but two handsome, rich, young men." But she knew that this would distress her friend so she said nothing. Instead, she listened to some of his plans for commanding Miss Bingley's attention. With gentle nudges, she helped steer Sir Walter to increasingly rational plans. After all, Miss Bingley was to stay for another five weeks at least, that was more than enough time to win her heart, or at least, her hand. She let Sir Walter know that Mrs. Taylor and Miss Bingley would be at the Pump Room that very hour, and he might go meet them there.

15
Caroline

He looked as handsome and as lively as ever **Northanger Abbey Ch 8**

Caroline Bingley was not expecting to see anyone of note at the Pump Room. After the awkward evening playing cards, she hoped to meet with some of her female friends for calm conversation, but it was not to be. No sooner had she entered with Susan and written down her name that she saw Sir Walter. He approached her immediately and requested her arm. Susan was quick to find a friend and follow at a reasonable distance.

""Sir Walter, I thought you were gone from Bath," Caroline began, "There was no word as to the where and why."

"There was urgent business at my estate. I was required to depart at once, without leaving apologies," he answered.

"I hope it has not been distressing business."

"No, only damage from a storm, but the repairs are already completed."

Caroline was very satisfied; this was the exact sort of thing she had hoped for. He had not forgotten her, nor left to supplant her: it was merely business that had taken him away. "I am glad you have returned; it seems the society of Bath is diminished without your presence. Though I must not forget Miss Elliot's efforts."

"I am glad to hear of it. Have you been having a pleasant time in Bath?"

"The evening that I spent playing cards with Miss Elliot at Camden Place was one of my more stimulating evenings," she said honestly, before turning to flattery "I have not been in such a large drawing room in Bath or viewed such handsome furniture."

Caroline was again perfectly understanding her partner and they spoke for some time on the merits of his establishment at Camden Place. He was very vain, she could easily see that, but he was enjoyable to listen to and his manners were refined. She found herself easily enjoying his company. She complimented delicately, flattered slightly, and exposed her own taste as often as she could.

After they had circled the room once or twice, Caroline began to wonder at the propriety of so long a tête-à-tête. She began to look for her friend and Sir Walter, sensing her desire, began to take his leave.

"You shall be at the theatre tonight, I am told?"

"Yes, we have been invited by Mr. Bertram," Caroline said, watching Sir Walter's reaction. He seemed to hardly notice.

"I will look for you and Mrs. Taylor there," Sir Walter bowed and departed.

Susan was immediately back at Caroline's side, "He has returned! And clearly to see yourself." Susan and Caroline watched as Sir Walter began speaking with a few other men.

"I believe so," Caroline was sanguine, he had seemed very attentive, but perhaps he had come upon her by chance. He could not have come only to see her; even Caroline was not that self-assured.

"If I am not mistaken, dear Caroline, you have the attention of three very eligible men. You are very clever, but you must be careful. You cannot hold them all at once."

"You must tell me what you think of each of them," Caroline pleaded, "I have my thoughts and preferences. And, have you heard of Miss Isabella Thorpe?"

"Yes, daughter of an attorney, now deceased. She used to be often in Bath, but there was a rumour she had a child in the country. I was surprised to see her again."

"Do you have any idea of who the gentleman involved was?" Caroline asked.

"No, there is no positive report. What I know is that Miss Thorpe was thought to be engaged to a Mr. Moreland, but then she was courting the attentions of Major Tilney, a captain at the time. I cannot recall everything that happened. I know the engagement was broken, though I do not know which party initiated the break. It is my understanding that she played a game and lost, ended up with a child and no prospects."

"This is my scruple with Major Tilney," Caroline said in an under voice, "I have reason to believe that he was the one at fault. I am not sure I can abide marrying a man with such vicious propensities;

what if something is discovered and I must live through the gossip and exposure!"

Susan shrugged, "He has managed to keep himself free of scandal; there is merit in that. Besides, I had a friend tell me once that only a silly woman can expect constancy from a very charming man."

"Well that sets me against him entirely! For he is both handsome and amiable; I do not wish to bind myself to determined inconstancy. I would feel myself in real danger if I suspected him of any principles."

"Well Mr. Bertram then? He is handsome but I would not call him charming."

"No, he is more direct, I almost wonder how often he speaks with the fairer sex," Caroline said.

"He is fair in complexion; you have always told me of that preference."

Caroline nodded, "Yes, I must own that I prefer light hair and eyes, but I could learn to change! I was ready to marry dark eyes before. Mr. Bertram is a rational choice."

"And Sir Walter?"

"I cannot entirely understand my own feelings. I know he is vain and spendthrift; if anyone has claims to vanity however," Caroline smiled; Susan giggled.

"A prudent wife can discourage mismanagement; a rich wife can prevent it entirely," Susan mused, "And there is no need for speculation about inheritance, that is the sacrifice of youth."

"I might need to stipulate something in the marriage articles about his daughter," Caroline sneered, "Her I cannot abide."

"And there is the sacrifice you make for a widower, to tolerate his children. In this case, children I suspect to be older than yourself," Susan said.

"If they are all like Miss Elliot, that may be a heavy duty," Caroline said gravely.

Susan smiled, "Whomever you choose, I think you will be doing right. No one, I would say, can see any disparity of fortune."

"There is always a difficulty for a woman wishing to marry," Caroline mused, "society calls the ambitious woman mercenary for wanting to marry high, despite her own fortune. If I have the wealth and merit to deserve a husband with a title, who are they to judge me? Tell me what is the difference in matrimonial affairs between the mercenary and the prudent motive? Where does discretion end and greed begin? I do not think myself evil for desiring what I have been raised to expect."

"Those are deep questions," Susan observed, "and not generally what I think on. It is in the interest of every woman to marry well, if she can. And what one may call ambition another may very well call avarice, but the choices before you are in so many ways equal. Whom shall you choose?"

Caroline realized that they had completed an entire circuit of the room without her feeling any more resolved, except for an emotional pull in Sir Walter's favour. Perhaps that was the beginning of love? She hesitated to name anything on so short an acquaintance. She decided to only remain as she was, without showing any marked preference, until she knew more.

16
Elizabeth Elliot

"At present I only want to keep Harriet to myself. I have done with match-making indeed." **Emma Ch 8**

Elizabeth Elliot was with Nancy, talking over their plans for the evening. If Elizabeth was more judicious, she would have done as her father had and consulted an intelligent friend, but Elizabeth was not prudent. She instead relied on the very limited experience of a woman whose greatest story of courtship was riding to London with a doctor who might have shown some interest in her. It had all come to nothing. Lucy had been the cunning one. Nancy only knew how to flatter and dress well enough to be admitted into the homes of the rich.

"I have fixed," Elizabeth was saying, "on either Mr. Bertram or Major Tilney. They are both elder sons. I must hope they are soon to inherit, and they are reasonably handsome. Major Tilney is the better of the two, but I must not be too particular. Though I have never cared for sandy-coloured hair like Mr. Bertram's. It is very unbecoming. Perhaps he would consider dyeing it black?"

Nancy could only reply with perfect candour, "Major Tilney is handsome indeed, one of the most handsome beau- gentlemen I have seen."

"Yes, but you must remember Nancy, that he is not titled. Mr. Bertram has the upper hand on that account."

"Why indeed, but surely you would be a desirable choice for either."

"That must be certain, though I am not sure why they were so engrossed with Miss Bingley. What is Miss Bingley to Elizabeth Elliot?"

"Nothing at all, I am sure," Nancy said dutifully, "If I can guess, her last gown was only eight shillings per yard and the gown you shall wear tonight was twelve, to say nothing of the gold threading."

Elizabeth tried to feel the compliment, but her plans for the previous night had failed. Miss Bingley, and not herself, had been the object of the men's attentions. She had only invited Miss Bingley because Major Tilney had hinted strongly at wanting her there. Elizabeth was determined. If her father was to marry quickly, as she now believed he would, she must secure whatever was best. She could not abide being the second woman at Kellynch Hall.

"Have you decided on a man for myself?" Nancy asked eagerly, "You have spoken of it many times."

Elizabeth looked at Nancy: plain, simple, old, and past any hint of bloom. She had never lowered herself enough to seek out a man who might enjoy Miss Steele's company. Elizabeth's needs were simple; she wished to be flattered and relieved of boredom. What gentleman would want the meagre offerings of Miss Nancy Steele? Certainly no one had yet!

"Of course, my friend, we shall examine the patrons of the theatre tonight," Elizabeth lied.

"I am so pleased!" Nancy smiled. Elizabeth almost felt guilty, but it passed quickly. She was offering Nancy the best life she could hope for already. Surely her new husband would not object to Elizabeth having a companion. Then she thought of a delightful plan.

"You Nancy, must try for one of them as well, I will ensure that Major Tilney and Mr. Bertram ask for you to dance at the ball!"

Nancy's eyes glowed with excitement, "Truly? Oh that is the most delightful idea I have heard ever in my life, I do think. You are the best of friends, Miss Elliot."

Elizabeth smiled sweetly. If the gentlemen were engaged to her unmarriageable friend, they could not dance with anyone else. She was sure of competition from Miss Bingley, but everyone else must be kept at bay. Nancy might prove useful; there was no chance of losing her prospects to such a woman!

17
Caroline
"We all talk Shakespeare" **Mansfield Park Ch 34**

Caroline and Susan arrived at the theatre with high expectations. Caroline had spent more than her usual good amount of time at her toilette and wore her newest and least-seen dress. She wished to appear every inch a lady. She caught herself; she was a lady. She was more than worthy of any of these men. The previous night and her conversation with Susan had made her bold. It did appear that Sir Walter, Mr. Bertram, and Major Tilney were all vying for her hand. The thought was intoxicating. She mused over the various fortunes and estates of the men, for every woman with twenty thousand pounds knows the names and wealth of the men she might marry. She tried to rate which one she would most like to preside over.

The theatre was full. There seemed to be great interest in this new player. Caroline and Susan found Mr. Bertram without too much trouble, despite the crowd. He took Caroline's arm and led her, with Susan following, to his box. Caroline spoke to him about the play and how much she enjoyed plays in general, all while she cast out a speculative eye for Sir Walter. She had not seen him yet and she feared that his box might be so close to hers as to make sight impossible.

"Are you in search of someone?" Mr. Bertram asked, with some amount of feeling.

Caroline blushed at her behaviour. Why was she not attending to the man before her? "Yes, just for the other friends we were to meet. It is a full house tonight."

"Anything is entertaining enough for the frivolous inhabitants of Bath," Mr. Bertram said, with a hint of longing.

"Are you not fond of Bath?" Caroline asked.

"I was once often in Bath or London, before my brother and sisters married. Now I find myself needed at home. I have planned a few pleasant diversions to pass my time, while I am here. I suppose I will spend the season in London when I am in parliament. Who can say when that might be?"

"You are very fond of the country then?"

"I have grown to appreciate it more than I used to. There is a comfort in the country that is lost in the crowd of London or Bath. There is more of a purpose to life, less frivolity."

Caroline took this as meaningful information: that Mr. Bertram meant to spend the chief of his time at Mansfield Park and that his future wife would be there with him. Caroline loved town; she did not see herself as the sort of woman who could reside always in the country. It lowered Mr. Bertram's appeal in her mind by a few degrees.

"Do not think that I abhor entertainment," Mr. Bertram was saying, "We often spend the evening reading a fine play. There is riding and exploring. I have come to enjoy these diversions more than I did in my youth."

"It has become more of an attraction to myself as well," Caroline said, smiling. Mr. Bertram seemed relieved and then turned his attention to the play as it began. Caroline used the time to look over the crowd again. Finally she spied Miss Elliot, but she was alone other than her constant companion Miss Steele. There was a chair beside them. Caroline watched it intently, finally Sir Walter appeared, as handsome as she remembered and took his seat. He seemed to be searching the crowd as well. Caroline snapped her attention back to the stage just as she saw Sir Walter's gaze settle on her box.

Caroline very intently watched the play, taking only two small glances towards the Elliot box. Both times Sir Walter was watching the stage. Caroline wondered at her own presumption; Sir Walter might not be thinking of her at all. He could have been searching for a friend: he certainly had many acquaintances in Bath. Caroline wanted to believe he looked for her, but she was afraid to assume too much. She had been convinced she had a chance with Mr. Darcy too.

The intermission began with the central players leaving and several singers taking the stage. Mr. Bertram and Caroline briefly joined in praise of the play, before Caroline begged to take leave. She had watched Sir Walter leave his seat. She joined the crush of the crowd, hoping to chance upon him. As she was jostled about and becoming quite cross, she was suddenly in the presence of Major Tilney, much to her surprise.

"I thought you did not come until tomorrow," she said, distracted from her goal and happy to be protected from the crowd.

"There was so much talk of this understudy, I could not stay away. Fortunately for myself, one of my friends had space in his box."

Caroline was surprised she had not seen him. "How are you finding the play?"

"I will concede the point, the new Lysander is an excellent player. I would add, however, that any man must play well next to such a charming Hermia."

"I am delighted by almost every player." Major Tilney was standing very close to her, Caroline suddenly realized, for the room did not allow anything else. She looked into his dark eyes and appreciated once more his handsome face. If only she thought better of his character!

"I am always fond of a play, when my duties allow. Mine however, cannot be a life of constant indulgence."

"I would have thought the life of an officer had diversions enough," said she.

"Nothing compared to Bath or London, but it must all be far superior to life in the country. I am there as little as possible."

Caroline smiled, "When I am in the country, I never wish to leave it; and when I am in town it is pretty much the same. They have each their advantages, and I can be equally happy in either."

"What a great gift to be content in any situation, it is no longer a wonder that you need not pursue your pleasure."

Caroline smiled, but she was distracted by Sir Walter walking past them. Caroline caught his eye, but he did not seem pleased and turned away. Could he have thought she was interested in Major Tilney? That could not be further from the truth, Caroline realized. She had no affection for this smooth-speaking officer, no matter how she felt about his fine eyes. There was a darkness behind them that did not suit her taste.

Caroline excused herself and walked with what speed she could towards Sir Walter. He was now with his daughter, speaking in a low voice. Her approach seemed to brighten his countenance and she greeted him warmly.

"Are you enjoying the play, Miss Bingley?"

"Very much," said Caroline. Though by now she almost wished she had not come after being requested to give her opinion so many times.

"I have not seen such a fine group of players in all my time in Bath. Handsome men and women every one."

"Do you not think," Caroline said, struck suddenly with a profound thought, "that there is nothing so superior as Shakespeare? It is almost a part of our constitution as English citizens. His thoughts and beauties are spread such that one touches them everywhere; one is intimate with him by instinct. We all speak Shakespeare, use his similes and describe with his descriptions."

Sir Walter looked startled and could only reply, "Yes, surely."

Caroline retreated back into the insipidity of normal discourse and they spoke for a short time on the size of the crowd, the costumes of the players, and the beauty of well-performed Shakespeare. Caroline reproached herself, where a woman wished to attach, she should always be ignorant. In fact, if she had the misfortune of knowing anything, she should conceal it as well as she could.

"Are you attending the next public ball?" Sir Walter asked, as the intermission was coming to a close and they were obliged, soon, to part.

"Yes, Mrs. Taylor and I shall be there."

"Would it be too bold of me to hope for the first two dances of the evening? Though I am sure that a superior dancer such as yourself will be much sought after."

Caroline watched his face, "I am engaged for those dances," she said, and saw disappointment, "but may I suggest that in my opinion, the superior partner wishes for the dances at the end of the set, that he might accompany the lady for tea,"

He brightened and amended his request. She accepted happily and made her leave.

Mr. Bertram seemed glad at her return; she had almost forgotten about him. He did not irk Caroline as much as Major Tilney. She suspected his past, though reckless and indulgent, was not quite as bad as other young careless men. Maybe it was that he seemed more repentant. Sir Walter's behaviour had been very promising, but she resolved not to cut short her choices. Despite his intentions of country living, Mr. Bertram would remain as a possibility.

As she suspected he might, Mr. Bertram also secured her hand for the ball. She accepted gracefully and he was clearly pleased. As they parted, the Elliots passed by, and Mr. Bertram stopped to speak with Miss Elliot. Caroline's eyes narrowed; Miss Elliot was suddenly all pleasure and charm. Caroline was certain that she was also vying for Mr. Bertram's attention. She could not be surprised. He was a young man of great future fortune, but she was worried. Caroline was wealthy, but she was not the daughter of a baronet. She reviewed her own merits carefully and judged them to be superior to Miss Elliot's. Calm returned, and Caroline again happily looked forward to the ball.

18
Lady Russell

"If we can persuade your father to all this," said Lady Russell, looking over her paper, "much may be done." **Persuasion Ch 2**

Lady Russell went to visit Sir Walter the next day. Mrs. Taylor and Miss Bingley had called on her that morning and they had sat together for more than half an hour. In the time that she had spent thus far with Miss Bingley, she was fully convinced of her worth. She meant to further encourage Sir Walter in his suit. As Lady Russell thought of it, she was forced to admit that the future Lady Elliot could not be as perfect as the first. No, her dear departed friend would always hold the first place in her heart, but Miss Bingley was certainly intelligent, worldly, and beautiful. She might not have much economy but she had wealth enough to make up for it. She was certainly vain, but Lady Russell thought that it would most likely suit Sir Walter. Miss Bingley might like him better than the former Lady Elliot had, and be happier for it.

Lady Russell arrived to find her old friend in no need of encouragement, his mind was entirely made up and he was miserable. "Lady Russell, I do not understand what I am about. With my late wife, everything was so simple. We met at her cousin's home in Somerset. We were engaged in six weeks and married shortly thereafter. It was so long ago; have the customs changed so much since then?"

Lady Russell was not expecting this and needed some time to gather her thoughts, "I do not think men and women ever really change. Only the words change, the clothes, and the manners. In essentials, everything is very much the same."

"I do not know if I am the first in her affections!"

"You have not given her enough time; you only just returned to Bath."

"That unlucky tree might have sealed my own fate. Mr. Bertram and Major Tilney have not been idle. She spoke to both of them last night and is engaged to dance with them as well!"

"There are other indications," Lady Russell said calmly, "I see some promising signs in Miss Bingley. She has been anxious to increase our intimacy. She visited a few times while you were away and she inquired into your absence. Miss Bingley has also sought out Elizabeth's friendship. Is this not all clear encouragement?"

Sir Walter seemed pensive. Lady Russell was amused. She was surprised to see Sir Walter so worried. Every other time he had made an offer -imprudently- he had been full of confidence. He must really like Miss Bingley to feel so much doubt. Or, and more likely, he was not used to competing against men with equal merit to himself.

"There are other young women in Bath-" Lady Russell began but Sir Walter held up his hand.

"I am quite determined. Miss Bingley suits my taste; I have not seen her equal since fixing upon her."

Lady Russell could see that he was resolved and promised to render what help she could, by receiving Miss Bingley and speaking well of him and Kellynch Hall. There was nothing to be done about the other men: Miss Bingley would make up her own mind. Lady Russell could only hope it would be in her friend's favour. She had very sanguine intentions for the restoration of Kellynch Hall, and those plans centred around Miss Bingley.

19
Caroline

Having only one minute in sixty to bestow even on the reflection of her own felicity, in being already engaged for the evening
Northanger Abbey Ch 7

    Caroline arrived at the ball prepared for an evening of both pleasure and duty. Her mind was now fully set against Major Tilney, but he still had a claim on her for the first two dances. She was resolved to be civil but no more. Mr. Bertram would be next, followed by Sir Walter. Caroline hoped there would be time enough to speak to each Mr. Bertram and Sir Walter and know more about their character. Susan could supply gossip and incomes to be sure, but she did not know either man intimately.
    Dancing with Major Tilney was not the labour she had anticipated. He seemed distracted, often doing what he had once accused her of doing, casting his eye about the room at other women. They only spoke as much as was absolutely required and Caroline was soon content that she was not the object of his affections. This suited her feelings exactly, and she made no effort to encourage any further intimacy.
    Mr. Bertram joined her next. Caroline was still unsure of her feelings towards him. He seemed very gentleman-like, but there were hints of a juvenile nature that she found less attractive. His manners were good and his dancing was what it ought to be, but Caroline found herself wondering if he would rather be doing something else. What else? With Darcy she had known, and his other interests had been entirely honourable though somewhat dull. Was it too much to hope that her brother might become intimate friends with another rich single gentleman, so that Caroline might observe him for several months together? Caroline tried to assure herself that she had time to decide, yet she was worried that she might not find another son of a baronet willing to marry anytime soon.
    Caroline brought her attention back to the conversation at hand. Mr. Bertram was saying something about his mother. She broke away from her reverie and focused on him.

"My mother is so dependent on my cousin, Miss Price, she has no fortitude for planning and administration. She is quite indisposed, has been for some time."

"I am so sorry to hear that, when did she become ill?"

"If it was an illness, I do not recall it. My memories of her are always the same. Continuously sewing, constantly elegant, but always seeming ill or tired. It was always my aunt who maintained the house; she has been gone these last two years."

"It must be difficult for your family," Caroline said kindly.

"It is not something I often speak of, you must understand. I feel like I could do much more at home, if I were to marry."

Caroline was surprised by how forward Mr. Bertram was, but she was also very interested in the proposition. To be the lady of the house in all but name was no small thing. Caroline missed the position she had held with Charles before his marriage to Jane. It mattered less that Mr. Bertram had not yet inherited if she would be the mistress of Mansfield Park.

"It is a great surprise to me that more men do not marry early, to establish the convenience of a wife to keep their house," Caroline said, "You are fortunate in your cousin, and my brother was fortunate to have myself at his disposal, but he was quick to find a more lasting partner."

Mr. Bertram was unable to reply, he was breathing heavily. Caroline observed with some concern that he seemed to be fatiguing. Whatever had happened to Mr. Bertram had had some lasting effect. He was struggling for breath and it was only their second dance. Caroline was not cruel, as they went down the set, she paused at the end.

"I am oppressed by the heat! I cannot continue without something to drink," she said kindly. She saw gratitude in Mr. Bertram's face as he bowed and slowly walked through the crowd to find her a glass of punch. Caroline found a seat and waited for his return. There was some time before the third set and she was happy to wait. She was not overly tired but she was indeed heated.

Mr. Bertram returned and they sat for some time in silence as he recovered from the exertion. Caroline thought it must be difficult for a young man, still in his prime years, to have experienced such an injury. She knew he must not wish to appear weak, so she continued with her complaint, "Thank you, Mr. Bertram, for the drink. I was nearly faint from this heat; the hall is far too crowded for comfort."

He readily agreed and they spoke for the last few moments about the weather and how a private, less crowded ball would have been superior to this public one. Caroline, content that she had left his dignity intact, but still unable to give much encouragement to his suite, excused herself to find Sir Walter.

He was already in search of her; Caroline noticed immediately his fine coat and splendid cravat. He looked nervous and she made efforts to smile more than was her habit. He visibly relaxed as they danced and Caroline made herself as agreeable as possible. After all, she had a philosophy: if a woman conceals her affection from the object of it, she may lose the opportunity of fixing him! Very few men have heart enough to really be in love without encouragement. In nine cases out of ten, especially when a very good prospect is at hand, a woman had better show more affection than she feels. Luckily for Caroline, this would not be difficult.

"You look very lovely this evening, Miss Bingley."

"There was no choice on my part, Sir Walter, I desired to match my partner."

"You dance so gracefully."

"A woman always appears graceful when her partner is so light of foot."

"Have you passed your time pleasantly since we parted at the theatre?"

"I would have been miserable without the promise of dancing with you again," Caroline said, with as much boldness as she could. She was beginning to doubt Sir Walter's regard. She was being as direct as she could and he still seemed nervous. Was this all in vain?

"Truly?"

"Indeed," Caroline said simply, "It is the hope of every woman to attend a ball already engaged to dance with the most desirable partner in the room." She was not sure how to be more obvious; had she been this transparent with Darcy? He had certainly been aware of her intentions, even if it had all come to nothing.

"I had thought that there were always things and people to entertain young ladies in Bath. I have found the city very diverting."

Caroline was unsure how to answer, she had been as direct as she dared. He must take her meaning or not. "I had the pleasure of calling on your friend, Lady Russell. She spoke very well of Kellynch and your daughter, Mrs. Wentworth. I feel I am already acquainted with her."

"Yes, my daughter was some time ago married to a man of good fortune, Captain Wentworth. A fine gentleman to be sure and they have been blessed with a son."

"You have another daughter I understand?"

"Yes, Mrs. Musgrove, she has been well-settled for some years now. Her husband is Charles Musgrove, the heir to Uppercross."

Caroline had hoped for a richer conversation but it appeared that with his younger daughters disposed of, Sir Walter did not have much else to say about them. This might have been more concerning if it was not the way of most men in the world. Daughters were always second to a father, especially if he had any sons. Yet, Sir Walter had no sons... Caroline rejoiced as she felt she had discovered his purpose, he must have decided he wanted one!

Sir Walter asked about her family and she described them, carefully emphasizing that both Charles and Louisa had recently been blessed with healthy children. The dances were finished and Sir Walter escorted Caroline to the tea, where they met Lady Russell and Susan, who had been sitting during the dance.

As Caroline talked of her last few days of activity and Sir Walter of his, Caroline noticed Lady Russell was attending her carefully. She was sure now; Sir Walter was uncertain of her regard and he had recruited his friend for advice. Lady Russell was not subtle; unfortunate Susan had a poor conversation partner.

Caroline gave the best coquettish smile she could to Sir Walter as she sipped her tea. She could not understand how he could be in any doubt, but that did not matter; she had time enough to convince him. The important thing was this: Sir Walter must be interested. Why else would he care? Thoughts of Mr. Bertram suddenly intruded. Should she now choose between them? She only had to be sure of her own heart.

As the music resumed, Caroline felt that she had made up her mind. Sir Walter stood, and seeming unsure what to do, he asked, ""Whom are you going to dance with?"

She smiled and met his eyes, "With you, if you will ask me."

"Will you?" said he, offering his hand.

"There is no one else," said she, as he led her back to the set.

20
Nancy Steele

This specimen of the Miss Steeles was enough. The vulgar freedom and folly of the eldest left her no recommendation **Sense and Sensibility Ch 21**

Nancy was delighted that Miss Elliot had secured her dances; these were some very handsome beaux! If she did say so herself. But she would not say so. Miss Elliot was always so insistent that she stop using the word beau. Nancy was determined not to embarrass her friend; she must very carefully watch what she said.

"Are you enjoying the evening?" Major Tilney asked.

Nancy took a moment to think, "I am enjoying it ever so much, thank you. I do love to dance."

"What woman does not love to dance?" he replied.

"Well I am sure I do not know, but my cousin told me that she knew a woman who felt faint every time she danced the quadrille. I do not think she was very apt to dance. I met a physician on the way to Barton once, who was telling me of the possible ailments she might have-" Nancy cut herself off and blushed violently. Miss Elliot would be so angry with her if she could hear!

"Miss Steele, do not be alarmed, I am in suspense."

Nancy looked at him in amazement, "Truly sir?"

"I cannot abide to hear more about the weather or the rooms, tell me about this fainting lady."

"Well he supposed it might be an affliction of the heart or the spleen; he recommended to me several remedies which I took down in my book. Yet, when I eagerly brought them to my cousin, she told me that the lady was now married and did not need to dance at all!"

"It is unfortunate her condition must remain undiagnosed."

"I wished to know what sort of man she might have married, who did not mind her fainting. You are right though, sir, the physician ought to have seen her anyway."

Major Tilney laughed and Nancy believed him to be enjoying the conversation. She was very pleased, perhaps Miss Elliot had been wrong all along! Her lessons for two years had yet to result in a handsome beau. Seeing him watching her with sparkling eyes, Nancy continued in good spirits, "You know my sister, Mrs. Ferrars, she loves to dance but her husband -he is a very wealthy man- well he stepped on her new worked muslin gown right as she was turning and it got a dreadful tear. She had to leave the ball immediately. I daresay she had thought twice before dancing with him again! And, It was nine shillings a yard!"

"That does indeed sound dreadful; quite an expense to replace a fine worked muslin."

"Do you understand muslins, sir?"

"Not as much as my brother, but I fancy myself to have a good eye for a fine fabric. Military men must have some proficiency. If a girl cannot be found in time, we must mend our own coats."

"Well that would be a thing I never did hear! A fine military officer doing his own mending?"

"Do not imagine, Miss Steele, that we are often at that sort of work, but a man must be prepared for a loose button or a torn sleeve."

"Those officers might find a wife who could do it for them," Nancy suggested, boldly.

"Indeed," Major Tilney smiled and Nancy smiled again. She was enjoying herself; it had been a long time since she had been able to talk so freely. Nancy was very grateful to Miss Elliot, she had been without a good situation since she had left her sister, but it was taxing for Nancy to live up to her standards. Even if nothing came from it, she would still mark this evening as one of her happiest.

21
Elizabeth Elliot

"And is such a girl to be my nephew's sister? Is her husband, who is the son of his late father's steward, to be his brother? Heaven and earth!—of what are you thinking?" **Pride and Prejudice Ch 56**

Elizabeth had spent the evening close by, dancing with Major Tilney and Mr. Bertram, while keeping an eye on her father. She had strongly suggested to both that they dance with Nancy as well. Elizabeth had been worried about Miss Bingley as a competitor, but her thoughts had materially changed.

"I must speak to my father tonight," she thought to herself as she watched him dance with Miss Bingley for the second time. She could not imagine what her father saw in that upstart, vulgar girl. She nearly burned with anger thinking that it would be a common woman from trade who would become Lady Elliot in *her* place.

"Miss Elliot?" Mr. Bertram said, as they were to resume dancing. Elizabeth broke her gaze away from her father and smiled at her partner. Her smile was not genuine, Mr. Bertram did not inspire any feelings in Elizabeth. He was five years her junior, not anywhere near as handsome as her father, and far less lively. She did not pity him for his illness; she saw only weakness. He had distinguished her in asking for a second dance; she was now certain he had done so when Miss Bingley joined the set with her father. Elizabeth could not stand to be a second choice.

Elizabeth watched Nancy dancing with Major Tilney, she wondered what he thought of her. Her friend was often vulgar, coarse, and silly. Was Major Tilney smiling? He must be laughing at her, there was no way such a man would like Nancy Steele. Yet, he was dancing with her again.

When it came to herself, Elizabeth was still undecided. Mr. Bertram would have the title, but while he seemed to have been handsome at one time, he had lost much of his earlier promise in his illness. It did not suit Elizabeth to have a husband less beautiful than herself, she was so used to appearing beside her father and thinking them the most admired pair in any room. His familial pride was admirable and his intentions to manage his estate were what she expected. He was not a bad option, as long as he came into his inheritance soon. She just did not feel that they were suited.

Major Tilney, however, only seemed to be flawed in one way, he had no title. Elizabeth had been living long enough in Bath to have heard the rumours of Isabella Thorpe and it gave her little pause. What kind of stupid, immoral girl allows herself to be seduced? Surely, Isabella had not been raised properly or well-minded by her parents. Major Tilney was one of the most striking and well-formed men Elizabeth had ever seen, besides her father. He was well-spoken and he flattered her assiduously. Elizabeth was certain she would accept if he made her an offer.

As the night ended, Elizabeth was again distressed to see her father in deep conversation with Miss Bingley. Lady Russell was standing nearby and seemed pleased. Elizabeth had always suspected that Lady Russell was a rather stupid, horrid woman and now she was entirely certain. Elizabeth approached her father, rather rudely cut Miss Bingley off, and half-dragged him towards their carriage. She did not care at all how it appeared to the presumptuous hussy, but she was not prepared for the indignation of her father.

"Elizabeth what are you about? Miss Bingley and I were speaking. You are not behaving in a proper manner fitting to your rank!"

"I am not! You are preparing to form an alliance with Miss Bingley, whose family made their fortune in trade and who boasts of a connection with the Darcys as if they were royalty? Are the shades of Kellynch to be thus polluted?"

"How can you believe that I would ever allow the proud Elliot line to be brought to disrepute? Miss Bingley is a very proper lady; her education and beauty far make up for her unfortunate family history. My intention to wed Miss Bingley can only bring greater honour to our family."

To hear her father pronounce his intent made Elizabeth incandescently angry. The rage that had been building within her all night spilled out, "For my own part, I must confess that I cannot see any beauty in her. Her face is too small; her complexion has no vivacity; and her features are not at all beautiful. Her nose wants distinction- there is no prettiness in it. Her teeth are regular, but no great feature; and as for her eyes, her eyes should be darker, I could never see anything astonishing in them. They have a haughty, quarrelsome look, which I do not like at all; and in her air there is a proudness without rank, which is intolerable."

Convinced as Elizabeth was that her father admired Miss Bingley, this was not the best method for dissuading him from affection, but angry people are not often prudent; and in seeing her father look grave, she hoped for greater success than she should have expected. He was still silent so she continued.

"When I first laid eyes upon her, I was amazed that anyone thought of her as a beauty with that dreadful hair colour. Somehow, she seems to have improved on you."

"Yes," Sir Walter disengaged his daughter's arm and regarded her with grave fury, "I thought she was beautiful the first time I saw her, but now I consider her one of the handsomest women of my acquaintance! I am going to apologize for your rudeness, you will wait in the carriage."

Sir Walter turned back to Miss Bingley, who received him with an overly welcoming smile. Elizabeth was left with all the satisfaction of having forced her father to say something that would pain only herself. She was both angry and mortified, to be ordered back to the carriage like a child! Elizabeth stood for a moment fuming before resolving to find Major Tilney and make herself as charming as possible. She would never return to Kellynch if Miss Caroline Bingley was to be its mistress.

22
Tom Bertram

Mr. Bertram's acquaintance with him had begun at Weymouth, where they had spent ten days together in the same society, and the friendship, if friendship it might be called... **Mansfield Park Ch 13**

Tom walked home from the ball and thought about his future. He was fairly certain Miss Bingley had chosen Sir Walter; he had offered Miss Elliot a second dance when he saw them on their way to the set. He had liked Miss Bingley, she was thoughtful and intelligent, but perhaps she was the wrong woman for him anyway. He should not be depriving other men of highly eligible young ladies. Miss Elliot had to be a better option, he did not like her (indeed, what was there to like?) but she would be acceptable to his father. He had no notion of her fortune, but as the daughter of a baronet, he was fairly confident she would have enough to pay his debts.

Tom had been trying very hard not to think about the events the day he had fallen off his horse, but now that he was considering marrying, he could not help it. He thought again of Charles Anderson, his first and only love. They had met at a molly-house in London, the single night Tom had dared to go and risk the reputation of his family. Afterwards, everything had been safer, Charles became one of Tom's many friends and they often stole away from company for clandestine rendezvous.

As far as Tom knew, no one had suspected them, everyone had only thought Charles to be his particular friend. When Tom visited the Anderson family, they were only too happy to consider him as the rightful property of one of their daughters. Having always paid little attention to women, Tom had accidentally made himself agreeable to one of the girls not yet out, but even that could not be too much of an affront from the eldest son of a baronet. He was welcomed there as long as he had wished to come. He had thought the two of them might go on like this forever.

But then there was that night, the horrible night. Charles had told Tom that everything was over; he was marrying and no longer was willing to risk exposure. Tom had been, was, devastated. He had returned to the party's revelry with utter despondence, drank until he could not think, and then in his stupor tried to ride after Charles' departing horse. He had fallen, taken ill, and certainly the heartbreak had contributed to how unequal he was to fighting the coming fever. He had not wanted to die, but he had neither wanted to go on living.

Now he was recovered, from the injury and illness at least, and he had thought of returning to town and finding another man to love. He could not bring himself to do it. Tom told himself that it was the reputation of his family that he was protecting, but he knew it was more than that. He was afraid of being left again; being destroyed again. Then there was the added danger of his falling back into gambling, which had already proved only too real a concern.

As for marrying, he had always known that at some point it must be done. The first-born son of a baronet must marry and produce a young Tom Bertram to eventually become Sir Thomas. Tom knew enough people in unhappy marriages to be fairly certain that his eventual marriage would not be that uncommon. He would not love his wife, he maybe could hope to esteem her or appreciate her, but not love, not in the proper way. His pleasures were not what they ought to have been. His own sister Maria had come to ruin because she did not love her husband, but there could be no ruin for Tom. Not when he had no opportunity to meet with ruin.

If he was to doom a woman to a loveless marriage it might as well be to a loveless woman. Tom had been watching Miss Elliot carefully. As little as he understood the fair sex, he could tell that she showed no real emotion when she spoke to him, despite her obvious intentions. If Miss Elliot was prepared to enter into marriage without affection to gain herself a title, Tom was only too happy to oblige her. She must be at least thirty years old; no one would wonder if they only had one or two children. He would have his debts paid, his heir created, and then he could keep to himself. Maybe he would find a way for that to be enough.

23
Major Frederick Tilney

"Even Frederick, my eldest son, you see, who will perhaps inherit as considerable a landed property as any private man in the county, has his profession." **Northanger Abbey Ch 22**

Frederick was extremely pleased with himself.

The ball had gone very well. He had made a long and careful study of women, he knew that Caroline was not in love with him, he had dismissed her as a prospect. He knew that Elizabeth was half in love, well, half in lust at least. Frederick was unsure about Elizabeth, if he was going to marry, he wanted to maintain some independence. Would her self-absorption be enough to make her blind? No, she thought so highly of herself, she might actually make life difficult if she discovered him in a liaison. It was nice to know that he *could* have her, if he wanted.

This, however, was not why Frederick was pleased. When walking home from the ball he had run into a very old acquaintance, Mr. Foxx, his father's trusted lawyer of many years. The man was drunk and staggering so Frederick had helped him home. The act of kindness had proved extremely advantageous. During the walk, as Frederick strained to keep the rotund man on his feet, Mr. Foxx had started talking about his younger brother Henry. Frederick soon learned what his father had never told him, the most glorious information that he could have ever heard: the General had been so enraged by Henry proposing to Catherine Morland that he had irrevocably settled his estate on Frederick.

Frederick's father had come to accept the marriage, but the act had already been completed. Frederick was basking in the freedom of this rash action. He had a profession, he hardly needed his father's paltry allowance, he was an entirely free man. Northanger Abbey, the entirety of its property, was entailed and destined to be his own, no matter how far he strayed from the General's wishes.

Never before had Frederick been so exhilarated. His father was a tyrant who had ruled his children with an iron will. Each of them had been constrained by their dependence on his fortune, His sister, whom Frederick truly loved, had been kept miserable for years, separated from a man she treasured by their father. Henry had been lucky; his living was secure and Catherine was so in love she would have married on as little inducement as fifty pounds a year! But the General could have made them wretched if he continued to oppose them. General Tilney was cruel, and suddenly, Frederick was determined to have his revenge. He knew exactly what to do.

It was fortunate that the action that would most infuriate the General would also be what would bring Frederick the greatest measure of happiness.

24
Sir Walter

Here Catherine secretly acknowledged the power of love; for, though exceedingly fond of her brother, and partial to all his endowments, she had never in her life thought him handsome
Northanger Abbey Ch 15

Sir Walter was angry enough with his daughter that he sent her in the carriage with Miss Steele and walked home by himself. She was being ridiculous! Miss Bingley was no upstart, she had the education and bearing of a lady and he was absolutely sure that she would do credit to the Elliot name. Her brother was a gentleman now, new as his purchase was. But this was all nothing to Sir Walter, the more time he spent with Miss Bingley the more he was convinced that she was the most beautiful woman (save one or two, maybe three) whom he had ever met. Here we must acknowledge the power of love, for while Caroline was indeed a fine lady, she did not have quite this magnitude of personal claims.

His daughter's concerns were fully dismissed; Elizabeth must only be worried that she herself had not yet secured a husband. Sir Walter had been so focused on his own prospects, he ought to ask his daughter about her wishes. That would smooth everything over. Yet, he would have to make it clear that disrespect towards Miss Bingley would not be tolerated.

During his apology, Sir Walter had been able to engage Miss Bingley for a walk the next day around Bond Street. He felt that everything must be going extremely well, but there was doubt. He was not used to doubt. This business of courting was piercing his nearly iron-clad self-confidence. Sir Walter was not blind, he could see the merit of Mr. Bertram and Major Tilney. Despite everything that had happened at the ball and Miss Bingley's rapid acceptance of the plan for a walk, he remained unsure of her affections. She might as easily choose one of the younger men. Maybe Sir Walter ought to encourage his daughter to get at least one out of the way...

The next day, Sir Walter set out to Rivers Street to meet Miss Bingley. He was certain he looked extremely well that day, he had spent extra time with his valet and wore his newest waistcoat. It was a handsome green with gold embroidery and it matched very well with his ensemble. He was ashamed to feel anxiety as he arrived on Rivers Street., but Miss Bingley was already outside with her friend Mrs. Taylor and Lady Russell. Miss Bingley joined him immediately and the other two women fell in behind.

"It is a lovely day," Sir Walter began, as he took Miss Bingley's arm. She was wearing a white muslin gown with a pink petticoat underneath. Her high collar was adorned with fine lace and her auburn hair was captured by a bonnet with blue feathers. It was fortunate it had not rained; the dirt would surely have ruined her dress.

"Very pleasant," Miss Bingley replied, "I am glad to be out of doors, the balls have been very crowded and hot."

"I have a preference for private balls, but in Bath we do not have a hall of our own," Sir Walter observed. He suddenly realized the source of his anxiety; he did not have access to Kellynch Hall! Sir Walter could only speak of its merits but he would not visit unannounced, no matter how accommodating he was sure the Crofts would be. Without his home, he felt he only presented half of his merits to Miss Bingley.

They passed several people on the street, who were startled to see Sir Walter, whom everybody knew, walking arm-in-arm with a woman who was not his daughter. It was a spectacle to be sure. There had been those who had seen Sir Walter at the ball, but this was an absolute confirmation. Sir Walter meant to marry. And unfortunately for several hopeful women, it looked like his choice was already made.

"Everyone's eye is upon us," Miss Bingley whispered.

"I have observed that this is the effect which a couple of decent appearance produces. I do not believe we could walk anywhere arm-in-arm without attracting such attention," Sir Walter said, congratulating himself for choosing such a handsome partner for his walk.

"They are starved for beauty; we have already passed nearly ten women and men without there being a tolerable face among them!" Miss Bingley said in a low voice.

"Yes, there were six women and four men, scarecrows all of them!"

"Let us observe the next two couples," Miss Bingley whispered, "Though I do not have high expectations."

The couples passed and Sir Walter lowered his head to speak to his partner, "I am in despair, we have now passed fourteen without a hint of beauty."

"How have you remained in Bath for so long, with such poor prospects?" Miss Bingley smiled up at him, "Though perhaps it is your duty to balance the proportions of beauties to frights."

Sir Walter liked this idea very much, "It is even worse in the winter." Two women passed them by, "there was a reasonably comely pair."

"We have passed by twenty-eight to find one acceptable couple," Miss Bingley observed, "Our presence itself has been a charitable service among this crowd."

"Your presence at least," Modest Sir Walter! But he was not allowed to escape.

"It is commonly thought that beauty is enhanced by contrast to plainness; I do not hold this to be true. Like a gallery that arranges beautiful pictures, one after the other, a handsome man on the arm of a lovely woman puts each to their best advantage. If they do look at me, it is only because I am well matched with my partner," said she.

For a moment Sir Walter thought this was an excellent sentiment, but still he worried. Did she rate his personal merits as highly as he did hers?

While he was lost in thought, Miss Bingley must have continued surveying the crowd, for she whispered suddenly, "I believe it is now two-and-forty to six."

"Yes, I agree," Sir Walter said, he had begun to relax when Major Tilney appeared, exiting a shop in front of them.

"Well this is difficult," Miss Bingley said quietly, "Even if a man is very well-looking, he may not suit the observer."

Sir Walter was finally assured. Here he secretly acknowledged the power of love, if Miss Bingley could ignore a man with so many personal attributes as Major Tilney. Sir Walter had evaluated his rivals carefully and he felt the greatest threat from that very man. His pride bolstered; he carried on with the walk in heightened spirits. How silly he had been! Of course, Miss Bingley was taken with him, how could she not be?

25
Elizabeth Elliot
"My reasons for marrying are, first,..." **Pride and Prejudice Ch 19**

Elizabeth was disappointed and cross. She had arranged to meet Major Tilney at the pump room, but he had not come. For nearly half an hour she had consoled herself, imagining that he was merely late, but it had been far too long. He had forgotten the engagement or something else must have delayed him. She fumed as she walked around the room with Lady Russell. She could not stand the conversation of her father's friend. How could Major Tilney neglect her?

She was watching the entrance, not bothering to attend to Lady Russell when Mr. Bertram entered the room. She sighed, there was no one else in Bath that was even near worthy of her hand other than Mr. Bertram. Perhaps she could accept marrying him. After all, he would inherit in time. He had mentioned something about his mother wanting relief from her duties. Elizabeth could hardly remember; he had been far too winded for much conversation when they were dancing.

Elizabeth approached Mr. Bertram and he readily offered her his arm, "Miss Elliot I must be frank," Mr. Bertram began, "You can hardly doubt the purport of my discourse; my attentions have been too marked to be mistaken. Almost as soon as I entered Bath, I singled you out as the companion of my future life. But before I am run away with by my feelings on this subject, perhaps it would be advisable for me to state my reasons for marrying—and, moreover, for coming into Bath with the design of selecting a wife, as I certainly did-"

"I must interrupt you," Elizabeth said, "While I am flattered by your address, I am not entirely certain yet of my own heart."

Mr. Bertram seemed quite at a loss of how to respond. They walked in silence for a short time. "Do your affections lie elsewhere?" Mr. Bertram finally asked.

"Our acquaintance has not been quite as long as I might like," Elizabeth said diplomatically, "for my opinion to be entirely formed. But I do not wish to dissuade you. If you were to be so good as to have tea with us tonight at Camden Place, and perhaps give me three days to understand my feelings?"

 This was acceptable to Mr. Bertram. Elizabeth was pleased, she wanted nothing to do with Miss Bingley, so she must be married before her father. Mr. Bertram, however, did not stir any feelings within her. This would give her enough time to inquire into the whereabouts of Major Tilney. Maybe he was only indisposed and had forgotten to send a note? Elizabeth could not imagine him settling for any other woman.

26
Nancy Steele
"I have burnt all your letters" **Sense and Sensibility Ch 49**

Nancy had remained quite alone at Camden Place that day. A note handed to her by an unknown boy had kept her in place, forcing Miss Elliot to ask Lady Russell to the Pump Room. She had kept the secret and told Miss Elliot she had a headache. Nancy waited anxiously, was Major Tilney really coming? She could scarcely imagine what a man so handsome and rich could want with her. Perhaps he meant to learn more about Miss Elliot? Nancy would have much to depose when it came to her character and way of living.

Major Tilney was announced and Nancy rose to greet him. He was the most handsome beau she had ever beheld. She waited for him to reveal his purpose.

"Miss Steele, in vain have I struggled. It will not do. My feelings will not be repressed. You must allow me to tell you how ardently I admire and love you."

This is not what Nancy had expected, though it had been the subject of several dreams. Indeed, many a lady has dreamed about a man without knowing of his affections first! She was too much surprised and delighted to respond.

"It is not a match, I fear, that my father will approve, but I have enjoyed your conversation more than any woman I have ever met. There is something so easy in your manners; something in being unrefined that makes you so fascinating and new. I cannot imagine marrying any other now that I have met you. I know your fortune must be small and your birth may be humbler than I had hoped, but you must do me the honour of accepting my hand."

Nancy was composed enough now to speak, "What shall we do? If your father will not approve."

"You must come with me to Gretna Green with all haste, we shall be married upon our arrival."

Nancy thought for a moment, Lucy had given her instructions for this very situation, what were they? If a man of wealth and standing proposes and suggests Gretna Green... she remembered, "You must write me a letter, to this effect," she said, "That I might cherish forever your tender feelings." Those were the words! Lucy said she must get a letter. Lucy also had another suggestion... she could not do *that* here. Not *now*.

"Of course, my love. When shall we meet again? I know I cannot linger here too long; Miss Elliot might return home."

"I will meet you tomorrow, on Bond Street by the glove shop. You know the one?"

"Yes, and then we will go? We must be wed before my father hears anything of it."

Nancy smiled, "Tomorrow night, you will come for me here."

Major Tilney smiled and taking her suddenly into his arms, kissed her, "Dear Nancy, you have made me the happiest of men."

Nancy looked at Major Tilney, saw his bright dark eyes and could not perceive anything of malice or cruelty. She almost believed he was in love with her. It did not matter; she would have her letter and that was all she required. She had a plan! Nancy was nearly one-and-thirty, married women had stopped being careful around her years ago. She knew the basics, she raised her lips back to his, and taking one of her hands, she suggestively played with the buttons on his trousers.

Withdrawing with a smile, she simply said, "Tomorrow."

27
Nancy Steele

"His marrying Miss Thorpe is not probable. I think you must be deceived so far. I am very sorry for Mr. Morland—sorry that anyone you love should be unhappy; but my surprise would be greater at Frederick's marrying her than at any other part of the story."
Northanger Abbey Ch 25

Nancy could not believe her good fortune: she was walking down the street, in Bath, with Major Frederick Tilney. Nancy was feeling very sly. She knew that Miss Elliot wanted to marry Major Tilney, she was wild about him, but Major Tilney wanted to marry her! They were just discussing the particulars.

"I will come to Camden Place at midnight, do you think you would be able to slip out?"

"Oh, I am sure I can, Miss Elliot is always in her room by that time. Sir Walter may still be sitting with one of his friends, but he hardly attends to me."

"It is a long journey to Gretna Green; you must bring sufficient clothing. We will need to stop several times at an inn. It is a three hundred mile journey."

"Can we not just wait for the banns? I am already in residence here; it would only take three weeks."

"No, my father would hear of it. He has too many friends in Bath."

"And you have what I have asked for?"

"Yes, my love," said Major Tilney said, taking out a sealed letter and handing it to Nancy.

"I need to buy a new pair of gloves, tonight at midnight," said she, taking her precious item and leaving Major Tilney on the walk. Once inside, she carefully opened the letter. It was exactly what she needed. She folded it up again and slipped it into her bosom.

Major Tilney had moved on and was no longer visible, Nancy looked around for gloves. A beautiful woman ducked in the door and walked directly to Nancy.

"Excuse me, Miss Steele, I must speak with you," she said.

"Speak with me? I do not think I know you at all. Whatever could you have to say to me?"

"My name is Isabella Thorpe," she said, as though that was some information. It took Nancy a few moments.

"Oh, you had a baby, yes, Miss Elliot spoke of you."

Miss Thorpe coloured, and Nancy realized that she had been far too indelicate. Her Frederick did not mind her impertinence; she was in the wrong state of mind.

"Yes, with Major Tilney. I do not think he will change. Has be made you an offer of
marriage?"

Nancy lowered her voice, "We are going to Gretna Green, his father would not approve. Oh, but I ought not have spoken. Frederick said it was a great secret. I am always telling secrets. You must not tell!"

"You have nothing to fear from me, I only wished to warn you. Major Tilney also once made an offer to me. He left me without a single hope in the world!"

"Well you must not have been very intelligent. Lucy, my dear sister, she told me that you always must get a letter; then no one can ever deny that you are engaged." Nancy patted her chest where the precious letter was stored.

"Nothing can be certain," Miss Thorpe pleaded, "General Tilney is a very powerful man and his son does not care who he harms."

"Miss Thorpe, this might be my only chance. I am going to go. Do you know what it is to not have a home? Where did you spend your confinement?"

"With my mother," Miss Thorpe admitted.

"My mother and father both died shortly after my sister's birth. We lived for some time with my uncle in Plymouth, until my aunt died and he turned us out. For nearly four years, my sister and I lived with whatever relations would take us in, for a few months at a time. I have not had my own home, my own room, in six years. I thought when my sister married- but it was not to be."

"Your own sister turned you out? How could any sister do such a thing!"

"It was not Lucy's fault, her husband hated me, I know not why. I took it upon myself to find a new situation."

Miss Thorpe said, "He may leave you with nothing. You will be worse off than when you started."

"Miss Thorpe, I know what I am about. If he leaves me with child, the letter will be enough for a magistrate. He will have to pay for the babe and I will have a small income and a comfortable home. I could be happy in the country by myself. Either he marries me, he leaves me indisposed, or I gain nothing. You must see, Miss Thorpe, I already have nothing. What do you care, anyhow?"

"I came to Bath to try and win him back," Miss Thorpe admitted, "My stupid brother! He learned from a drunken lawyer that Major Tilney's inheritance was irrevocable. When Tilney left me, he told me that it was a matter of his inheritance that we must separate. I had believed him; I thought he might wait for me. Then I learned that my brother had spread the word of my ruin in some ill-advised attempt to reconcile us. Major Tilney already got what he wanted from me. I stayed in hopes of saving someone else. I ruined my own chances because of that man."

"I do thank you, Miss Thorpe, for your kindness. You ought to take that stupid brother and make him bring you someplace new. You are very pretty and your gown is very fine, seven shillings a yard at least! I am sure you can find a young man to be your beau. There are no such options for me."

Miss Thorpe looked pensive, she gave Nancy a bow and headed for the back of the shop. Nancy took the first gloves she saw and paid for them. She was determined, she *would* leave the city tomorrow with Frederick and if she was lucky, she would never return, unless her name was Mrs. Tilney.

Isabella Thorpe left the store a few moments later. It was over. She must no longer regret Major Tilney; she would make herself anew. It would only be a month later when she would set out for Newcastle with that same irksome brother. She would form a fast intimacy with a young officer's wife, Mrs. Lydia Wickham. Lydia knew all about getting husbands, and good to her word, Isabella Thorpe was married by the end of the winter to a charming young soldier with an income of about four hundred a year. When she did return to Bath, there was a material enough change in her looks and name, that no one remembered who she had once been.

28
Elizabeth Elliot
"What a letter is this, to be written at such a moment!" **Pride and Prejudice Ch 47**

Elizabeth woke up that morning and went to breakfast, fully expecting to see her friend Nancy in her usual place, sewing something of little importance and less beauty, but she was not there. Instead, Elizabeth saw a letter, in Nancy's hand, sitting on the seat cushion. She opened it.

My dear Miss Elliot,
You will laugh when you know where I am gone, and I cannot help laughing myself at your surprise to-morrow morning, as soon as I am missed. I am going to Gretna Green; I have got myself a handsome beau and he does not mind being called so. I shall never be happy without him, so think it no harm to be off. What a surprise this must be! I have left my best filigree basket for you to remember me by. I thank you for your continued friendship; I hope you will drink to our safe journey. When we meet next in Bath, I will be delighted to hear you call me Mrs. Tilney.
Your affectionate friend, Nancy Steele

One cannot imagine what a great shock it was to Elizabeth that the man that she intended for herself had eloped with Nancy. *NANCY? HER!* Nothing could have been further from Elizabeth's mind; no circumstance less anticipated! If she had heard of him engaged to a rich heiress, she might have borne it better, but this was beyond all acceptance. Nancy Steele! An unknown country bumpkin, whose claim to gentility was through a dead minor clergyman and a mother from trade. Nancy Steele, who had but a thousand pounds to her name and no connections beyond herself and a multitude of cousins. Major Tilney of Northanger Abbey had thrown himself away for this?
Elizabeth marched into Nancy's room, which was empty of any trace of her, save the basket laid caringly on the bed. Elizabeth took

it and ripped it to pieces. She took the nearest vase, one she had chosen herself, and smashed it on the floor. The letter she threw into the fire grate, which was unsatisfying given that in the summer heat there was no fire, so she drew it out again and ripped it into pieces as well.

Her father and two servants arrived at the door, drawn no doubt by noise of the smashed vase. Elizabeth suddenly realized that it might pierce her thin soles and she threw herself upon the bed to avoid the danger.

"Elizabeth what is the meaning of this?" Sir Walter demanded. Elizabeth sighed, it would do no good to be angry; it was done. Even if she wrote to General Tilney, there was no way he could stop the couple; they would be too far ahead. Somehow Nancy had beaten her, Miss Bingley had beaten her, she was going to be displaced. She had only one option.

"Nancy has left us," Elizabeth said calmly, "She has gone to Gretna Green with Major Tilney."

"I am sorry, Elizabeth, I had fond hopes that he would address you," Sir Walter said.

"No, do not be sorry. Mr. Thomas Bertram has made me an offer. Will you receive him to ask for your approval?" Elizabeth said. She was seething in anger still, but she would not show it. Mr. Bertram would do. She would not live through the mortification of living in Kellynch with a new mistress.

"Of course, you shall be the wife of a baronet, which is what I had always wished for you. Mansfield Park is a handsome property, I have heard, though I have not been there myself."

"Father, I wish to marry at once. Perhaps Sir Thomas can purchase a common license and we may go at once to Northamptonshire?"

Her father did not seem to like this plan, "I will speak to Mr. Bertram and see what may be done."

Elizabeth, seeing that the vase was gone, got off the bed and quit the apartment. She headed to Mr. Bertram's lodgings. It was still early; she was hungry but she was also quite resolved. The servant admitted her, Tom was taking his breakfast.

"Miss Elliot!" he said in surprise.

"I have decided," she announced, "if you wish to continue your offer."

Tom still looked quite startled, he began slowly, "Miss Elliot, um Elizabeth, would you do the honour of accepting my hand?"

Elizabeth, never one to miss an opportunity to be flattered, replied, "You must first tell me of the things that you admire."

"Yes... you are exceptionally beautiful and a fashionable dresser and a prudent manager of your household, and a gracious host. I would be honoured to have a woman such as yourself as my wife and future companion." Tom had forgotten his prepared address; it was far too early in the morning.

"I accept," Elizabeth said, "my father is waiting to receive you." Tom gestured at his unfinished breakfast, "You may come when you are finished then."

With that Elizabeth left the room and Tom was left wondering what he had gotten himself into.

29
Tom Bertram

*He was now esteemed quite worthy to address the daughter of a foolish, spendthrift baronet, who had not had principle or sense enough to maintain himself in the situation in which Providence had placed him, and who could give his daughter at present but a small part of the **share** of ten thousand pounds which must be hers hereafter. **Persuasion Ch 24***

Tom proceeded to Camden Place later that morning, with a fair deal of apprehension. He had assumed that Elizabeth Elliot had a handsome dowry, in accordance with her rank, but he had been informed that very morning by one of his friends, who he happened upon while on his way, that the Elliot girls only had ten thousand pounds between them, and only guaranteed upon their father's death. Tom could not believe his bad luck! He knew that Elizabeth was void of proper feeling, but he had not expected her to be poor! How was he to pay his debts of honour on the promise of three thousand pounds after the death of a very healthy man?

He knew his father would be exceedingly angry if he betrayed the family honour, so he continued on to Camden Place. He could only hope that his friend was misinformed. He needed at least a thousand pounds of ready money to pay his debts. What would his father think if he came home with a penniless bride and debt besides?

Sir Walter received him with cordiality and Tom said what he was expected to say, however little he felt any of it.

"The lawyers will begin their work soon," Sir Walter said, "I have already brought my agent, Mr. Shepherd, to Bath for- he is here. He will accompany us to Mansfield, once I have a few things in place. Do you believe your family would be amenable to a common license? I would like to be back in Bath as soon as I can."

"Of course," Tom said, not really knowing what his father would think, "As for the small matter of your daughter's fortune? You have a reasonable idea, I would think, of my eventual inheritance."

"Elizabeth is to have six thousand pounds upon my death, her share of her mother's fortune, but I do not think more than a thousand will be available now. However, there is a legacy of ten thousand from Elizabeth's late uncle and that will go with her."

Tom was confused, if the uncle had died after the other two daughters' marriages, it would be sensible for the money to go to Elizabeth, but why did she have a greater portion of the other amount? His own sisters, Maria and Julia, had each had equal fortunes, though, well, their marriages had both gone rather strangely. But if each had married as they should it would have been the same amount.

Tom decided to inquire and Sir Walter readily explained.

"Elizabeth is the oldest; when she told me that it was proper for her to have the greatest portion of the ten thousand, I saw no harm in it. We had always thought she was to marry her cousin and return the wealth to Kellynch. Besides, she is the most beautiful of my daughters."

Tom found this rather disgusting but he made no show of it. It only served to further sink his opinion of his future wife. Sir Walter had other things to discuss. Tom had imagined that he and his wife would dwell in the Mansfield cottage, made for the very purpose, but Elizabeth clearly had other ideas.

"My daughter was under the impression that you would make your home in the great house and assist your mother in management. Elizabeth is very used to a certain station in life, so I am pleased that your family would accommodate that wish."

Tom could only assent, since he had given hints of that very thing himself. He was growing increasingly worried. The more he learned about Elizabeth, the more he was convinced that she would not be very acceptable to his father. He had been blinded by his debts! He was beginning to think that he ought to have returned home and begged for forgiveness instead of entering into such an ill-guided alliance. It was too late. Tom could only agree and hope that as usual, he had misjudged his father's wishes.

30
Caroline

She was just in time to ascertain that it really was Mr Elliot, which she had never believed, before he disappeared on one side, as Mrs Clay walked quickly off on the other; and checking the surprise which she could not but feel at such an appearance of friendly conference between two persons of totally opposite interest-
Persuasion Ch 22

    Caroline hardly noticed that a week had passed. She and Susan visited Lady Russell, were invited twice for tea at Camden Place, and attended a concert with the Elliots. Caroline felt secure in Sir Walter's affection, though his daughter was another story. Caroline was certain that Miss Elliot despised her, though she was civil when her father was present. During their second evening at Camden Place, Sir Walter had left to speak with a friend and Miss Elliot stood and turned her back to Caroline. She could see Lady Russell's embarrassment, but she realized that instead of anger she felt pity for Miss Elliot. She must be feeling a great upheaval. How long had she been the mistress of her father's house, fifteen years? Caroline would be kind, Miss Elliot could not resent her forever and since she was to marry Mr. Bertram, who lived quite far away, it hardly mattered.

    Caroline was not enough in love to be insensible of others, she knew that the residents of Bath considered her and Sir Walter very nearly engaged, if not engaged already. Caroline considered this talk to be to her benefit, it must help convince Sir Walter of her intentions. Caroline might not have been as merry if she had been privy to some of those conversations that had done her so much good. There was a great deal of discussion of how this young woman had drawn Sir Walter in and what arts she might have used to attract his attention in only three short weeks. These voices, however, were not the majority and soon enough they would be silenced by the stronger wisdom: that if no woman had accomplished the task of arousing Sir Walter in fifteen years, then it must have been he who finally decided to fall in love.

That morning Sir Walter was to meet Caroline in the Pump Room. She had arrived slightly early with Susan, who wished to meet one of her many particular friends. They were walking arm in arm, with Caroline following a short distance behind when she was approached by a very elegant man, who by every appearance must have been a gentleman. Caroline was surprised, as she was certain they had never been introduced.

"Beg your pardon, madam, but I take the liberty of family, as I have heard you are soon to be engaged to my cousin, Sir Walter."

Caroline was immediately more at ease, "Good morning, sir, Miss Bingley."

"Mr. Elliot. I have only just arrived in town, I have only just left my card to inform him of my arrival," he offered an arm, which Caroline readily accepted.

Susan had walked on and did not notice Caroline until she rounded the room and saw her speaking with a man that Susan herself knew at once. Her eyes widened and she was immediately concerned. With all the speed she could command within the bounds of proprietary, she rushed towards Caroline, but they were on opposite sides of the room and the swell of parading patrons blocked her progress.

Elizabeth, at that moment, entered the room, begrudgingly, to carry out her duty and bid "dear Miss Bingley" wait some time longer for Sir Walter. Sir Walter, much to her disgust and indignation, was selecting an item from the family jewels to give to her, which would seal the dreaded engagement. He had been unable to decide which necklace might "best adorn her slender neck" -she remembered with disgust - and had stopped at Rivers Street to ask Lady Russell's opinion. Elizabeth had been sent to give his apologies and beg Miss Bingley to wait a little longer. She looked around and her eyes rested on a very familiar face. She raised her hand to her mouth in a gasp, her cousin! With that very woman on his arm whom her father was determined to marry. Mr. Elliot smiled at Elizabeth.

Caroline heard the gasp and saw Miss Elliot. Suddenly, she felt her partner stop and his arm wrapped around her. As she tried to pull back, she found herself unable to free herself from his grasp. Caroline was gripped with fear, Mr. Elliot was smiling but his eyes were stone cold. Caroline with horror what he was about to do, he was dangerously close to kissing her and she was almost too shocked to react. She could hardly hear anything, someone was rushing towards her but everything else was still, everyone would see. Why was he doing this!

Caroline's mind was working quickly, she had to escape his grasp if she wished to be seen as an unwilling party. If she tried to fall, his arm would still support her, his hand was up her back, holding her head in place. Her arms were her own, but she had been pushing against his chest already and he was not giving way. She suddenly remembered an incident from her childhood, where she had been playing with Charles, she had been very young and she had accidentally...

With seconds left, Caroline brought her knee up directly between Mr. Elliot's legs with as much force as her small body could command. It slammed into the un-gentleman-like gentleman and a second later, Caroline found herself crashing to the floor. She landed on her bottom, her hands, which had grasped his waistcoat for added force, were not quick enough to break her fall. The stone floor was hard and cold and Caroline was forced to suppress her wail of pain. This must look bad enough already.

Susan was at her side, helping her up and away from Mr. Elliot. Caroline turned her head, but Elizabeth was already running out the door. Mr. Elliot was bent over in pain and surprise, but he was trying to move towards an exit. The room, once still, was erupting in movement. Women were gasping and men were moving towards Mr. Elliot with honourable intent. Caroline was trying to catch her breath.

"Caroline, I am sorry," Susan was saying, "I wish I had seen him in time."

"Who was he?" Caroline managed.

"He is Sir Walter's heir, but something happened between them two years ago. They are not on speaking terms!"

Caroline's mind was racing. If Sir Walter married her and produced a son, the heir presumptive would be left with nothing. Whatever had happened between them, Mr. Elliot must be trying to prevent Sir Walter from marrying. Miss Elliot had seen them together; she was sure to believe the worst-

"Susan, I must get to Camden Place."

"Caroline, you must sit back down. Let me get you a glass of the waters."

"No," Caroline started towards the exit. She left Mr. Elliot behind and, nearly running, was out the door and onto the street. Miss Elliot was still in sight, hurrying towards Camden Place, Caroline had every hope of overtaking her before she could reach that far district, but she suddenly turned. Caroline realized that she must be heading to Rivers Street where Lady Russell was lodging. That was a much shorter distance and she was in too much pain to walk faster. She knew she would not catch up in time.

Caroline, her lungs burning and her body sore, watched Miss Elliot at a distance as she ducked inside. The door was still open, the servant announcing Miss Elliot as Caroline rushed in behind her. She could not say a word, Sir Walter and Lady Russell stared at them both in wonder as Elizabeth began to nearly scream.

"Your precious Miss Bingley is with Mr. Elliot! They are working together; I saw them in the Pump Room! He kissed her!"

Sir Walter looked at his daughter in shock, could this truly be? Was this another plot by his vile cousin? He turned to Caroline, who was visibly shaking and flushed with exertion. For a moment, all he could think of was how lovely her complexion appeared with exercise, but his daughter's words soon returned to his mind. Sir Walter looked from his love to his daughter with no clear idea of what could be going on. He was disposed to believe Caroline, though his daughter's assertion was heavy on his mind. He decided quickly, there was no possibility that such a beautiful woman should prefer odious the Mr. Elliot to Sir Walter, Caroline was not a traitor.

"I have never seen that man in my life," Caroline spoke in a gasping whisper, and then she looked at the people around her, considered her options, collapsed on the floor, and burst into tears.

Elizabeth continued, "I went to the Pump Room, as you requested, and I saw Miss Bingley, walking with Mr. Elliot. They stopped and when I saw them, they were to every appearance in league together. I left at once. They must have known one another already! Miss Bingley must have known him before, they must be plotting against us, like Mrs. Clay!"

Caroline had begun to cry on purpose, but now she was finding it difficult to stop. Her courage was failing her and she was truly frightened by the recent events. She could hardly look up as Sir Walter knelt down to help her into a chair and gave her a fine embroidered handkerchief.

"Why would she come here directly, if that was the case?"

"I caught them together!"

"No," Caroline managed.

"We were entirely taken in last time. I doubt Mr. Elliot would be so foolish."

"She would be!"

Sir Walter spoke in a low furious tone, "You are to return home, Elizabeth."

Caroline looked up long enough to see Miss Elliot turn white and retreat from the room. She had just enough presence of mind to momentarily gloat at her defeat. Lady Russell, who had gone, returned with a glass of wine for Caroline. Sir Walter was sitting beside her, watching her intently.

"What happened?" he asked gently.

Caroline composed herself as much as she could, and meeting his gaze, replied, "I was approached by a man who introduced himself as your cousin, newly arrived. I was put at ease and we spoke for a minute or two, when Miss Elliot entered the room, he tried-"

Caroline found herself weeping again. What had he tried? What might have happened if she had not broken free?

Lady Russell whispered to Sir Walter, "He knew what Elizabeth would think if she saw them together, he was trying to convince you that Miss Bingley was in league with him."

"No scheme is too black for that man," Sir Walter cried, "I must find him."

Caroline said softly, "I believe him to be already gone from the Pump Room."

There was a knock at the door and Susan entered. The story was again told as Caroline listened and attempted to compose herself. That Sir Walter had already acquitted her was a great relief, Susan had witnessed the interaction, and told the story faithfully, discreetly suggesting what Caroline had done to win her freedom.

"Mr. Elliot is gone, he was almost overtaken, but his carriage was at the ready and those who might have sought retribution were denied it," Susan finished.

Sir Walter put a hand on Caroline's arm; she felt the warm comfort, "I ought to have been with you already," he said.

"I did not think him capable of this," Lady Russell exclaimed, and she seemed faint herself. Susan began to help her upstairs, leaving Sir Walter and Caroline alone.

31
Sir Walter
Ready to die if she refused him **Emma Ch 15**

Sir Walter was a widower with three daughters, but he was not experienced with crying women. His wife had rarely come to him for comfort or consolation, she had gone to her dearest friend, Lady Russell. His daughters, except Elizabeth, had gone to their mother until her death, and then followed on their mother's well-worn path to that same lady. Sir Walter did not know who Elizabeth turned to, but it was absolutely not himself. To see Miss Bingley - could he dare to call her Caroline?- wretched before him was untenable. He was completely at a loss. Having done what propriety demanded by supplying a chair and his best handkerchief, he found himself at the end of his abilities.

He decided it must be best to sit beside her. Almost unconsciously he laid his hand on her arm. She did not recoil or withdraw her arm and from that encouragement he thought it was the right thing to do. Caroline was no longer sobbing; that must be an improvement.

"I am sorry," he said softly, "It was on my account that Mr. Elliot acted with such malicious intent."

Caroline turned to him, "Why?"

Sir Walter had hoped to never speak of the events that occurred two years ago. He had been deceived and he was ashamed that he had not understood it at the time. "Mr. Elliot is indeed my heir, it is a long history, but some time ago, he re-established himself within our family and gave every indication of interest in one of my daughters. She was luckily- it was so strange a circumstance- informed of his true nature and after he left town, she made it known to myself."

"What nature?"

"He had only renewed the relationship because he feared that I would marry. He is desperate to secure his inheritance. Yet in truth, he despised us all. It is unaccountable, I know. Last I inquired he was settled in London, with Elizabeth's former companion in his protection."

Caroline looked up, and Sir Walter was for a second surprised that she could look so charming despite her red eyes, "There has been talk of- of you in Bath."

"Yes, he must have heard that I was to be- and thought that he was too late to prevent the connection any other way."

"You did not believe Miss Elliot? Not for a moment?"

"It is natural that when she saw you together, she would assume the worst. However, Mr. Elliot is clever, if you were somehow in league together, he would be more careful not to be seen. He is more likely desperate; the report is new and he wants to prevent-" he trailed off.

Sir Walter watched Caroline as he spoke, she still appeared shocked, though she was no longer crying. This must be an encouraging sign. She set her empty glass on the table and rose, Sir Walter standing with her. She seemed to be thinking and then suddenly embraced him.

Sir Walter was a man of the world, a not-insignificant part of his debt was accounted for by some very well-paid women of a particular occupation, but it had been a long time since he had held a lady that he admired that closely. There were several particular feelings that were assuring him that he had indeed made the correct choice in a future wife and that his inclination to marry her quickly would be prudent. He wrapped his arms around her as gently as he could. He could smell her, hints of lavender, and he could feel the warmth of her chest against his. He directed his thoughts away from any other feelings with effort.

"This is a compromising position," he felt obligated to say, though he had no inclination to end it as long as Lady Russell and Mrs. Taylor were out of the room.

"If I am going to be compromised," Caroline replied softly against his coat, "I would prefer to choose for myself."

Sir Walter was not overly pleased by the situation that had led to this moment, but he felt assured enough to continue with: "Dear Caroline..."

32
Caroline

Do not consider me now as an elegant female, intending to plague you, but as a rational creature, speaking the truth from her heart.
Pride and Prejudice Ch 19

"You did not believe Miss Elliot? Not for a moment?" Caroline said, with a great hope that the terrible events that had just occurred would not ruin her chances.

Caroline was beginning to calm down. Sir Walter's explanation of the events had not helped as much as she had hoped. She now knew the why Mr. Elliot had attacked her, but her heart was still racing and she felt on the verge of tears. She had cried enough. Sir Walter was close to her, closer perhaps than proprietary allowed, but it was not sufficient to her feelings. She wanted her brother: Charles would have understood what to do.

She finished her wine, laid the glass aside, and stood, knowing that Sir Walter would follow. Years of manners were dismissed and she did what she felt she must, wrapping her arms around him. He did not immediately reciprocate, she briefly wondered if she had been wrong, but soon enough he responded in kind. She could feel her body relaxing, despite alarms in her head that warned that Susan or Lady Russell might return any moment. What did it matter? He had believed her, whatever Mr. Elliot's intent, it had come to nothing. This was what she wanted.

"This is a compromising position," Caroline heard. The tone was different, low and perhaps, lustful? Caroline felt no inclination to pull away.

"If I am going to be compromised, I would prefer to choose for myself," she replied. Sir Walter pulled away himself, slightly, enough that she could see his face.

"Dear Caroline, I am convinced you are a person with every worldly perfection: you are beautiful, fashionable, and well-spoken. You are, in fact, the only woman in the world who I can ever think of as a wife. Your loveliness of face and figure, your taste in dress, your sweetness of voice, all recommend you as the most exemplary lady in all my acquaintance. Your beauty, how shall I describe it? Of all the women I have observed in the course of my life, only perhaps three or four could claim a greater portion of charm, elegance or delicacy. But to have combined all this with you other merits, numerous as they are, no one can be considered your equal.

"I offer you myself, my home, and my love, if you will but accept it, I will be the most fortunate of men."

"Yes," Caroline replied without thinking, and then continued to say exactly what she ought, as a lady always does. Caroline knew what she wanted and it was to stay in this embrace forever. His words broke so many of the bonds of modesty upon her anyway, she took her hand and touched his face. If she was going to be kissed, she would prefer to choose for herself. She pulled him towards her, standing on her toes to reach until he saw what she was about and lowered his head to meet her.

Caroline had about the same amount of experience with anything outside of holding a man's gloved hand at a ball as the average unmarried member of her sex. She had, upon the marriage of her older sister, demanded to know the particulars of a married woman's duties, and Louisa, knowing that her deceased mother would be unable to complete the task, eventually relented and explained as much as she could. Caroline knew most of the mechanics, but she had not anticipated the feelings. She had been embraced before, though even that had brought new sensations which she had not felt with members of her family or close female friends, but she had never kissed anyone. She had no idea at all what she was doing or how it might be taken by Sir Walter. Her motivation was not entirely pure, a man, wholly unknown to her had almost taken this liberty with her, had almost ruined forever an action that ought to be only done between a husband and wife. Caroline had created the memory she wanted, the kiss that she wanted to be her first.

Her mind was then overcome with feeling, warmth, pleasure, and desire. She could feel heat in her body, in places she was not often aware of. Something spread from the centre of her chest out to her entire body, excitement? Caroline broke away and saw emotions she had never witnessed before in Sir Walter's face. She could still feel the sensations on her lips, she felt weakness and exhilaration. It was perhaps best, she realized, to resume a more proper position. She released her hold and slightly pushed away from Sir Walter. To her great relief, she was immediately free from his embrace. Blushing, she took a few short steps away from him.

Caroline stood there unable to speak. She had surprised herself, and Sir Walter, if she had any ability to read his expression. Too much had happened in the span of an hour. Where was Susan? Had he really proposed? Was she to be Lady Elliot!

Susan found them moments later, standing in still suspense, "Caroline, you must want to rest."

"Please allow me to escort you," Sir Walter offered.

Caroline accepted his arm, though it was only a few minutes' walk to her door. She was unable to speak at all. Her thoughts were running wild.

"You are recovered?" he asked, as they came to the door of her lodgings.

"Quite," she said, though it was certainly untrue.

"Will you come tonight for tea? If you feel that it is within your power."

"Yes, yes of course. I will come."

He seemed to be waiting for something else but Caroline was not enough in control to say anything beyond, "I will write to my brother by express post; he will see to the marriage articles. Good morning, Sir Walter."

33
Charles Bingley

Between him and Darcy there was a very steady friendship, in spite of great opposition of character. ***Pride and Prejudice Ch 4***

Charles Bingley was hosting the Darcys for one of their frequent visits when the letter from Caroline arrived.

"You will never believe this Darcy," said Charles, "Caroline is engaged! To Sir Walter Elliot of all people."

"Sir Walter of Kellynch Hall? Has he not been a widower for over fifteen years?" Darcy said, clearly surprised.

"My sister does not lack in charms," Charles said, somewhat offended.

"You mistake me, Bingley, it is the gentleman that confounds me. I have met Sir Walter several times in London; he is the most vain man I have encountered in my existence. Seemed to think he was worthy of a duchess."

"Well he must have been taken with her; she has hardly been in Bath for a month!"

"There is no question; for it to happen so quickly he must be very much in love. It's a prodigious match, Charles," Darcy said.

"Would you say so? I had heard he was living in Bath to discharge debt."

"There is nothing singular in his case, especially among those first families. It's a common affliction. This is undoubtably why he wishes to marry."

"There is no debt among the Darcys."

"We are an exceptional family and I have a very economical wife."

Bingley laughed, "Yes, I am sure all the credit goes to Elizabeth."

"It ought to," Darcy said, "Imagine my profligacy if she had turned me down."

Bingley, who now knew the entire history, could not think of a response that might not go further than teasing. He instead replied, "I am sorry, I must depart as soon as I can."

"Is the wedding to happen so soon?" Darcy asked.

"Yes, please accept my apologies. I only hope that Mr. Wolfe, my attorney, will be available at such short notice."

"I would say that I am surprised by the rapidity, but a woman's desire does jump quickly from love to matrimony."

"Are Jane and Elizabeth out of doors?"

"I believe they are in the shrubbery, whatever do you require them for?"

"You know the state of my writing, Darcy, when I have to write a letter of business, I have Jane write them. I must say, everything has run more smoothly since she began."

Darcy laughed and set out to find his wife and sister-in-law. Charles began the preparations; he could be in Bath in three days if he rode post. Mr. Wolfe resided in London; Charles would send his request by express to meet him in Bath. Everything in Caroline's letter spoke of urgency, he would come as quickly as he could.

34
Sir Walter

"Let me call your maid. Is there nothing you could take to give you present relief? A glass of wine; shall I get you one? You are very ill."
Pride and Prejudice Ch 46

After leaving Caroline at her lodgings, Sir Walter went back to call on Lady Russell and determine if she was over her shock. He was received immediately, "I am glad to see you in spirits again, Lady Russell," said he.

"Even with the information that your daughter Anne gave us," Lady Russell said, "I did not imagine your cousin quite so bad as this. It was a shock, to be sure. You must forgive me the liberty of detaining Mrs. Taylor. Are you engaged to Miss Bingley?"

Sir Walter was surprised, "I am," he sputtered.

"I am glad of it, it seemed the best solution, given the situation."

Sir Walter was amazed by his friend's foresight and judgment; she had left them alone on purpose! But he was still in some distress himself, "You must tell me, Lady Russell, what is to be done for a crying woman?"

Lady Russell sat across from Sir Walter and gave him a knowing look, "You ought to have her sit, bring her wine, and remain silent until she begins to tell you of her problem. Then you must continue to listen. Unless it is a rare case where the issue can be immediately solved, it is better to refrain from attempting to give advice or assistance. Instead, offer your condolences. If propriety allows, it is often best to extend a hand or an arm."

Sir Walter nodded, "I was at a loss."

"I may not be an easy distance from your house forever. I do not mean to quit the neighbourhood; I merely speak of the normal passage of time. You are to have a new young wife and she is not my intimate friend, as much as I like her. Sir Walter, you must do better by Lady Elliot this time."

"Do better? Whatever can you mean? I held my late wife in the highest esteem! Her every wish was granted."

"Your late wife, my very dear friend, told me a great deal of your marriage before her passing. I had resolved to make some things clear to you before you entered into another alliance. If you wish to make Miss Bingley happy, you need to listen to some advice."

Sir Walter was to discover a few deficiencies in his performance as a husband that left him in wonder that Lady Russell might be so frank and explicit. He spent a full half hour listening to everything she had to say, and left the house feeling very foolish that with all his worldly experience, his friend, who had been widowed for fifteen years, was the first to bring this... *problem*... to his attention.

35
Caroline

When that business was over, he applied to Miss Bingley and Elizabeth for the indulgence of some music. Miss Bingley moved with alacrity to the pianoforte **Pride and Prejudice Ch 10**

Caroline was feeling quite recovered, at least from the distressing attack in the pump room by Mr. Elliot. How she felt about what had happened afterwards was still undecided. She knew she was exceedingly pleased to be engaged but she was not certain how she felt about her audacious behaviour afterward. What could Sir Walter think of her? Caroline felt it was very wrong, but she could not stop thinking about how it felt. Whatever she had felt for Darcy, it had been a more rational understanding of his worth. This was something else entirely. When she remembered the moment when she had turned and beheld him for the first time, there was something very irrational in this attraction.

Susan and herself were second to arrive among the guests at Camden Place. Elizabeth greeted Caroline with far more civility than usual; her father must have explained the circumstances of the morning to her. Strangely, the doors between the two drawing rooms were closed, and Elizabeth brought both women immediately to the room on the left. Lady Russell was already within.

"Miss Bingley, we were hoping you might play for us this evening, the pianoforte is set in the other room. Would you be so good as to select some songs from the collection?" Lady Russell asked.

"Of course," said Caroline, though she was strongly reminded, for a moment, of Charles laughing about Mrs. Bennet contriving reasons to separate Jane from her sisters. The inclination proved to be correct, she entered the other drawing room to find Sir Walter waiting for her. He was looking unnaturally grave and taking her gloved hand, directed her towards a seat. He sat beside her, so close their legs almost touched. He was holding both of her gloved hands in his own.

"Forgive me the presumption, Caroline, but I wished to speak to you alone, and ensure that you had recovered from the odious events of the morning."

"I have quite recovered, I assure you. I only worry that he might return," said she.

"I do not think Mr. Elliot will dare show his face in Bath. If he is to return, you will not be so ignorant of his motives."

"That is true," said she. She was also glad to know that the "odious events" only included the actions of the cousin, and not those of herself.

Sir Walter still looked more serious than Caroline had ever seen him, "I feel it incumbent upon myself, to apologize for any liberties I may have taken-"

Caroline interrupted him, "No, you did not take any- the liberties were my own." She blushed and looked away.

"Oh," Sir Walter was silent. A few moments passed before Caroline looked at him, and saw that all hint of gravity was gone from his expression, he seemed rather content. She felt that she owed him some explanation.

"Be assured Sir Walter," she began, "I have never before felt the inclination to welcome the sort of marked attentions you showed me. And never in my life have I even been in fear of losing the ability to bestow my affections where I decided they ought to be. It seemed proper, that the man who was to be my husband..."

"A man that you esteem? I must hope."

Bold as she could be, Caroline could no longer meet his gaze, "A man that I love."

"I am fortunate to be loved by the most beautiful woman in the world."

Caroline could not find any words to say, but she looked into Sir Walter's eyes and saw the same expression he had before, when she had not known what it was. It must have been love. She had even risen in his estimation of beauty! She raised her hand carefully to touch his face, and felt him lean into her hand. She was emboldened, she moved as close as she dared, hoping for a repetition of what she had felt before. She was not disappointed.

He kissed her again and with more passion than before. The same warm feeling spread in her chest; the same emotions flooded her mind. Only a closed door was hiding them from disgrace, but Caroline did not care. She had tasted passion and she wanted more. She wanted him. Inexperienced as she was, she had a good idea that he wanted her too.

Caroline soon found herself wrapped in surprisingly strong arms, pressed against Sir Walter's chest and learning that there were more possibilities in their current activity than the mere pressing of the lips. She had no notion of how long the embrace lasted but finally she felt a growing certainty that this activity could only lead to others, and she drew back. Sir Walter released her as soon as she wished and she felt a small pang of relief, a potent reminder of how very frightened she had been of Mr. Elliot.

"I should return to my friend," she said softly, having caught her breath.

"I will join the party in a moment," Sir Walter said, standing and moving from her to gaze out a large window. Caroline thought back to her sister's descriptions and smiled; she might have had more of an effect than she bargained for. She left the room and returned to the women, who carried on as if she had never left.

36
Charles Bingley

"Younger sons cannot marry where they like."
"Unless where they like women of fortune, which I think they very often do." **Pride and Prejudice Ch 33**

Charles arrived in Bath after a long journey and almost immediately was met at the hotel by Mr. Wolfe, his attorney. Charles had a card sent to the Elliot house at Camden Place, indicating that a meeting ought to take place and giving his address. The card was not sent in vain, for in half an hour, just as Charles was washed and dressed, Sir Walter himself arrived. Charles had not met Sir Walter personally and he was immediately struck by the gentleman's appearance. He did not look at all his age, with thick black hair, skin unblemished by his years, and a quick lively step. It seemed that time had quite forgotten about Sir Walter, and Charles, who was not often vain, wished for a moment to have such good luck at six-and-fifty.

Introductions were made and consent, as superfluous as it was now that Caroline was in control of her fortune, was readily given. Charles had little doubt that his sister was serious and Sir Walter's quick arrival was a good recommendation in his mind. Of course, he would speak to his sister alone as soon as he was able, but he saw nothing to object to as of yet.

"There is some debt I believe," Charles said, as the regular civilities ended and business began.

"Yes, my agent, Mr. Shepherd has a better idea of the particulars, but I believe the remainder is nearly two thousand pounds."

"It is your expectation, I presume, that my sister's fortune shall provide relief?"

"I believe the elevation of your sister, to the honour of a wife of a baronet and the lady of Kellynch Hall, will make up for a small contribution from the fortune which she brings to the alliance."

Charles was familiar enough with these negotiations, his father had thought to include him for Louisa's marriage settlement and he had been in charge of his own. He knew that the marriage contract had little to do with affection on either side. This was the business of marriage, affection came afterwards and hopefully before, if the couple was lucky.

"I have great respect for the honour my dear sister is to receive, it shall be accounted for in our negotiation. However, it is my duty to ensure that she should be well provided for, in the unfortunate event of your passing. I suggest only a life's interest in the remaining fortune, which would hereafter be her jointure."

Sir Walter smiled, "I see it will be a long negotiation, shall we leave it to our men and engage in more enjoyable pursuits?"

"Mr. Wolfe will expect your agent in the offices here. I must see my sister before we meet again."

"Unfortunately, my daughter has also been recently engaged and I am required to accompany her to Northamptonshire. After the first draft is completed, I beg your patience as I dispose of my daughter."

"I cannot see any great difficulty in that. Have the banns been read for the first time?"

"No, we awaited your arrival and consent."

"Excellent, then we have at least the three weeks or however long the lawyers must argue. I will have Mr. Wolfe prepare to meet your agent."

"Your sister may not have told you," Sir Walter said, in a low voice that made Charles alarmed, "There was an incident in the Pump Room, my cousin accosted her. She was able to escape, but I worry that she thinks of it still."

"Your cousin?" Charles demanded and Sir Walter explained. Charles set out for Caroline's lodging at once. She greeted him excitedly and wished to know if he had seen Sir Walter already.

"Sir Walter called on me, we shall leave the rest to the attorneys, but he told me what happened with Mr. Elliot. Why did you not write of it?"

"I did not wish to cause you distress. Nothing came of it; if anything, it secured my engagement," said she, with little emotion.

Charles was not content, "You must have been frightened. I wish I had come with you to Bath. Or that Louisa and her husband had come"

"You have a family now Charles, you have other responsibilities. Susan was nearby, I was not alone."

"You are my sister, Caroline, it is my duty to protect you," Charles argued.

"I release you; Sir Walter will take your place soon enough."

"Caroline," Charles took her hands and looked her in the eye, "Are you truly recovered?"

Charles watched his proud sister try to reply, but tears took away her voice. Charles embraced her.

"It happened so suddenly Charles, I had no idea what to do. If I had not recalled-"

"I heard what you recalled," Charles said dryly. He could still remember what had happened when he was a child.

"He might have taken something from me- that I could not recover."

"He was a fool; his actions were too overt to be believed. I do not imagine it would have stopped your engagement with Sir Walter. The man seems too much in love."

Caroline smiled, "Yes, I do believe he is very much in love."

"I only hope you can be wed as quickly as you wish, my marriage was simple. The income of the Kellynch estate alone is nearly six thousand pounds. Between your fortune and Sir Walter's debts I am sure the lawyers are having a properly long discussion."

"You will be proud of me Charles; I have saved enough to buy my own wedding clothes."

"I had meant to pay for it," Charles said gallantly, "In place of our father."

"No, save it for your charming daughter. She will need her own portion soon enough."

Charles was pleased to hear his sister speak so well of her niece and thought of it no more, "So you truly love him? He is certainly handsome enough; you'll be the lady of a grand estate."

"Yes, I have been lucky to love where I wish to wed. You did give your consent?"

"Of course, you made yourself very clear in the letter. I only wish you had told me of what came before."

"I should have. I did not wish to write it."

"I understand. You must tell me what to say about it if I am asked; I am sure it is widely known by now. Have you written to Louisa?"

"I have," she said.

Charles saw that Caroline would rather not speak any more of the incident and he felt that he had done everything within his duty to her. Sir Walter had assured him of Caroline's protection and his efforts to find Mr. Elliot. It did not seem there was anything more to be done.

"I will be here until the wedding, have you set the date?"

"Sir Walter is speaking to his tenant, Admiral Croft, but he believes the Admiral will be willing to give up the lease. Of course, we might wed and spend some time at Camden Place, but I would prefer to remove to Kellynch. You know one only ought to spend so long in Bath."

"Sir Walter has been living here for almost three years, he seems content."

"Sir Walter also decided to marry after fifteen years a widower."

"An excellent point," Charles conceded.

"You must come with us to Camden Place tonight, I assume Sir Walter invited you?"

"Yes, for dinner at six."

"Oh, dinner too! The Elliots do not usually give dinners; few people in Bath do!" Caroline observed.

"He must truly like you, then, if he is endeavouring to impress your brother," Charles said.

"I believe he does," Caroline smiled at him, "I want to tell you: I finally understand why you married Jane. I am sorry I ever interfered; it was beyond my comprehension until now."

"Thank you," Charles said seriously, "Your friendship since our marriage has been apology enough, but it is good to hear."

"There are feelings that overcome cold prudence, as I ought to have learned already," Caroline sighed, "I may never love your mother-in-law and I can only hope to see Sir Walter's daughter Elizabeth as seldom as you now see Mrs. Bennet."

Charles laughed. Content that his sister was reasonably well and pleased with her choice in marriage, he set out for his rooms. Charles liked his sister, though their temperaments were not very similar. That she had aided Darcy in separating him from Jane he had long forgiven. It appeared that despite everything, Caroline would marry the best of all of them. She must be delighted.

37
Sir Walter

"I have been waiting for you at least this age!" **Northanger Abbey Ch 6**

Sir Walter called on Caroline the next morning at Rivers Street to take his leave. Caroline, knowing this would occur, had given a hint to Susan that it might be best to visit Lady Russell for part of the morning. When Sir Walter arrived, Caroline's friend discreetly said her goodbyes and left them alone.

"I will be travelling by post," Sir Walter began, "I hope to conclude the chief of the business within a week, I will return in ten days at the utmost."

"I know it is your duty, but it feels like an age," Caroline observed.

"Yes, it is an imposition. Though, I have happier news as well, I have heard from Admiral Croft. He and his wife are happy to depart from Kellynch Hall at their earliest convenience. They have been meaning to visit my daughter Anne and her husband, Captain Wentworth. He is Mrs. Croft's brother."

"We are able to remove after our marriage?"

"If you wished to wait, we could be married at the Kellynch Chapel."

"No," Caroline said, perhaps too quickly for her sense of decorum, for she knew they must start the reading of banns again if they moved to another parish, "Unless you wish to purchase a licence; I am happy to be married in the city where we met."

"That is all I desire," said Sir Walter. He took Caroline's hand. She gave it readily, though they both wore gloves, and it was not all she wished for. They were sitting on the same sofa, though far enough apart that no one could fault them.

"That is not all that I desire," said Caroline in almost a whisper, as she closed the space between them. He seemed to have anticipated her intentions and she was in his arms and he was kissing her. The same feelings she had been seeking burst again within her. Her mind was solely focused on passion, save one lingering notion. For the first time, they were truly alone. Susan was gone, Charles was to come later on, and the man was to say that she was not at home if any visiting friends tried to call. There was no one to disrupt them or to stop them; even Caroline's ladies' maid had requested a day's holiday.

"Caroline-" he breathed. She felt a twinge of pleasure as he said her Christian name. Caroline freed a single hand from its glove and stroked his face. His hand covered hers, she noticed in passing that he must have discarded his gloves as well. She began to think of how many layers of clothing she was wearing. The thought was enough to jolt her back into decency. She pulled back, enough to see his face.

"I will miss you terribly, Sir Walter" she said, trying to regain some shred of her former modesty. She realized her hand was still intertwined with his; she did not have the will to let it go.

"Sir Walter- you still call me "Sir Walter", yet it is formal. I want you to call me something else, but I do not know what."

Caroline blushed, but speaking from a sound knowledge of his character, which she had been able to form in their short time together, she said, "You must not think me mercenary, but having found a husband with the double blessing of beauty and baronetcy, I feel I must retain my warm respect and devotion to the "Sir" that starts your name. It feels somehow wrong to separate your Christian name from its honourable title."

She had in no way anticipated the effect of her statement, for she found herself again in a very intimate embrace and unable to speak as her mouth was suddenly employed. Caroline was somewhat proud of herself for understanding her intended so exactly; though she had spoken nothing but the truth. She was extremely pleased to have secured herself a title.

"When we are alone, shall I call you Caroline or Lady Elliot?" he said.

"Walter," she tried, "My own baronet?" He was running his hands down her bare arms. Caroline found herself wondering if she was even capable of taking off her gown, her maid usually needed extra time to do up all of the buttons. Caroline blushed and drew back again. What was wrong with her?

"I believe I was wrong, use Sir Walter as much as you wish," he said.

"Caroline will do, until I am Lady Elliot complete. I will eagerly await your return," she stood as she spoke, it was best for him to leave.

"I will think of you constantly, my love," Sir Walter said, as he held her hands in his own and brought them to his lips. Caroline smiled, she appreciated that title nearly as much as Lady Elliot.

"And I you," said she.

"You may expect the Crofts to call. The letter indicated that they wished to take leave of Lady Russell and myself. I will send my excuses."

With that, Sir Walter left. Caroline remained to reflect that it might be a better thing for him to be a two day's journey away, if she was going to maintain any modesty before the wedding!

38
Major Frederick Tilney and Mrs. Nancy Tilney

I am going to Gretna Green, and if you cannot guess with who, I shall think you a simpleton, for there is but one man in the world I love, and he is an angel. **Pride and Prejudice Ch 47**

Frederick and Nancy crossed the border into Scotland with little difficulty and were wed in Gretna Green. It was a surprise to both of them. Nancy, when they returned from the church with the legal document, burned the letter she had held for the journey as proof. She had thought for a good portion of the journey that Frederick meant to ultimately abandon her. Nancy had made every effort to carry out her original plan and now found that it had not been needed.

Frederick had resolved to marry Nancy in a fit of pique to disoblige his father. While he had every intention to marry her when he set out, he began to have doubts as the several days' journey went on. Yet, he was finding that he actually liked her. Nancy was hilarious! Her misinformed mind gave every story a ridiculous perspective and she had lived with so many different sorts of families that he suspected he had yet to exhaust a quarter of her recollections during their long days in the carriage. And then there were the nights.

Frederick had indulged himself frequently when it came to carnal enjoyments, but he was used to very different women. He had always enjoyed winning hearts and then abandoning women once the chase was over, but this was something new. Nancy had no reservations; she was willing and eager. She did not have a lovely face, but the rest of her certainly served. If he had not confirmed her as a maiden on the first night himself, he would never have believed that she was inexperienced.

Nancy, in finding him irresistible, was becoming so herself. Without any clear idea of how long they would be together, she sought to make the most of every opportunity. She had imagined the process of making a child to be unpleasant based on Lucy's reports, but was excited to discover it could be quite the opposite. Perhaps it helped that she adored Frederick; he was one of the few people who listened to her. She could not imagine that Lucy felt any esteem for her vain and conceited husband.

After the rapid pace of their journey to Scotland, they stayed for a week in one of the better inns before beginning their slower progress towards Frederick's home in Gloucestershire. Frederick was resolved, he had properly married Nancy and he intended to present her to his father, but he was reluctant to actually do so. The fear a child has for the anger of their parent runs deep; he had only partially overcome it. His imprudent marriage would either cause an irreparable breach or begrudging acceptance. He was slowly moving towards an uncertain future for the first time in his life.

Nancy understood the situation, but it did not bother her. She would have a home either at Northanger or within Frederick's regiment; either were acceptable to her. She had lived without parents and family for a very long time, all she needed was him.

39
Caroline

"We will not say how near, for fear of shocking the young ladies." Then, lowering her voice a little, she said to Elinor, "She is his natural daughter." **Sense and Sensibility Ch 13**

Caroline and Susan paid a visit the next day to Lady Russell, who had resolved to stay in town until the wedding took place. Caroline was growing intimate with her and was pleased that after she was transplanted from her usual home with either her brother and sister, that there would be at least one friend in an easy distance. Susan had promised to visit once Caroline was well settled, as she wished to see Kellynch and its grounds.

"I would not come for a few months however," Susan said, "I do not think you will want for diversion for the first few weeks."

"I must agree," Caroline replied, "I have kept house for my brother but it will be nothing to an estate like Kellynch. To know what to do and to learn to do it are very different things."

Susan and Lady Russell gave each other a knowing look. Susan replied with a coquettish smile, "You mistake my meaning. I have seen you two together, I daresay that making an heir will take up the chief of your time."

Caroline blushed, she had not thought she was so obvious, "I do not think a day can be *filled* with that activity," she scoffed.

"That all depends on the man," Susan replied, "Has anyone spoken to you about it?"

"I had my sister explain it," Caroline said, "I have an adequate understanding, I think."

"Unfortunately," Lady Russell began, "A good deal of women enter marriage with no true idea of what the process entails or how they might enjoy it. Susan and I are going to tell you the truth of the matter, though our confidence shall not leave this room."

Caroline felt her cheeks growing warmer, "I understand."

"I am very glad to see that you are in love," Lady Russell said kindly, "and a good stout love can only be improved by the intimacy between a husband and wife. The more you understand about yourself, it will be more a thing of joy than of duty?"

Susan added suggestively, "There is far more to the marital act than duty."

"How do you know of it?" Caroline was unsure of the ultimate usefulness of the two women in this domain, one having been so long a widow.

Lady Russell said, "When a woman decides to establish herself as a widow; by abstaining for the proper number of years from anything in the way of engagement or marriage, she comes to discover that there are a number of young or widowed men, who have moral rectitude enough to avoid women for hire- but you know how men are. Women are not so very different." She shared a knowing smile with Susan.

"What if you become... indisposed?"

"Unfortunately, that was never to be in my case," Lady Russell said, "But you only need to take a trip to the country for a few months. Most widows have a sister or someone in need of a child."

"Susan?" Caroline nearly shrieked, looking meaningfully at her friend.

"My sister needed an heir; I might have been indisposed. As far as anyone knows, a baby boy was born on the estate and he will one day inherit it," Susan said mildly, "I shall visit whenever I please and be dear Aunt Susan."

This revelation completed, Caroline spent the rest of the visit violently blushing, as Lady Russell and Susan spoke fondly on topics that Caroline had never thought of before. She had imagined, as a young girl, that widows remained as they were simply for the freedom of movement and money. She had not imagined that they could have more control in... other areas.

"Do not worry though Caroline," Lady Russell said as they were preparing to go, "I have already taken the liberty of speaking with Sir Walter about this as well."

"Thank you, Lady Russell," Caroline managed.

"Anne, my dear," Lady Russell offered, "I am anticipating your continued friendship."

Caroline accepted the offer of Lady Russell's Christian name graciously (though dear reader, for clarity, we shall continue to call her Lady Russell), "Of course, I look forward to the day that I might visit you as the lady of Kellynch Hall. Allow me to say, I am honoured that you consider me worthy of the former position of your dear friend."

"The former Lady Elliot will always have a place in my heart, but I have also long wished for her to be replaced by a suitable candidate. You have a proper appreciation of the duties of a lady of the rank you shall ascend to. Most of all, I believe you will make Sir Walter happy. He does not realize it, but I do not think he has been truly happy for a long time."

"I am flattered," Caroline said, "I can only hope that I will be happy as well."

"I believe you will be," Lady Russell said, "My friend, she was an excellent woman, but her temperament was not suited to Sir Walter. She was never as content as she might have been. You are a very different sort of woman and you are perfectly suited for Sir Walter. I believe you will do very well. I might go so far as to think that no other woman in England would do so well."

Caroline walked back, arm-in-arm with Susan but unable to meet her gaze. She was thinking of her feelings and of what she had been told. Caroline had a strong desire to retire to her room. There were things she needed to think over.

40
Sir Thomas Bertram/Tom Bertram

Maria had a moment's struggle as she listened, and only a moment's- **Mansfield Park 21**

Sir Thomas Bertram of Mansfield Park had experienced the disastrous effects of two very imprudent marriages among his children, His first daughter, now rarely spoken of, had married a man she did not love at all and it had resulted in her ultimate ruin and banishment from the family. His second daughter, Julia, had eloped with a foolish young man, who had at least adequate fortune to recommend him but little sense or principle. It was not the most happy marriage, but he suspected it was within the general norm. Though certainly not what he had wished for his daughter.

He had been luckier in his son Edmund, who had very recently married his cousin Fanny. It had taken Sir Thomas some time to realize Fanny's true worth, her goodness and strong moral character, which his son had perceived long before himself. The marriage was the best his family had yet achieved, for while Fanny did not have a penny to her name, he could see that Edmund was truly happy and Sir Thomas was proud to call her his daughter in place of the one who had been lost to selfish desire.

When Sir Thomas first met Elizabeth, he had high hopes. She was beautiful, had refined manners, and was the daughter of a baronet. This must all recommend her in marrying his son, but his estimation of her worth fell quickly. He soon was thinking more of Maria than Edmund. Elizabeth was not the sort of woman he might have chosen for his oldest son. He had hoped for an upright lady, who might maintain Tom's reformation from frivolity to duty, but he perceived nothing of the sort. Elizabeth treated Tom with poorly disguised indifference. Her character seemed to begin and end in vanity and pride. She had regarded their home, his very Mansfield Park, with thinly veiled disgust, only caring how long it had been since they redecorated the drawing room and or claiming they had a very small breakfast parlour. Sir Thomas was beginning to feel that his son was somewhat out of his proper mind.

With solemn kindness, Sir Thomas addressed Tom, told him his fears, inquired into his wishes, entreated him to be open and sincere, and assured him that if he regretted his choice in any way, they might find a way to break the engagement. He could act for Tom: by complicating the wedding articles, drawing out the discussions, and suggesting to Elizabeth's father that she might not be entirely happy with the familial situation at Mansfield.

Tom had a moment's struggle as he listened, for he did not wish to impose a woman that was so disgusting to his father upon the family, but he was already resolved. He realized now that his sanguine plans of Elizabeth being a help to his mother were not to be. Elizabeth's fortune, long coming as some of it was to be, would be more than enough to discharge his debts without his father's knowledge. He had already spoken to their lawyer, Mr. Herd, to ensure that the debts were paid quietly.

He thought that perhaps Mansfield would cure her. The country and the separation from her father could make Elizabeth better. He knew that she did not love him, but love Tom did not require. She loved his rank and consequence and that must be enough. Tom thanked his father for his attention and kindness, but he was quite mistaken in supposing that he had the smallest desire of breaking his engagement.

Sir Thomas was forced to accept that Elizabeth would be very soon bound to the family. Since Tom's letter had arrived and laid out the circumstances surrounding the engagement, Sir Thomas had taken it upon himself to purchase a license. The marriage would be carried out in a mere four days, if the lawyers could come to a quick agreement. Sir Thomas would only need to be vigilant; he knew the only too common fate that the Elliots had fallen into. His investments were thriving, his wealth was now secure. He must ensure that Elizabeth's frivolity did not destroy his efforts.

41
Tom Bertram

There is one thing, Emma, which a man can always do, if he chuses, and that is, his duty **Emma Ch 18**

Tom was not one to dwell on misery but he did have a tendency to shirk his duties. He kept one eye on the light coming from his wife's room. He had been hoping she would fall asleep. It had been a late night celebrating their wedding, was it too much to ask that she be too tired for anything else? He looked at his watch and determined he could not dally any longer. He would need to consummate his marriage at some point...

In the course of his life, Tom had in fact slept with a total of two women, just to make sure that his lack of desire was not inexperience. It had never gone very well. The first time he had been simply curious and the second time he had been extremely drunk. He had decided against being inebriated this time, the last time that had made everything worse. Instead, he was trying to determine how best to get the job done.

The trick was, he needed to think of someone he actually found attractive. Elizabeth was decidedly not his type. Not only was she extremely womanly, but even in a man he did not usually appreciate that sort of dark beauty. He would need to try and not look at her as much as possible. He would need to think of someone else, not Anderson, that would make him sad. Maybe Charles Maddox, now there was as gentleman-like a man as one will see anywhere! If only there was any way to find out if there were any men in the region with similar proclivities as himself.

This was not a train of thought that he should dwell on tonight, he had a job to do and it would be done. Tom tried to imagine that all across the country there were many other men treating this interaction as a mere act of obligation. He would simply need to close his eyes and think of England

42
Elizabeth Bertram
She was fully satisfied of being still quite as handsome as ever
***Persuasion* Ch 1**

Elizabeth was sitting perfectly still at her vanity, trying to define her tumult of emotion. Thoughts flew about unbidden; Lady Russell was a contemptible liar! She felt incandescent rage, revulsion, and resentment. She was trying to find the proper word, the proper way to think of what she felt.

Mortifying. This evening had been mortifying.

Elizabeth had suddenly been fully aware that her own husband did not find her attractive. It was as plain as day! What a mortification to a woman who had always prized her beauty. How could she not be attractive to anyone? It was past all rational belief. She turned to her mirror and was assured again that she was still as handsome as ever. More handsome, in fact, then she had ever been. Apparently, she had married a blind fool.

Elizabeth took a deep breath and tried to think more rationally. It had not been so very bad, just awkward and uncomfortable. Maybe things would improve? Elizabeth wondered if that was even possible. Instead, she began to think of all the ways she might defer that particular activity from happening again. She understood, on some level, the necessity of getting children, but she was completely unwilling to encourage it. She began to imagine that headaches, or fatigue, or a hundred other complaints that might defer a recurrence. Maybe she could just pretend to be asleep! Elizabeth had no abhorrence of disguise; falsehoods were generally very useful.

She was quite resolved by the time she was falling asleep; she would do everything in her power to avoid her husband. Elizabeth generously calculated that she had many years ahead of her in which the creation of a child would be possible. Had not Nancy spoken of a woman having a child at two-and-fifty? She was certain that it would happen eventually; he would insist on her acquiescence sometimes and that would result in a child. Luckily for Elizabeth, her deferral seemed entirely acceptable to her husband.

With that cause of anxiety over, she had every confidence in maintaining all her foolishly undervalued good looks.

43
Caroline
But the clothes, the wedding clothes! **Pride and Prejudice Ch 49**

Caroline was busy during Sir Walter's absence. She had wedding clothes to purchase, which must be fine enough for her new station, letters to write to friends, and enjoyments to be had before she departed from Bath. Sir Walter had indicated an intent to spend a good deal of time at Kellynch after his long absence. This suited Caroline well enough; she had spent enough time in London and Bath for a year at least, but it did mean that she ought to finish what shopping she wanted before her departure.

She also spent the greater portion of one day perfecting her signature as Lady Elliot and many more embroidering the same name into a wealth of handkerchiefs.

Caroline was lucky enough to meet the Crofts, who called to take their leave of Lady Russell and deliver a few items of business to Camden Place. Caroline saw in them the very picture of marital felicity she had observed in her brother and Jane and it gave her sanguine hopes that such a love could last decades of being together. The Crofts were plainly very happy. They spoke of their time in Kellynch: riding around the country together most days and visiting whatever sights were within an easy distance. They planned to find another situation much the same, where they could stay in comfort and explore the countryside. Caroline informed them that Netherfield, a very eligible house for their purpose, had recently become available in Hertfordshire. She nearly laughed as she said it, the childless Crofts would not suit Mrs. Bennet's hopes for her remaining unmarried daughters!

Caroline spent what time she had left with Charles, who would certainly be able to visit his sister, but saw it as a distant event. It was an endeavour of several days to travel between Somersetshire and Derbyshire and of course, Charles was now a father. He doubted Jane would wish to travel when their daughter was still so young. Caroline assured Charles that Sir Walter would likely want to travel to London for a few weeks every year, which would be more convenient for each of them.

Sir Walter arrived back in town with Mr. Shepherd and the lawyers were set back to work. The eagerness of each led to a few concessions on both sides. The papers were signed, the banns were read, and they were to marry early that Monday morning.

44
Sir Walter

His good looks and his rank had one fair claim on his attachment; since to them he must have owed a wife of very superior character to any thing deserved by his own. **Persuasion Ch 1**

Sir Walter was nervous. This was an incredibly foreign feeling. Was Caroline as in love with him as he hoped? Had he not held Caroline in such high esteem it might have been better, but he was very much in love. Obviously, if a woman was worthy of his love, she must be a very excellent person. Sir Walter wished he had been able to arrange things more exactly at Kellynch. He had no time to ensure that everything was in perfect order, as much as he trusted the Crofts.

He was in a near panic the day before the wedding as he realized that he had not nearly enough time to have a new coat made. His current selection of clothing was entirely inadequate; his newest coat was nearly three months old! Why had he not planned for this when he resolved to marry! It was an inexcusable oversight. He was certain, *absolutely certain* that Caroline would be dressed in the very latest style, in the best that her ample fortune would allow. How could he have been so careless?

He had his valet search again through his closet, which only was maintained within its limited space because, generally, anything older than six months was cast off. He dismissed each option with equal disgust. Too worn, too simple, the wrong colour for the season, why did he even still own that? Then his valet reached a coat he had quite forgotten about. He had had it made for his daughter Anne and Captain Wentworth's wedding and out of sentimental value (that is, because he had been complimented so many times while wearing it), he had kept it, despite not wearing it again. The cuffs would need to be changed, but that could be done at once, otherwise, there was nothing objectionable; it was a very fine coat. The gold thread embroidery had been done by a
particularly skilful woman in town. He sent it to one of his maids for alteration.

That decided, Sir Walter had a bath, had his hair trimmed, and was shaved. The wedding was at ten in the morning the next day, so as much was done that evening as possible. His valet offered specific lotions and ointments from Sir Walter's large collection for his hands and face. Sir Walter was never seen without a hat outdoors and he gave every possible attention to his youthful looks. He had determined that it was best not to accept any invitations for this evening, he meant to go to bed as early as seemed rational, that he might be looking his best tomorrow. He could not have any blemishes under his eyes.

The morning arrived. It was to be a small affair, with Lady Russell and Mr. Shepherd the only ones present on his side, Mrs. Taylor and Charles Bingley attending for the lady. Sir Walter had informed his two younger daughters of the marriage but as both were out of the county, neither would attend. There was to be a wedding breakfast before they set out to Kellynch Hall with Sir Walter's many friends in Bath attending.

Sir Walter waited anxiously for Caroline to arrive. He felt that she must be as happy as he was; but he found he could not entirely be sure of her intentions. She could have chosen anyone! He did what he could: ten solid minutes in front of his best mirror had assured him that he looked very handsome that day. He had set out for the church in all his state and grandeur.

Caroline came! She was everything he had ever imagined. The silk gauze of her dress was pure white without blemish with patterned blue leaves in flossed silk. It was trimmed with silk net and rich blue satin. She wore a trimmed cap with blue feathers and net; and fine white slippers, untarnished by dirt. Her hair was elaborately styled about her head in long auburn braids and curls. It was her face where his attention was to rest, bright light eyes, a shapely nose, and a joyful smile. He imagined that her face had no need of preservers or beautifiers: she was perfect. Her brother was at her side, though Sir Walter only attended to him long enough to accept the bride.

Caroline, Lady Elliot hereafter, was beside him, speaking the vows that would bind them irrevocably together. Sir Walter could feel her delight, in her words, her face, and her manner. He ought not have been so worried. Yet, there was still the wedding night, he could not hide behind his fine clothes then. The anxiety that he had so recently dismissed returned in full force. This was all Lady Russell's fault! At least he had the day's travel to contend with the mounting sense of dread.

45
Caroline or Lady Elliot

Matrimony was her object, provided she could marry well.
Mansfield Park Ch 4

    Caroline took her husband's arm and they left the church. The wedding breakfast was to be held at Camden Place only a short walk away. The party gathered for the wedding followed behind them and more friends and acquaintances, from Sir Walter's long stay in Bath, were invited. The two ample drawing rooms were full of guests by the time they arrived. Sir Walter seemed unwilling to release Caroline from his side and she was happy to remain. She imagined that he wished for everyone to see what a handsome couple they made and that was an enterprise she wished to participate in.
    Caroline was particularly pleased by those people who were new acquaintances as she was introduced to them for the first time as Lady Elliot. The title covered over her birth and rank, only hinting at her lower origins by the lack of her Christian name. She was now in society as a married woman of unimpeachable rank. She happily imagined her next trip to London as Lady Elliot. There must be other reasons for her delight on this day, but her new name was very high in her esteem.
    The breakfast was lavish, with hot rolls, breads, ham, eggs, and butter, all laid around a fine cake and there was chocolate in addition to tea and coffee. Caroline greeted everyone with Sir Walter before excusing herself to eat. They had the journey to Kellynch ahead and were expected to arrive for dinner. Caroline was hungry and tired, having slept very little the night before, she had eaten nothing before heading to the church.
    Caroline tried to eat her food but she was such a mixture of excitement and nerves that nothing was appealing. She was setting off to a home she had never seen: to a new neighbourhood and new responsibility. She was not worried about the wedding night, there was more excitement than anxiety, but it would be novel. She only hoped that Sir Walter would not be disappointed, there is only so much one can learn from lessons without application.

Before their departure, Caroline saw Sir Walter leave the room and she followed, not entirely certain why. He had gone up to his chamber; she lingered in the hallway. As he left the nearly empty room, furnished only with what was not his own, he was startled to see her standing there.

"I wanted to spend a moment alone with you," she said, "before our journey." She took his hand in hers. He took her into his arms, as she kissed him, she felt the promise of what was to come. They would not be truly alone until nightfall; her heart ached as she thought of it. She almost resented that her maid, Aliénor, would ride with them to Kellynch Hall.

"We must be going," he said, stroking her cheek with his hand, but instead of letting go, he resumed kissing her. Caroline's feeling rose, she wished to enter his chamber, but it was empty now. They had to go.

"I am eager to go home, my love," said she, as they finally parted.

"I am pleased to hear you speak of Kellynch as home," said Sir Walter, as he released her and they went down to take their leave.

Soon Caroline was embracing Charles, with tears in her eyes, and bidding farewell to the other guests. The house, so long the residence of the Elliots, had already been emptied of personal items and would perhaps serve as the home of another indebted member of the gentry. Caroline was helped into the carriage and four. Sir Walter was looking out at Bath as they left, perhaps saying goodbye to the city that had served as his home for so long. Soon they were out of its sight and driving along open fields.

46
Sir Walter

"Their house was undoubtedly the best in Camden Place; their drawing-rooms had many decided advantages over all the others which they had either seen or heard of, and the superiority was not less in the style of the fitting-up, or the taste of the furniture."
Persuasion Ch 15

They were nearly at Kellynch Hall. Sir Walter was holding Caroline, who had fallen asleep against him. Her head was resting on his heart, her hair smelled of lavender. He wished that he could free her auburn locks from their braids but it would not be right to be in a state of undress when they made their entrance at Kellynch. Besides, their personal servants were present as well. Sir Walter contented himself with admiring the construction and material of her dress; Caroline had a very keen sense of fashion. He was reminded again of his failure to order a new coat, though it did not seem that she had noticed. That was fortunate; he hated not looking his best.

In thinking of Kellynch, Sir Walter had remembered, quite suddenly, that the chamber that had been his late wife's had not been updated since her death, and some items even long before. She had changed very little when his mother removed to the dowager cottage, claiming that she was content with the furniture and decoration. Sir Walter had found this extraordinary, but since it was her private chamber and was not open to viewing, there could be no harm in its less than fashionable appearance. There had been no protest made by Mrs. Croft, so nothing had been done for over-thirty years? Sir Walter was mortified. Why had he not delayed the wedding?

He knew that the house was in good condition, he had visited a few weeks ago, but he knew nothing had been done in the way of improvement. Elizabeth had been wanting to redecorate the drawing room, what else ought to be done? He could only hope that Caroline knew what to do, she certainly knew how to select gowns. Her education was pristine, she must know how to lay out a room. This was enough to do away with most of Sir Walter's anxiety, what woman would not love to decorate a room in their own style?

"Caroline," he said, "We have crossed into the estate."

She roused and looked out the window. There was a handsome forest on one side and fields on the other. Sir Walter was elated to be returning; he excitedly pointed out various landmarks. His holdings were large and he was endlessly proud of them. It was only proper that it now had come back to his full possession. Let us kindly forget, for his sake, that nearly every field was still mortgaged.

He was mildly ashamed of how paltry the assembled party of servants appeared; it appeared that the Crofts had lived more simply than he thought proper of *his* distinguished status. Caroline did not seem to mind; she was watching with a bright smile. The carriage stopped and Sir Walter helped his wife down. The introductions were made before they went into the house to wash for dinner.

Sir Walter led Caroline to her chamber with trepidation, "It is not in the latest style," he said quickly, as he opened the doors, "I did not think of it, I hope that you can manage until there is time to decorate it."

"It is charming," Caroline said smiling, "It is not exactly to my taste, but the furniture is so handsome, I cannot think that it would need much alteration."

"The furnishings must be older than yourself," he said, wondering if that was a prudent thing to say. She might be reminded of his age. Sir Walter did not like anyone to think about *his* age.

"Whomever set up this room," she said, running a hand over a fine wooden desk, "Purchased with great taste. These are well made pieces, with real elegance in the construction. I would be remiss to cast aside such things. This desk is truly well designed."

Sir Walter had decided already that he had complete confidence in Caroline's discernment, so he quickly followed, "I only worried they might not be to your taste."

"I have time enough to make the changes I wish for," Caroline said mildly. She turned to him and said with a mischievous smile, "After dinner, we may properly appreciate my chambers."

After nearly an hour with their respective servants to dress, the married couple descended for dinner. Sir Walter was again displeased. The meal did not suit what he had expected, but at least Caroline seemed happy enough. There was only one course, though it generously covered the table. He was used to two courses at Kellynch, the Crofts had ruined his servants! They never would have dreamed of serving this sort of meal before he had left. He regretted again his rush to marriage. He ought to have come before Caroline to set everything to rights. She must be blinded by love not to be greatly offended by the lack of servers and food. He only hoped that she would enjoy setting his house in a proper order.

47
Caroline

"But I would really advise you to make your purchase in that neighbourhood, and take Pemberley for a kind of model." **Pride and Prejudice Ch 8**

Caroline had entered the house in great curiosity. Her education had been very good (if she did say so herself); she had no scruples about her ability to manage such a house. Sir Walter, she had determined, had not been very involved in the keeping of the house beyond his own dressing room. This suited Caroline. On the approach, she saw Kellynch Hall was of older construction, though it was well situated and maintained. The gardens were modern, though more ostentatious than she liked. Her model of perfection was Pemberley, though she should not have been surprised by the difference in taste, she had not married a man near the sense and discernment of Mr. Darcy. Fortunately, it was more enjoyable this way.

She was keenly aware of the number of servants as they were introduced, it seemed entirely proper to the size of the house, as she imagined it to be. It might even be generous, though she must speak to the housekeeper before she made her final decision. A good housekeeper was worth her weight in gold, her mother had always said. The housekeeper looked old enough to have been selected by the previous Lady Elliot, not Elizabeth, and Caroline had a notion that anything Elizabeth touched might be overly pretentious. She did not realize just how correct she would be.

As she entered the house, Caroline was- well... not entirely surprised. The house itself was magnificent, but the decoration and furniture were gaudy and disorganized. As they passed through rooms, too quickly for a full assessment, Caroline began to suspect that Elizabeth had decorated them one by one, regardless of any accordance in the room before it, each room was in a "latest style". She went through rooms overly done in the fashion of ten separate years, in a random order. The sheer amount of gold leaf was hurting her eyes. A quick glance told her that the true improvements had been neglected, the windows were showing wear and likely would need to be replaced. It was imperceptible in summer, but she was confident drafts would plague them in the winter.

Sir Walter had stopped and he looked exceedingly nervous, Caroline deduced they must be at her chamber. She suspected this room had been untouched by Elizabeth which made her fairly excited. The doors were opened and she instantly relaxed, the rooms were exactly as she had hoped. They were ample and well-fitted, with timeless dark wood furniture and elegantly painted walls. The style was consistent through the sitting room, dressing room, and bedchamber, a welcome relief from the juxtaposed extravagance behind her. There was a handsome bookshelf, but it appeared that most of the books had been removed. Perhaps by one of the daughters? She had yet to meet Anne or Mary, she doubted Elizabeth read much at all.

Sir Walter made excuses but Caroline rushed to assuage his concerns, the room suited her exactly. The primary colour was green, she preferred blue, but otherwise she saw very little that needed to be changed. Caroline cared very little for the actual style or size of the room, it was the apartment of Lady Elliot. This was to be her own, at least as long as Sir Walter lived. If she bore the son he desired, she would be secure forever.

Sir Walter seemed relieved by her obvious enjoyment of her chambers. He left through an adjoining door in her dressing room. Caroline could not see beyond it, as Aliénor entered to help her wash. Her toilette was already arranged as she liked it, with her various creams and tonics to maintain her glowing complexion.

Caroline was quite hungry and was happy to see many dishes she liked served for dinner. She had no inclination to hire another cook; the meal was delicious and well-served. She was anxious to be alone with her husband, but her trained eye was conscious of the servants and surroundings. The decoration in the room was again overdone, but the table at least seemed to be an older piece; preserved, no doubt, because it was so large.

"Do you wish to see the manor?" Sir Walter asked when the meal was over.

"I would prefer to retire to my chamber," Caroline said, smiling meaningfully, "There will be time enough tomorrow to view Kellynch, and in better light." He offered his arm and Caroline felt nearly giddy with excitement. They parted briefly to undress. Caroline's gown removed in favour of a nearly sheer nightgown and her long hair released from its braids. Sir Walter entered her chamber through the adjoining door.

"I cannot describe how beautiful you looked today, Lady Elliot," said he, taking her hand.

"There was no choice on my part, Sir Walter, I desired to match my husband," Caroline said coyly, recalling her response from the ball and knowing where it might led. She was not disappointed; she was in his arms again. She let go of all her reservations and propriety: they had served their intended purpose. Her emotions were running wild.

Who can be in doubt of what followed? It was exactly what can be assumed to arise from very strong feelings of love (or maybe lust) on each side. Caroline had begun with high, but rather abstract expectations, and she was as fully satisfied as anyone in her position could be. This is the great preserve of new husbands everywhere: their wives have no possible means of comparison.

"I have acquired the most exquisite object in the world," he said, when it was over.

Caroline tried to think but it was difficult, "I wanted you from the first time I saw you," she said simply. It was true. Why had she even considered the others? She finally had everything that she had ever desired.

48
Caroline

She could have said more on the subject; for she had in fact so high an opinion of the Crofts, and considered her father so very fortunate in his tenants, felt the parish to be so sure of a good example, and the poor of the best attention and relief, that however sorry and ashamed for the necessity of the removal, she could not but in conscience feel that they were gone who deserved not to stay, and that Kellynch Hall had passed into better hands than its owners'. These convictions must unquestionably have their own pain, and severe was its kind. **Persuasion Ch 13**

    Caroline was determined to do her duty as the new mistress of Kellynch. She arranged to meet with the housekeeper after breakfast the next morning. Mrs. Martin was an older woman, perhaps near Sir Walter's age (though Caroline would never have said that to her husband). Caroline liked her very well by the end of their hour together. Once Mrs. Martin had realized that Caroline was interested in her opinion, she had been straight forward and rational. Caroline understood quickly that Mrs. Martin was heavily prejudiced towards the management of the Crofts and against Elizabeth. Given how little Caroline liked Elizabeth, this suited her opinions exactly. She was inclined to agree with Mrs. Martin.

    Mrs. Martin had brought with her the ledgers for the last year, under the Crofts, and the most recent year of Elizabeth's oversight. Caroline sat to study them; she took pride in her abilities; she had kept Netherfield well within her brother's income and the ball had been very well within her ideal budget. It had been a full display of their wealth without waste, a triumph indeed! She opened the two ledgers at once and compared them. By the end of the first page she was nearly laughing, no wonder the Elliots had fallen into debt!

    She could see that Elizabeth and Sir Walter were more likely to entertain than the Crofts, but that did not account for the difference. The orders of food were massive, even with a greater number of servants a good portion must have gone to waste. Caroline had a deep respect for the title that she now shared, but the spending was as gaudy as the decorations. The number of servants employed made her wonder what half of them could have been employed doing!

The budget for clothing was also massively ridiculous; did Elizabeth think herself royal? Caroline thought she had spent a good deal on new gowns, but she had always stayed within her generous income. She was not enough in love to entirely excuse her husband: his tailoring bills were also obscene. It had never occurred to Caroline before that so much money per annum *could* be spent on fabric.

Looking up at Mrs. Martin, she said, "I am partial to Mrs. Croft's management, I do not see too much need for alteration."

"I retained this as well," Mrs. Martin looked relieved, she took out a sheet of the ledger book that had been torn out, it looked like it had crumpled but was now smoothed. Caroline looked it over; it was a household budget, quite austere, but one that would have spent far less than Kellynch's income.

"Who drew this up?" Caroline asked, the writing was not like either ledger.

"Lady Russell and Mrs. Wentworth," Mrs. Martin said with some pride.

Caroline smiled, Mrs. Wentworth was the second daughter, Anne, who would have still resided at home before the move to Bath. "At least Sir Walter has one rational daughter," thought Caroline, she was already convinced of Lady Russell's sense. She could see why it had failed to be accepted, however, Bath was preferable to such strict economy.

"Mrs. Martin, this has been very elucidating. I have no intention of again removing to Bath or diminishing the name of Kellynch Hall in the neighbourhood. I will rely on your experience and wisdom in the coming weeks," she said. Caroline had a great appreciation for the distinction of rank, especially now that she had attained a high degree of rank herself, but she had long known to respect a competent housekeeper.

"Thank you, Lady Elliot," Mrs. Martin said. Caroline smiled for a moment, enjoying the sound of her new title, but then she had another thought.

"Mrs. Martin, my room, I notice, is in a different style. Is it possible that other items have been retained before Mrs. Bertram's efforts?"

"Yes, ma'am, would you like me to show you to the storage?"

"Please."

Caroline followed eagerly, almost all the furniture and decoration in the house were new and modern. The home lacked the distinction of the seat of an ancient family. Elizabeth's misguided attempt to make the house grander had robbed it entirely of its history, only some art and family portraits remained. Mrs. Martin led her past the offices and into an older part of the manor. In a few disused rooms remained nearly all the old furnishings, carefully arranged and covered in cloth. Caroline liked Mrs. Martin even more, she had obviously thought to preserve these herself. Her opinion of Elizabeth, if it were possible, fell further.

The housekeeper began to show Caroline the best pieces, which were handsome and well-made. Yes, some were far out of style, but many only needed to be covered again or painted. They were certainly more elegant than many of the pieces currently on display. Caroline was already forming plans to restore much of what was saved to former positions of prominence. She recalled some designs that she had worked on with Georgiana Darcy, certainly this card table could be restored.

"Would you have this table taken to be stripped?" Caroline asked, "I am not yet familiar with the offices. I suppose I have been going about in a random order, I should first ask for a proper tour."

Mrs. Martin gave direction to a nearby man, and then promptly led Caroline on a very detailed tour. The manor was large, though not as large as Pemberley. The entrance and front half were newer, though still almost a century old, and the back section had been built much earlier than that. The rooms had good light and the layout was reasonable for a house of its age. Mrs. Martin focused heavily on her domains, showing Caroline more of the offices than galleries. They finished in the library.

"I am afraid the library has been neglected," Mrs. Martin said, "The late Lady Elliot and Mrs. Wentworth were more attentive to its upkeep."

"There is no enjoyment like reading!" Caroline said, seriously. She had always wished to have a grand library, but she was not miserable to see that she did not have an excellent one at Kellynch. It was only another thing for her to improve.

"Indeed, ma'am," said Mrs. Martin.

"Was there a collection removed from my chamber?" Caroline asked, remembering the strangely empty shelves.

"Yes, the late mistress has a collection of novels and poetry that she read often. Mrs. Wentworth requested them when she wed and Sir Walter made no objection."

"I will need to replace them," Caroline said. She had another thought and asked, "You have been with the family for many years?"

"Since Mrs. Bertram was only a year old; I began as the head nursemaid."

"You have remained all these years?" Caroline asked diplomatically, knowing that Mrs. Martin was too professional to speak plainly.

"Perhaps there are not many who have stayed so long; I have long felt a duty to the Elliot family. The late Lady Elliot was an excellent woman, her daughter Mrs. Wentworth was very much the same. She was more attentive to the needs of a household. Besides, my husband is the butler. Where else would I go?"

Caroline internally translated, this daughter Anne must have made sure to show proper concern for the servants and tenants. Caroline had been taught that it was the proper duty of the lady of the house to act in such a way, but she had seen its effect living with Charles and Jane. She would not admit it, she hardly understood it herself, but she had learned from Jane's kindness. Caroline had every intention of living up to the example of her predecessors; she would be a benevolent Lady Elliot.

Mrs. Martin and Caroline parted with warm feelings on each side. Caroline had employment and confidence that the household had been kept for some time in good hands. Mrs. Martin was relieved that Sir Walter had not married a woman too much like Elizabeth, who might have reversed all the prudent management of Mrs. Croft and the Lady Elliot before. Mrs. Martin had truly dreaded the idea of another unfit manager, without the counteracting goodness of Anne. It was for Anne that Mrs. Martin had stayed for the long eleven years under Elizabeth. If Caroline proved to be as reasonable as she appeared to be, Mrs. Martin was willing to remain.

49
Sir Walter

The party drove off in very good spirits; Sir Walter prepared with condescending bows for all the afflicted tenantry and cottagers who might have had a hint to show themselves **Persuasion Ch 5**

    Sir Walter had been awake nearly as long as Caroline, but he had not yet left his chamber. He had finally returned to Kellynch; he needed to look his best. He selected his clothes with all the care as his wedding day, ordered a bath, and spent a good deal of time in front of his favourite mirror. He was feeling better than he had in quite a long time. The whole business of courting had been nearly disastrous; he had begun to doubt his own merits! It was a concept so foreign to him; he was certain it would not have ever happened if he had not feared that Caroline was attracted to that sallow Tom Bertram, with his sandy coloured hair or- Sir Walter decided not to try and compare himself to Major Tilney, he respected natural beauty too much; but he was a baronet and Tilney would never be.
    He went down for breakfast and found Caroline at a writing table composing a letter. She looked exquisite, a light blue dress with silver brocade highlighting the lovely colour of her hair. She looked up at him with her keen light eyes and smiled.
    "I have met with Mrs. Martin," she said, "but I was sure you would want to show me the house and grounds."
    "I would be delighted; have you been pleased with what you have seen of your new home?"
    "It is a very handsome manor," Caroline said, "I could not be more honoured to be the mistress of such a fine house."
    Sir Walter was extremely satisfied. Caroline was saying exactly what he liked to hear, for Kellynch in his mind was merely an extension of himself, and he was very nearly perfect. He congratulated himself on choosing a woman of Caroline's background: she could never look down on a house such as his own.
    "After a tour, I thought we might visit one or two of the prominent families of the neighbourhood," Sir Walter very much wished to show off his wife. He had a wonderful plan of riding in an

open carriage. She was his choice, and therefore she was an extension of himself. She was very nearly perfect. He was certain that the loss of Elizabeth, with all her beauty, could not be that difficult for the community to bear with Caroline's striking features presented in their place.

"Of course," Caroline said, and returned to her writing. Sir Walter ate and when he had finished, he offered an arm to his wife, who had by now folded her letter.

"Where do you wish to begin?" he asked ceremoniously.

Caroline turned to him with a coy smile, "Perhaps we might begin in my bedchamber? I felt that we did not quite finish last evening."

Sir Walter was startled. He was not accustomed to the initiation of marital relations coming from anyone but himself. It was not unwelcome but it was unexpected. Sir Walter had imagined himself for some time as a good husband, who did not require regular admittance into his late wife's chamber beyond what must be necessary for the getting of heirs and his own satisfaction. He had settled somewhere around thrice a week. He seemed to have found a different sort of woman; one that he had not entirely believed existed.

After a moment's pause, he led his wife to her rooms, but another problem was then presented. They were both already dressed and he did not wish to delay their plans too much. Their personal attendants were most likely taking their own meal. Sir Walter did not have long to think over this problem, as Caroline was already working on his trousers.

"I like your coat," she said, running her hands over the fine embroidery. Of course she did! How could she not? Her morning dress was hardly any barrier, though he must be careful not to rip or wrinkle it; it was clearly new and quite stylish.

The difference that had caused this sudden inclination on Caroline's part, Sir Walter supposed, must be in Lady Russell's advice. Difficult as it must be, he tried to remember the instructions. They could be summarized in two general rules: slow down and make sure *she* is enjoying herself. It had taken Sir Walter a significant amount of time to accept that there might be *any* problem with *him* at all, and then still more convincing to accept that a widow could supply the solution, but in time he had been persuaded. Everything had clearly gone so well the night before; he thought it best to follow his friend's wisdom a second time.

Lady Russell was of course, entirely correct, and therefore in a reasonable amount of time, the newly married couple were feeling that this was an enjoyable way to start their day. Caroline began to rearrange her gown. Sir Walter quickly eyed her dress and hair; it had not been damaged by their activity. She smiled at him as he fixed his own appearance. In no less than twenty minutes, they were back on schedule, Sir Walter began the tour with his apartment. He had never seen his wife so impressed; she must be admiring his mirrors.

50
Major Frederick Tilney

I leave it to be settled, by whomsoever it may concern, whether the tendency of this work be altogether to recommend parental tyranny, or reward filial disobedience. **Northanger Abbey Ch 31**

Frederick had now spent nearly a month in the intimate company of Nancy and he was surprised every day that he still did not tire of her. She had spent the last few days, on the leg of the journey that brought them within an hour's ride of the Abbey, telling in minute detail how her sister had come to marry Mr. Robert Ferrars. The exploits of the Dashwood girls were told, the silliness of Mrs. Jennings, the hospitality of Sir John and Lady Middleton; and the predicament of Mr. Edward Ferrars. When Mr. Robert Ferrars was introduced, Nancy described him so candidly, from his uppity manners to his carefully selected and overly-ornate toothpick case, that Frederick could not help but laughing until he nearly wept. Nancy was not overly skilled in the telling, for she took long detours to describe frivolity and gave personal opinions of every person who was introduced, but to Frederick it was all delightful.

They stayed for one more night at an inn, it was a Thursday and Frederick was particularly desirous that they arrive at Northanger Abbey on a Friday. He was entirely resolved in his plan to spite his father, he was far too pleased with Nancy to even think of casting her off, but he wanted to temper the rage he was certain his father would feel by the presence of his brother. Henry and his wife Catherine dined nearly every Friday at the Abbey. It was a weekly engagement that he was certain brought very little joy to either side, but it served to maintain a cordial relationship with their father. It was perhaps not overly kind to use his brother's presence as a shield, but Frederick was not one to often consider the comfort of others.

Nancy, for her part, was very desirous of seeing the Abbey and surrounding neighbourhood, which she hoped would hereafter be her home. If everything went as well as it could, Frederick had expressed a wish of giving up his commission so that they might settle. Nancy was only nervous that her powers of persuasion would by no means equal her sister's. It was always Lucy who had used words to the greatest advantage, talking her way into the good graces of everyone. Nancy was not very proficient; she was not certain she could convince the General of her worth.

Frederick was very diligent in the timing of their arrival, they dressed and washed at the inn and were on the road with only ten minutes to spare. They arrived at the Abbey, Nancy ogling out the window at her future home. Frederick had only a few minutes to dispose of the horses and carriage and be announced before they were all summarily seated for dinner. Frederick had requested that the man only announce himself, and they entered the room together. They found the family party at their seats and the General hardly kept his countenance as he began to realize who the lady accompanying his son must be. A servant quickly set an extra place.

"Father, Henry, Catherine, this is my wife, Nancy," Frederick said with a forced pleasant tone. The introductions were made in due course and once the civil formalities of names and titles had been completed, no one had anything else to say. Catherine gave her husband a meaningful look, and with a set smile and slightly sardonic tone, Henry began.

"From where do you hail, madam?"

"It is somewhat hard to say," Nancy replied, in a serious tone, "I was born to a rector in Longstaple, Richard Steele, but when my father died, we went to live with our uncle, Mr. Pratt, he runs a small school at Plymouth. Nearly six years ago we left his care, my sister and I, and we lived with various relations. Two years ago, my dear sister married. Since then I have been living with Miss Elizabeth Elliot, and her father, in Bath."

This history seemed to soften the manners of Henry and harden those of the General. Henry continued, "Really? How much of the country must you have seen?"

"When I was with Lucy, I should say Mrs. Ferrars now, I travelled a prodigious amount I would think, we were so often staying with cousins here and there around Devonshire and Dorset. Why, when we were staying in Exeter, we met a cousin, Mrs. Jennings, and spent some months at Barton with Sir John Middleton. After Lucy was married, I even went as far as Sussex."

"You are related to Sir John of Barton Park?" General Tilney finally spoke.

"No, I believe our only relation is through his mother-in-law, and a distant one at that. Well, Lucy was always better at remembering these things than I," said Nancy.

"What of the Elliots?" the General continued; his tone was too mild to be believed.

"I- well you mustn't tell her- I met Miss Elliot quite by chance when I arrived in Bath and- well I told her and she believed me- but I do not think we are related at all. I cannot even recall what I told her."

At this Henry burst out laughing, his wife looked at him in confusion and Frederick looked smugly at his brother. Henry caught his glee and after taking a breath said, "You convinced the Elliots that you were a relation? Sir Walter must sleep with his copy of the baronetage! You are better than you think."

Nancy was flustered, "Well, Miss Elliot does not like to look at it. And after we met, she never inquired again and I never spoke of it. I was fortunate I suppose, I have a hard time keeping secrets."

Frederick looked at his brother and he could see that Henry had a very good idea of what sort of woman he had married. With a quick glance to their father, Henry smiled and shook his head slightly.

"You have a very lovely gown," Nancy said to Catherine, "Where did you purchase the fabric?"

"In Bath actually, the last time we visited," Catherine smiled, "My husband helped me choose the fabric, he says I never pay attention to how well it will wash."

"Oh yes, it is very important to select something that will not fray," Nancy agreed readily.

"Mrs. Tilney, I believe that you and I will get along charmingly," Henry said, lifting a glass to her. "Catherine is always too enchanted by a sprigged muslin that cannot be washed safely."

"Frederick said you were a great connoisseur of fabric," Nancy said seriously.

"There is nothing that recommends a man more," Catherine said lovingly. The conversation continued for a few more minutes in relative gaiety, until the General spoke again and his children fell silent.

"Who are you actually related to, madam?" he asked.

Frederick corrected him, "Mrs. Tilney, you mean."

"You truly mean to uphold your clandestine marriage to this woman?" he demanded, "I am certain my agent could have it annulled. You must have been out of your mind."

"No, not at all," Frederick replied. "In fact, I had Mr. Foxx, whom I met on his yearly retreat to Bath, write up my marriage articles. Everything is quite legal and binding, I assure you. You might even say *irrevocably settled.*"

Frederick had never seen his father so openly angry, for all at once the General understood what Frederick knew and had done. Everyone at the table, save for Catherine, had a nearly perfect comprehension of what Nancy was. Frederick had married to disoblige his family and he had done it spectacularly. Nancy could not be further from what the General had wished his eldest son to marry, she was old, plain, poor, ill-mannered, and without consequence. She was a half-rate con woman. (This assessment of course, left out Nancy's many redeeming qualities). The General and Frederick alone knew the final truth: there was nothing his father could do about it.

"I have been meaning to give up my commission," Frederick continued, "I no longer believe in professions for elder sons. Nancy and I would very much like to reside here, in the village. With your permission of course."

"I do not think it would be prudent." General Tilney had returned to his usual feigned civility.

"Well if you will not have us, I mean to dwell in London. The interest on my commission is enough to rent a fine house somewhere, perhaps near some of your friends. I am sure they would be very pleased to meet my wife," Frederick speculated thoughtfully.

General Tilney was calm, he had entered a negotiation and this was something he understood. Unfortunately for himself, he knew that his son held nearly all the cards, "I do not think that London is a suitable place to start a family."

"I think so much the same! It would be best to raise the children in the country, I am exactly of your mind," Nancy said enthusiastically, though she did not quite understand the discussion.

"Of course," Frederick agreed, "Would you want your dear grandchildren so far from you? Where is little Harry today besides?"

Henry answered quickly, "With his nursemaid, he has a cold."

"I am sorry he could not be here, I am always distractedly fond of children," Nancy said. Catherine smiled. She continued, "I love to see children full of life and spirits; I cannot bear them if they are tame and quiet."

"Harry is a quiet sort of child, and I ought to know, having grown up with so many younger brothers and sisters myself," Catherine replied, "I am one of ten, you see, the first girl after three older brothers."

"Ten! It was always just myself and Lucy. I have often wished to have that many children myself, though I am afraid I will spoil them terribly."

"I cannot think that number would be possible for you," said General Tilney coldly.

"I am but one-and-thirty," Nancy retorted, "You would not believe, I lived with a lady for some months, Mrs. Hill, she was one of my distant cousins, on my mother's side if Lucy told me rightly, and she had a child at two-and-fifty! Why I could hardly believe it myself, for a lady of that age. It was her eighth babe and he was growing very well when I visited again, three years later. He was full of monkey tricks! He tore off my hat one day, and it had a great pin in it. I was so very alarmed; he took out the pin like a small sword and stabbed it right through a seat cushion. I knew not how to act, but his mother merely drew it out and returned both to myself, though my hat was badly crushed, and gave him some apricot marmalade to calm down his distress. I never saw anything like it, I declare."

Henry and Catherine were staring at Nancy in wonder, General Tilney was nearly red, and Frederick was, as usual, highly amused and nearly laughing. Nancy simply continued.

"Well he had gotten it into his head that hat pins were a great toy, the next I saw him he had found the lot of them, in his mother's dressing room, and stuck them all through a chair with great vigour. It looked nearly like a hedgehog and the boy was wailing as his mother tried to draw them out, but he had been very determined in his actions. The chair was destroyed and the pins all stored very high up from his reach. Yet, that was not the entire end of it: for a maid had to reach so high when she tried to fit her mistress into a hat that one day she tumbled and, I tell you the truth, she broke her arm. I never heard of a child causing quite so much mischief as that young boy."

"How have you not told me of that lady already?" Frederick laughed.

"I did not think of it until someone mentioned my age," Nancy shrugged.

Catherine, beginning to understand the joke, smiled at her new sister-in-law, "You must come have dinner with us at Woodston, may I call you Nancy?"

"Of course, I hope that we will be great friends, Catherine. You know I quite relied upon my own sister and Miss Elliot was a poor replacement."

Henry Tilney added, "Yes, you must come to Woodston. I ought to inform you however, that Miss Elliot is no more, she is Mrs. Bertram now. It was in the papers."

"How good for Mrs. Bertram! *She* was one to quite forget her own age you know. Put on airs like she was a ripe young woman of twenty," Nancy replied.

General Tilney suddenly stood and left the table. His children watched after him and when he was out of sight and hearing, Henry lifted his glass, "Nancy, I welcome you to the family, such as it is. And as for you Frederick, you have certainly bested me in filial disobedience, though I am not sure I meant to recommended it!"

51
Sir Walter

"What! every comfort of life knocked off! Journeys, London, servants, horses, table--contractions and restrictions every where! To live no longer with the decencies even of a private gentleman! No, he would sooner quit Kellynch Hall at once, than remain in it on such disgraceful terms." **Persuasion Ch 2**

About a week after they arrived at Kellynch, Sir Walter, on perceiving no material change in the number of servants or bounty of the table, was determined to speak to his wife. There were no guests, so after dinner they retired to the drawing room. Caroline offered to play and Sir Walter listened to her Italian songs. He had married such a beautiful, intelligent, and accomplished woman! He fancied, for a moment, that Caroline was just as accomplished as his daughter Anne, who had certainly been the most studious of his daughters. The thought quickly passed, for Sir Walter thought very meanly of his middle daughter and he thought far too highly of his wife for a just comparison to be made. When Caroline finished and they sat for a game of cribbage, Sir Walter brought up his concerns.

"Have you begun to hire more servants?" he asked. His wife looked somewhat surprised for a moment, but then smiled.

"Oh no, everything is running so smoothly, we may need another groom but I shall trust your judgement in that domain," she said.

"You do not realize that this is not the style of living that I am used to at Kellynch. I wish you might have been here before we removed to Bath," Sir Walter said. His wife simply did not grasp the problem.

"The Crofts have done us a great service, I think, in leaving us such well-trained servants. You were so very clever to get a family from a navy background, who I am sure think nothing of getting a house in order when they must command a ship usually. Normally, a house such as this might need many more servants, Somehow, we are getting by with what we have. But please, if there is something that you have noticed amiss, I will set it right."

Sir Walter agreed that he had been very clever in finding a navy family, it had all been his own doing he was sure. Sir Walter tried to think of any particular that he had found lacking, but nothing came to mind. He was simply used to... more.

Caroline continued, "It was a different sort of household before you left for Bath."

"Not so very different," Sir Walter scoffed, "Myself and Elizabeth." (There was no occasion for remembering Anne.)

"Yes, before it was you and two women, not so very different, but they were unmarried daughters. It is natural for you to keep a house in a grander fashion while you are focused on finding husbands for your children. Now, however, it is only you and your wife. There shall be no reduction in hospitality, we shall host all the dinners and guests you wish, perhaps two balls in the winter?"

Sir Walter was satisfied enough with this response. It was, after all, Elizabeth who had managed the household, Sir Walter hardly knew a thing about it. Caroline must know what she was doing, though she had not lived in a home quite as grand as Kellynch.

"And as for the dinners, they are not in the style I remember. If I had not married in such haste- I hate to think that you are offended."

"Offended by a fine ragout? Never! The table is exactly as it ought to be, I must compliment whomever hired that capital chef. I assure you; I will order a better dinner if we are to entertain, but with the family party only, I cannot see a smaller table as an evil."

Sir Walter reflected once again that he had married a very exceptional woman, she had very pretty notions. He was not sure who had hired the cook, but he imagined that he had played a part in it and therefore it was a compliment to himself. Accepting her arguments, he focused once more on the game. He was losing badly; Caroline must be very clever indeed!

52
Caroline
"I am quite in raptures with her beautiful little design for a table"
Pride and Prejudice Ch 10

Caroline looked at the smaller drawing room with pride; her first project as the proper lady of a manor was completed. All of Elizabeth's purchases were disposed of, most of them to market, though one or two vases had been nice enough to keep on display. She was careful not to displace anything of sentimental value, samplers from each of the girls remained prominently over the fireplace. She had added one of her own drawings to the opposing wall, a landscape she was particularly proud of. Nearly everything had come from storage, some items refinished. It was no longer uselessly fine; the room had less splendour, and more real elegance in her estimation.

She only hoped that Sir Walter would approve, then she could proceed with the rest of the house. Caroline wanted to restore Kellynch to its former beauty, but she also was very determined to strip the rooms of every remaining hint of Elizabeth's detestable taste. If it was somewhat spiteful, Caroline did not mind, she had no love for Mrs. Bertram.

Her own chambers remained much the same, she had ordered them painted and added a few of her personal pieces to the walls. Her own small collection of novels and poetry were on the bookshelves, which still looked too empty, but there would be time enough to fill them; she was busy. The two younger daughters of Sir Walter, Anne and Mary, were returning soon to the county and would be visiting together. She wanted to be ready for their arrival.

She felt very fortunate to have taken over from Mrs. Croft rather than Elizabeth. The house was already running very smoothly, she merely had a few adjustments to make to the servants and purchasing. Sir Walter had finer taste in food and they kept more horses. She was conscious of the expenses in a way she had not been before; a house that has fallen into debt might do so again, even with the additional funds her fortune provided. Caroline was determined to maintain her place as Lady of Kellynch Hall. *She would not be reduced to renting in Bath.*

There was one concession that Caroline made to Elizabeth's taste, her flower garden was exquisite. Caroline always had beautiful flowers to fill the rooms and to walk in the garden itself was magnificent. Elizabeth seemed to have chosen both for scent and beauty, the smell was intoxicating and the sights were dazzling. Caroline mourned that the garden could only be seen from the side of the house where the three girls' bedrooms had once been, her window faced a different prospect.

Sir Walter came looking for her. He had been out riding for the morning. He looked over the room critically. Caroline waited with mild anxiety; she had a good idea that she would be able to talk him into the design if he was displeased. If not, she could always distract him. He stood before her painting.

"This is yours?" he asked.

"Yes, of the park at Pemberley. You know of the Darcys?"

"I have met Mr. Darcy a few times in London; I knew his father but I have not met his wife. I am told you are connected to the family?"

"My brother and Mr. Darcy are close friends; they each married sisters two years ago, Jane and Elizabeth Bennet. They are both very good women; I am intimate with young Miss Darcy as well," Caroline spoke mildly, as much as she had despised Elizabeth at first, she no longer felt any strong feelings towards her. Caroline was far more suited to Sir Walter. She realized now that she would have never been so completely the mistress of Pemberley. Caroline had a feeling that Sir Walter would make no objections to her desires in respect to the house and grounds. He already seemed willing to surrender almost all of the management of Kellynch without much thought to it himself.

"The Darcy family lacks only a title to be truly respectable; I am surprised one has not yet been granted. You will invite them to come to Kellynch?"

"I will, but your daughters are to come soon," Caroline reminded him. She knew that Sir Walter loved Elizabeth, but she was still trying to determine how he felt about Anne and Mary. The relationship did not seem particularly strong. She also did not wish for the Darcys to visit until she had Kellynch looking as she wanted. Maybe there was a lingering amount of envy or pride.

"Yes of course. You will like Captain Wentworth I think, he was in the navy but you would not think it. His complexion has not suffered in the least! I have never seen a man in the navy but he is course and weather-beaten, but Wentworth has escaped it. He is a very respectable match for Anne."

"I am anxious to meet Mrs. Wentworth as well; Lady Russell speaks very highly of her," Caroline tried.

"Anne is... just Anne. Though she looked very well last year, before her confinement. I am told the child is a handsome one."

"Nothing can be more important," Caroline agree sardonically.

Sir Walter looked about the room and turned to Caroline, "It is exactly as I like. You must continue, do not spare any expense. I am fortunate to have a wife with such an excellent eye for elegance."

Caroline beamed, "Perfect," she thought. And then said, "Do not be alarmed, I will continue without any extravagant spending." She actually suspected that when the other pieces were sold, she would have more than when she began. Nearly everything was from storage, the restorations had only cost her time and effort, from herself and the servants.

Sir Walter pulled her close and kissed her. Caroline had not expected her body's response to remain so strong, "My rooms have just been painted," she said.

"Mine then?" Sir Walter whispered. Caroline nodded. She followed her husband to his dressing room; and stopped for a moment to admire herself in the full-length mirror. They did make a handsome couple indeed!

53
Sir Walter

Mr. Elton was actually on his road to London, and not meaning to return till the morrow, though it was the whist-club night, which he had been never known to miss before; and Mr. Perry had remonstrated with him about it, and told him how shabby it was in him, their best player, to absent himself, and tried very much to persuade him to put off his journey only one day; but it would not do. **Emma Ch 8**

Sir Walter spent at least two of his evenings a week at the chess club established among the gentlemen and half-gentlemen of the county. Mr. Musgrove and his son Mr. Charles Musgrove were members as well and were excited to see Sir Walter's return, as Admiral Croft had been trouncing them for nearly three years. Mr. Northam, a man of moderate property was always present, the country parson, Mr. Eaton, was never known to miss a meeting, and several other men attended when they could: Mr. Terry, the apothecary, Mr. Cole, a man of low birth made rich through trade, Mr. Charles Hayter, and Mr. Shepherd.

One might not imagine that Sir Walter would be interested in chess, and indeed he was not, but a gentleman must have something to do and his father had established the chess club long before. Sir Walter prided himself in having the most handsome ivory and ebony set and in purchasing the finest sherry for the group. They gathered at a hall in town, attached to a small inn, in a room used for assembly balls.

The foremost of these men, Musgrove, Northam, and Eaton, had all received visits from the principal couple and had all paid their respects to the new bride. By the second week of Sir Walter's return to Kellynch, everyone, with the exception of Mr. Charles Musgrove, who was out of town, had met the new Lady Elliot and Sir Walter was anxious to hear their opinion of his new wife. The feelings of each of these men were as follows.

Mr. Musgrove was happy to visit nearly anyone. The new Lady Elliot had a pleasing address and while her manners were formal, she had spoken very kindly to his wife. She had also received his younger daughters with interest and promised to hold and attend a few balls during the winter. This was everything that he could desire in a neighbour.

Mr. Northam, a married man with a young daughter and another child on the way, was friends with nearly everyone he met, so his approval was hardly worth notice. However, his wife, who had been governess to the Elliot girls, was more discerning and she had been greatly flattered by Lady Elliot's admiration of her baby. This was more than enough for Mr. Northam to greatly desire to see both the residents of Kellynch Hall on a regular basis.

Mr. Eaton was a man of some small property and he held the living of Kellynch. He had several private thoughts about Lady Elliot and meeting her reminded him that he really ought to find a wife. He was a young man living alone without much liking it.

The opinions of the lesser men were unimportant to Sir Walter. He would have them at the club, but they would not likely visit his house or he theirs. Sir Walter's respect of rank was too much for him to expand his circle. Only those who were truly respectable, in his eyes, were worthy of his condescension. While this had long restricted his enjoyment of the neighbourhood, it was something he would never cast aside. He was sure Lady Elliot would agree.

Sir Walter lost nearly every match that evening, but he did not mind. He won enough, perhaps by the contrivance of his companions, to be safe from discouragement and he drank enough to hardly notice. They allegedly played high, but the payments were so loosely demanded that Sir Walter most often called for a round of drink and put his debts behind him. So it was that night. He returned home rather late and rather drunk, pleased in the knowledge that everyone was in great envy of his wife. No man is offended by another man's admiration of the woman he loves, and since his wife only had eyes for him, there was nothing of torment.

54
Mrs. Elizabeth Bertram
Fanny was indeed the daughter that he wanted. **Mansfield Park Ch 48**

Elizabeth could not think of a time in her life when she had enjoyed herself less. She was very used to being out in society, as thin as it had been at Kellynch Hall, and celebrating in the distinction of her rank. Sir Thomas and Lady Bertram did not often mix in society, preferring their small family circle. Lady Bertram had no interest in anything beyond her Pug and sewing. And Susan Price. Elizabeth had no idea why a woman with Lady Bertram's status would be so devoted to a niece with no fortune, no education, and no proper manners. How was it that Elizabeth Elliot of Kellynch, the daughter of a baronet, was second to a poor cousin from Portsmouth? Nothing made any sense.

Then there was Fanny, the new wife of Sir Thomas' second son, Edmund. At least the couple no longer lived at home. Every time Fanny and Edmund visited, which was at least once a week, everyone was delighted. Elizabeth had no idea why. Fanny was small and inconsequential, and by birth she was nothing but the older sister of Susan. Fanny hardly said anything to Elizabeth, beyond what manners demanded, and Edmund spoke of nothing but his work and his home. Elizabeth was not at all diverted by the work of a country parson but the Bertrams listened with rapt attention. Who cared if Mrs. Nobody was sick or if Mr. Nothing was injured and could not work?

It was all backwards, Susan and Fanny ought to have been recognized as lower, insignificant beings, like Nancy; grateful for every scrap of notice they received from their august relatives. Susan was completely unwilling to cower or simper before her new cousin-in-law and Elizabeth found it reprehensible.

As for diversion, it might have been possible for Elizabeth to mix more with the neighbourhood if Tom wished to, but he did not have much inclination for it. He spent most of his mornings either with his father, attending to the plantations and tenants, or riding about the country. There were some visits from the neighbourhood to herself, as was duty to the bride, but Elizabeth was to find that the circle of the Bertrams was very small and they seemed to like it that way.

Almost as disappointing to Elizabeth was the house and people within it. No one seemed to have the proper idea of what was required to demonstrate their rank and consequence. Sir Thomas did not consent to a single alteration, beyond Elizabeth's own apartments and the small drawing room given to her use. She had tried to persuade them to purchase new carriages, and furnishings with no success. While she had once commanded most of her father's income, she was confined to the exact amount stipulated in her wedding articles. That portion even was smaller than she liked, why had she married a man in debt? She hated everything about Mansfield, everything in Northamptonshire, and most of all, she hated the Price sisters.

"Will we go to town in the winter?" she asked, as the family sat for supper.

"I am to go," Sir Thomas said, "But we no longer keep a house in town. Tom may choose to accompany me."

Elizabeth looked at her husband meaningfully, "No, I prefer to stay here and attend to the estate," Tom replied.

"How am I to know the newest styles and order new clothes?" Elizabeth demanded.

Sir Thomas replied, "My daughter Julia will be visiting in due time, I am sure she would be happy to tell you of the styles. We have adequate enough shops in Northampton."

This was not what Elizabeth had hoped to hear, later that evening she attacked her husband "I am sure the steward would be sufficient," she said to her husband, "And your brother is often here. Do you not think we could go, for some weeks at least?"

"No, I am set against it," Tom replied. He thought for a moment, "The air in town is not conducive to my health."

Elizabeth glared at her husband, but said nothing. Tom never wanted to do anything. She could not imagine a time in her life that had ever been so dull.

"Would you like to learn to ride?" Tom asked, "I would be happy to teach you. Then you could go out with Susan."

Elizabeth had never learned to ride, she saw it as quite beneath a woman of fortune, and she had no desire to accompany the ill-bred Susan Price! As for her husband, the less time she spent with him the better. He had nothing of interest to say, as he seldom spoke about her. She snapped angrily, "No thank you, I do quite well on my own."

Elizabeth had been regretting her decision to marry since almost her first week at Mansfield. This was torment, she wanted to go home!

55
Tom Bertram

Lady Bertram, sunk back in one corner of the sofa, the picture of health, wealth, ease, and tranquillity, was just falling into a gentle doze **Mansfield Park Ch 13**

Tom was not heartless; he could see that Elizabeth was unhappy but he was not sure what he could do to help her. He only knew that he needed to avoid London and therefore she could not go either. If he went to London, he was sure to run into someone who would take him to the races and once he was there, he was sure to make a wager. He was determined to stay away. So, he decided to talk to Elizabeth and find her something to do.

He found her that evening in her small drawing room alone, and began his interrogation, "Are you certain you do not wish to ride? There are many fine prospects in this area."

Elizabeth was in a particularly sour mood, "No, I have no inclination to ride."

That was a problem, Tom did not know of many other diversions, other than hunting, and women were not often permitted to partake in such sport. He was quite fond of a play, but Elizabeth had no love of reading, "My mother sews, Fanny does as well, and Susan likes to play piano. What other diversions could you desire?"

Elizabeth glared at him again, but decided to answer, "My father and I liked to ride in the open carriage and visit those within our neighbourhood who were deserving of our presence. I am used to hosting, dancing, and cards. Your family visits so few other people, my gowns are wasted here!"

"We play cards," Tom offered.

"Your mother is more liable to fall asleep than follow the game," Elizabeth snapped.

"Susan is a good player," Tom tried, "And my sister Fanny."

Elizabeth did not reply. Tom almost thought he heard her mumble something about "d---ed Prices" but he must have been mistaken.

"I know some great ladies visit the poor," Tom said.

"That is a job for the housekeeper, I hardly see your mother condescending to visit those filthy people."

"Well Susan takes care of that now, I understand. I think my Aunt Norris did it before, on our behalf, my mother is always too indisposed."

Elizabeth made no reply. This was not going very well.

"You know we have a hot house," Tom said finally, "Your father said something about flower gardens that you kept. I must think it too late in the year to attempt anything out of doors, but you may do something there."

Tom was gratified to see his wife finally look interested. "You think Sir Thomas would agree?"

"As long as you do not disturb the foodstuff, but my mother likes to have flowers in the winter, I think he would approve."

Elizabeth did not look very convinced and Tom was forced to admit that he rarely knew what his father truly wanted, but to his great fortune, the plan was approved. Elizabeth was shown to a section of the hot house for her own particular use. Seeds were purchased, pots and soil were prepared, and for the first time since arriving at Mansfield, Elizabeth was *slightly* less disagreeable.

56
Caroline

Mr. Bingley was unaffectedly civil in his answer, and forced his younger sister to be civil also, and say what the occasion required.
Pride and Prejudice, Ch 9

By the end of the month, Caroline had the house almost entirely put to rights. Except for Sir Walter's own rooms and the billiards room, which seemed to be his own design, Kellynch Hall had been restored to respectability. Sir Walter seemed very pleased with the changes, though he might have just been experiencing nostalgia. Almost everything had been liberated from storage and Caroline had used the profits from the sale of the new furniture to buy a few new items. Jane would be so proud of her economy. Lady Russell had come several times to visit and Caroline was pleased to see her approval.

The shrubbery and gardens were another matter entirely, Caroline would attempt to tackle that in the spring. She wished to change some of the park to reflect the new style and more closely resemble her model of Pemberley. Elizabeth's flower garden, however, would remain. While she expected to incur some cost in the outdoor improvements, she was not worried. Caroline knew how to keep to a budget.

Caroline's biggest personal expense had been resetting several of the Elliot family jewels. She had been quite happy to restore to Kellynch the selection that Elizabeth had brought to Bath. Caroline had no interest in creating discord between Sir Walter and his daughters, or herself, but she had been spurned by Elizabeth. To recover the jewels from Elizabeth's possession had been a small measure of revenge. Elizabeth should not have believed they were intended for herself; they were for Lady Elliot after all.

Mrs. Wentworth and Mrs. Mary Musgrove, with their families, were expected soon, Caroline went to her chamber to dress. Aliénor arranged her hair and she selected the gown she had worn on her wedding day for the occasion. It was perhaps too fine but she believed Sir Walter would like it.

"Ma'am, you have not had your courses since you came to Kellynch," Aliénor, her lady's maid said, as she finished with the gown.

"It is nearly time to find a midwife," Caroline said happily, "I am sure Mrs. Martin will know who I might request. However, to be certain, I will wait at least another fortnight." Caroline had very sanguine hopes, after all, she knew the action for getting children and she had been vigorous in committing it. However, right now there were other things to think of, she wanted Sir Walter's daughters to like her. She wished them to be excellent society since they were some of the only people of note within an easy distance.

Mary was the first to arrive with her husband, two older sons, and a very young daughter. Caroline was introduced, but she already knew their names.

"Have you yet been to Uppercross?" Mary asked.

"I have been, though at your request we have waited for your return to dine there. I would be delighted to visit your home and family," Caroline said obligingly.

"We do not yet live at Uppercross, we are in the cottage. You must not expect my small cottage to host much entertainment, but we are always going to the great house for some distraction," Mary said.

"How happy you must be to be near your family," Caroline said.

"We are near enough to Uppercross," she sniffed, "but not enough for them to visit us often."

"That must be difficult I am sure."

"The neighbourhood is very sparse, as I am sure you have found. There are so few people to visit."

Caroline was surprised how quickly Mary had moved from greeting to complaint, "Now that your father is back in residence you will be able to come here."

"We do not keep our own carriage, we hired one for the trip to London."

"Now that you have returned to the country, I will be happy to extend an invitation for dinner. If you wish to come; we might send our own coach for you."

Mary brightened, "That was not something that my father has ever thought to offer, he is always forgetting me."

Caroline had not yet brought the guests inside when Captain and Mrs. Wentworth arrived in a handsome landaulette. Anne did not look like her father at all, Caroline guessed her to be a picture of her mother. She was small and had soft instead of striking features. She was carrying a baby boy, the nursemaid followed. She greeted Caroline warmly as Mary collected her children.

"Lady Russell wrote to tell me about you," said she, "I am pleased to finally make your acquaintance."

"Our mutual friend spoke very highly of you as well," Caroline smiled, "I have a great hope that you will find my alterations to the manor much to your liking."

Caroline brought the party inside and watched the two daughter's reactions to the house carefully. Mary seemed hardly to notice; she was busy disposing of her children to the care of a nursemaid and banishing them back out of doors. The girl, who could not be older than two, stayed with her mother while the boys ran back outside. Anne, however, was looking about the room with an expression that spoke of longing and remembrance. Caroline was pleased, this was what she had hoped for.

"It is very much to my liking," said Anne, with some emotion.

"The estate has always had those who properly maintained its dignity," Caroline hinted, "though they may not have been noticed." Anne looked at her in a way that confirmed the compliment. The women sat in the parlour while the men proceeded to the billiards room.

"This is young Frederick?" asked Caroline, motioning towards Anne's son. She smiled and offered him to Caroline.

"Yes, he is but six months old," Anne said proudly. Caroline smiled down at him, she had only meant to ingratiate herself with Sir Walter's daughters -she had even learned all their children's names!- but the baby was very adorable and was smiling up at her. She felt an aching for a child of her own, not just to stop the entail, but for herself. She suddenly was understanding her sisters.

Mary was not to be left out and after only a few moments of letting Caroline hold Frederick, she burst out, "You must see my daughter, little Mary. Is she not a very pretty girl?"

Caroline handed Frederick back to his mother, who accepted him with a well-worn grace that gave Caroline a hint of the relationship between the sisters. The toddler was placed on Caroline's lap. Little Mary smiled for an instant before grasping one of Caroline's curls and pulling with all her strength. Caroline tried to free herself, while also trying not to scream or lose her precious hair.

"Mary, you must not do that," her mother said uselessly, as Anne flew to Caroline's assistance. The hand was unwound from the curl and Anne, still holding her own son, handed the girl a biscuit. Little Mary began to happily eat it, leaving Caroline with a lap full of crumbs, which she judged as preferable to damaged hair. Crumbs, of course, could be cleaned.

Mary began to ask Caroline about her family and Caroline soon had a strong suspicion that Mary was establishing, for her own satisfaction, her own primacy in birth if not in rank. This was an inclination that Caroline could easily understand and she was determined not to pay mind to it; as the current Lady Elliot, her rank was firmly set above the wife of a mere squire. Mary was very soon satisfied, as Caroline knew she would be. Despite her current circumstances, Caroline had been forced to remember that her father's fortune had been gained through trade.

When Mary was done, she yielded to Anne who asked with real interest if Caroline was finding the country and house to her liking. This vein of conversation proved to be rich, as whatever Caroline talked of, Mary was able to add her superior knowledge to its description and Anne could speak of pleasant past visits and memories. Mary's constant quest for supremacy even in conversation was odd to Caroline, since Mary was among family, but she graciously smiled at each possible insult and pretended not to hear what might have made her angry.

Lyme, where the Wentworths now resided, was not overly far from Kellynch and Caroline was invited to visit at her leisure. The Wentworths had taken a property called Greenlea, very small from Mary's description, just outside of the town. Caroline knew of it only from Sir Walter's description and she was very inclined to go. She only hoped they could while it was still warm enough to visit the Cobb.

"I will take you to the Cobb, if you promise to be careful on the steps," Anne smiled. Caroline suspected some story behind her words, but she would not hear it from Anne. Mary claimed the right to tell the whole of their time in Lyme and Anne yielded again to the interruption. Caroline had been determined to like both of the girls, but Anne was the one she knew she would truly esteem. Anne reminded her so strongly of Jane that she suddenly missed her brother's wife. Her constant employment during the past month had distracted her from her lack of friends and family.

Caroline was coming to understand that Mary was the sort of person who saw herself as very unfortunate and neglected, whatever the circumstance, and she was prepared to enter into whatever conversation would make Mary the most at ease. This seemed very acceptable to Mary. Caroline did not know if Mary would be overly pleasant company, but the neighbourhood was sparse and the Musgroves were second only to the Elliots. It was certainly a connection Caroline wished to promote, no matter Mary's worth as a friend.

By the time they sat for dinner, invitations were given on both sides and another dinner was decided upon at Kellynch, in about a month. Caroline was happy enough to have met Sir Walter's daughter of greatest worth, she would just need to tolerate the other two. She was more than glad to see Mary's frightful children set off that evening and was very determined to visit Anne as soon as she could contrive it.

57
Sir Walter

"I should recommend Gowland, the constant use of Gowland, during the spring months." **Persuasion Ch 16**

Sir Walter had gained much less satisfaction from the visit with his daughters' families than Caroline. Neither Anne nor Mary had ever been high in his affections and their marriages, while granting some trivial importance, had not made his regard more acute. His chief concerns had lain in finding his daughters still handsome, as much as they had never been quite as striking as Elizabeth, they had always been very fine girls. He was always prompt to remind them to stay out of the sun and he had even purchased new hats for each along with tins of Gowland. He was very disquieted by the information that Captain Wentworth had purchased a small boat and that his daughter had deigned to sail. This could do nothing for her complexion and he began to despair that he had not purchased her a hat with a wider brim.

No, what had occupied Sir Walter's mind the morning after his children had visited was the discovery of a single grey hair amid his thick, healthy, black locks. Sir Walter was inordinately proud that he had lived so long without the usual tarnish to his good looks but now he was distressed. What could be done? He considered that it might be plucked, but he was not certain that it would not just return.

Sir Walter consulted his valet and it was very discreetly suggested that he might obtain a black dye. This had never occurred to Sir Walter before, there had been no need! However, it seemed like the best solution. Sir Walter had discarded wigs as soon as they had fallen out of style, he had always wished to display his natural, glorious hair. Now he almost wished to return to those days. But no, he could obtain a dye. It was out of the question to look nearby; he could not have the local apothecary know that he wished to purchase such a disgraceful potion of age. He would go to Taunton.

He went out to find that Caroline had already engaged the coach to deliver food in the village. He was not deterred; he would take the barouche. He was already wearing a hat, which must have disguised his purpose as he spoke to her. She did not ask any questions as to his endeavours and he did not supply any. His activities must be completed in utmost secrecy. He was forming plans for the purchase of the dye the entire time he travelled.

Sir Walter went to the best apothecary in Taunton and made his request. He had the perfect plan. He claimed the dye to be for Mary, for she was the only one of his daughters who shared his exact colour of hair. He wished he had concocted a plan that did not involve a member of his family, though perhaps it would not be thought that the greying hair was from his side, after all, his hair was magnificent. He could hardly be faulted for it changing at so late an age! The item was purchased and Sir Walter knew he would need to wait a few days to ensure that no nasty gossip would be heard in the village.

Sir Walter reflected, on the ride home, that this had been one of the most trying days of his life. To find his own beauty diminished was a constant fear. The day of Caroline's attack by Mr. Elliot had been distressing, yes. The day they had discovered his cousin's deception two years previously had been galling indeed! But it was nothing to this. There was little that bothered Sir Walter beyond his own reputation and appearance. His life had been easy and his upbringing happy. Perhaps one can understand his lack of perspective on matters of true importance and consequence. Or not.

58
Caroline

She had had many a hint from Mr. Knightley and some from her own heart, as to her deficiency—but none were equal to counteract the persuasion of its being very disagreeable,—a waste of time—tiresome women—and all the horror of being in danger of falling in with the second-rate and third-rate of Highbury, who were calling on them for ever, and therefore she seldom went near them. **Emma Ch 19**

Caroline spent that morning preparing the carriage with food baskets for the village. She had spoken to the parson, Mr. Eaton, over the last month, and had a good idea of whom should receive the extra food from the previous dinner. She had been warned, curiously, to visit Miss Gates and her elderly mother last. Caroline was not sure why. She had been about the village a few times, bringing food to the sick and poor, but this was the first time she had enough extra to make a general delivery. The Gateses had only just returned from Bath themselves and Caroline had yet to meet them.

Sir Walter happened to pass her before she set out and stopped curiously, "What are you about?" he asked.

"I am bringing food parcels to the village," she said smiling.

"Personally? Whatever for? Elizabeth always had the housekeeper do it," Sir Walter scoffed.

Caroline corrected him in her head, she was pretty certain that Anne had taken over that particular duty. She gave her best smile, "It is among the duties of a lady of my stature, I understand. If you do not wish for me to go- but I do enjoy it."

Sir Walter seemed confused but replied, "If you wish to, I cannot object, but it is not something I have ever enjoyed. I would much prefer not to deal with the tenants and inhabitants of the village at all. I leave that to my agent and steward. They are so... un-genteel."

Caroline was unsurprised: Sir Walter did not have any inclination to mix far below his class. Socially, Caroline was of one mind with her husband, but when it came to charity she had no such scruples. Had it not been trained into her by her mother and school; she would have learned rightly from Jane that to visit the poor and sick was her duty. She hoped that she was good enough to enjoy charity for its own sake, but she also enjoyed the recognition and appreciation that was shown to her. She would not begrudge a morning or two devoted to such an effort.

She was driven out and visited each house with some pleasure and little trouble. At last, with her final basket, she came upon the Gates establishment, in some small rooms, and was let in by the maid. Mrs. Gates was the widow of the former parson, with a small income and a grown, unmarried daughter of about forty who lived with her. Their maid let Caroline in and Miss Gates cordially rose to meet her.

"Oh, my dear madam, I am sorry we have not yet made your acquaintance- Oh! Such a beautiful basket. You are too bountiful."

"You are welcome," Caroline replied graciously.

"Oh, but I must get you some tea, please sit. My dear Lady Elliot, as my mother says, people are always only too good to us. If ever there were people who, without having great wealth themselves, had everything they could wish for, I am sure it is us. We may well say 'our lot is cast in a goodly heritage'. Well, Lady Elliot, you must take some tea. It is not the finest but we did bring it back from Bath just this week. Mr. Eaton must have been good enough to have informed you of our return. We were in the Westgate buildings, very near the hot baths- have you been to the hot baths? It was a very simple situation for we only brought our maid but we had a wonderful nurse the sister of our landlady. She was called Nurse Rooke, a nurse by profession indeed, and who had been chanced to be unemployed when we arrived. She was ever so attentive to my mother, most kind, and very obliging. Why, without her I doubt that my dear mother would have truly been set to rights but there she was. Helping us with the cure and telling us all that was going on about town. But you have just been in Bath, I am sure there is nothing to tell that you have not heard. Well, Sally is to wash the kitchen and then I will have all this put away. You are too good, Lady Elliot. Would you like a scone?"

Caroline, who had stopped listening some time before, started, and seeing the offered plate, accepted a scone. She wondered how soon it would be within her power to quit the house.

"Is your mother at home?" she asked politely.

"Oh yes, she is just lying down. When I heard the knock, I sent Sally to let you in- I wanted to check on Mrs. Gates- dear mamma- but she was very out of sorts and could not come. So- there was a slight delay of letting you in- I am ashamed- but somehow there was a little bustle- I had not expected anyone to be coming. And when Sally announced who it was, I was sure dear mamma would wish to see you- but she is so very indisposed. I am so sorry and ashamed that she is not here to greet you. Do not think the cure in Bath has gone ill, I believe it to be the effect of too many minced pies yesterday."

"No, no," Caroline cut in, "If your mother is doing poorly it is no affront to me. I am only glad that I might have come to meet you. I fear I must be going," Caroline searched her mind for a reason, "I still must call on Mrs. Clark and ask what she needs for the new child." This had been her previous visit.

"Oh yes! Mrs. Clark is expecting again and we have heard now upon our return-"

"Good day, Miss Gates," Caroline said, offering her hand cordially. Miss Gates grasped it and continued.

"You are too kind," Miss Gates continued, "So very kind, Lady Elliot. I am so very pleased to have met you. Why Mr. Eaton did stop by when we returned and he told us of the wedding. But then we heard all from Nurse Rooke. The sudden departure of Sir Walter has been talked off all over Bath. I must thank you again for the basket, it will be just what my mother needs. She has very bad fits sometimes but some vittles will set her back to rights."

Caroline rode back to Kellynch Hall feeling that she had indeed done a very great service to the poor of the village that day, if only by enduring Miss Gates. She made a note that perhaps it might be better to send future parcels to that particular home via Mrs. Martin. Caroline reproached herself, she knew it was right to do it herself. At least next time, she would be prepared. She would need to figure out how to politely refuse entering.

Sir Walter was returning to the hall around the same time as Caroline. She immediately covered any lingering annoyance in her face with a look of placid contentment. When Sir Walter asked her how it had been, she replied cheerfully, "It was a very pleasant trip, I think we ought to invite the Gateses to dinner sometime."

For the first time since their marriage, Sir Walter questioned his wife's judgement.

59
Lady Russell

Herself the widow of only a knight, she gave the dignity of a baronet all its due **Persuasion Ch 2**

Lady Russell returned home after a visit to Kellynch more than usually pleased. She enjoyed being right, as much as the next person, and she had been entirely correct about Caroline. The new Lady Elliot was exactly as she wished her to be.

It had long been a desire of Lady Russell's to restore the name of Kellynch and Elliot to their proper place, but she saw that Elizabeth was unequal to the task, extremely unwilling to act as a true patroness to the village and a gracious host in her own home. When Mr. Elliot had seemed enamoured with Anne, Lady Russell had rejoiced. Anne already acted as a proper lady ought and she would have set everything right. It had been a disappointment to learn that Mr. Elliot was unscrupulous and cruel. Since that time, Lady Russell had tried to encourage Sir Walter to find a wife, but until his recent urgency, she had not succeeded.

In talking to young women of high and lower rank, Lady Russell had become convinced that a lady of lower birth would be preferable. That sort of woman was taught the proper duties of a lady as a matter of course, but did not have the upbringing to know that it was easy to discard those duties without consequence. Caroline's notion of a lady was formed from reading, school, and her sister-in-law, Mrs. Bingley, whom Lady Russell wished to meet, and these ideas were pure and naively idealistic. Caroline might not be truly benevolent, but she was determined to play a lady and therefore she acted the part. That would be enough, until she actually grew to love the people she would help.

Lady Russell now found herself almost entirely content. Elizabeth was finally gone, though she spared a thought for the new village that Mrs. Bertram was undoubtedly ignoring. Anne was married and happy, and if only she had settled somewhat closer it would have been entirely perfect. Kellynch Hall was being restored to its former glory. Lady Russell had stood for a moment before leaving the house, admiring one of the pieces that her dear friend had loved, and imaging fifteen long years ago when they had been together.

If only Caroline could produce the blessed heir, everything would be entirely perfect. Lady Russell had finally persuaded everyone to do as she wished!

60
Caroline

Mary, often a little unwell, and always thinking a great deal of her own complaints **Persuasion Ch 5**

It was not long after this that Sir Walter and Caroline dined with the Musgroves at Uppercross. Mary had not thought it right for them to sit for dinner without her, and had told her father so. Mr. and Mrs. Musgrove had called on the Elliots frequently since their return and those visits had been returned. The Musgroves were the second family in the neighbourhood and were the most acceptable acquaintances within the distance of a morning visit. For that reason, Caroline was determined to like them, though they were not the sort of people she would have sought out if they had been in town and in a greater variety of company.

The Musgroves only had two daughters at home. The eldest two, Mrs. Hayter and Mrs. Benwick, were married and settled. The first not far from Uppercross and the second was at sea with her husband. Catherine and Isabella Musgrove were eighteen and seventeen, the youngest recently done with school. Caroline learned that there were two more young boys, still away for their education, in addition to their eldest son Charles, Mary's husband. Caroline thought it quite amazing that Mrs. Musgrove had lived to have eight children, to see them growing up around her, and to enjoy excellent health herself.

Caroline was occasionally chagrined by the informal manners of Mrs. Musgrove, who did not always attend to the distinction of rank, but she had very easy and open manners. While the elder Musgroves were not as educated as she might like; the daughters were intelligent and well-read. Caroline enjoyed their company. If Anne reminded Caroline of her dear sister Jane, then the Musgroves reminded her of Charles. Caroline looked forward to a time when her brother would visit and she might host them all together. They were the exact sort of people that Charles liked.

Mary had insisted that they come to the cottage first, to distinguish her rank, before they proceeded to the great house.

Caroline was again unwilling to cause discord in the family, so she complied.

"They have been ignoring me all day," Mary complained when her guests arrived, "Since they are to host there is no reason in their mind to consult me, even though you are my family and I ought to have a hand in the planning. I have taken it upon myself to remind Mrs. Musgrove that you are to lead the way, as Lady Elliot, with myself behind. She is never remembering that I am to lead when we dine."

Caroline had not been worried, for when Sir Walter visited, the Musgroves were always properly attentive to their guests. She did not know why Mary expected the Musgroves to stand on ceremony when it was only the family circle. Charles joined them and he and Sir Walter began to speak of guns and dogs, leaving the ladies to their own discussions as they crossed the park to the great house.

"I am glad we thought to leave the children at home," Mary said, "for their grandparents are always giving them too many sweets and then they are sick and cross for me."

"I cannot think it strange that the Musgroves would dote upon their grandchildren," Caroline replied mildly.

"It makes them behave so terribly for me, as I am not always indulging their every demand. They hardly listen at all- and Charles is no help."

"That is certainly difficult."

"Walter and Charles would be no problem at all if I always had my way with them, but I must send them to the great house or they would be very cross with me. It is no great help to me."

Caroline smiled and agreed that this all sounded very problematic. With her brief knowledge of Mary's parenting, chiefly formed while Mary's daughter was attempting to rip out a lock of Caroline's hair, she had determined that the problem might lie another way, but she said nothing. There was never anything good that had come from a childless woman instructing a mother in how to attend to her children.

"When will little Charles and Walter attend school?" she redirected instead.

"I do not think we will send them away," Mary retorted, "We will have a tutor here, I am sure no expense will be spared. I cannot stand to have them away from me."

Caroline sensed this was an insult to her hosts and so she tried again, though it was not a subject that she would have tried if she had any other option, "I have heard you are often unwell."

Caroline had determined rightly; Mary quickly began to list her symptoms and the dreadful state that her husband often left her in when she was feeling poorly. It was not a subject that anyone really desires to hear about, but it left Caroline able to be a neutral party. This discussion covered the time they walked to the great house, at which point civilities cut Mary off, who was by no means done.

As Caroline had met them all before, the introductions were quick and largely for the benefit of Mary's strict sense of propriety. The dinner was lively, the girls had young men and dresses to speak about, the men discussed hunting and politics, and Mary, unwilling or unable to enter more fully into the loving family she had married into, sat next to Caroline and said very little that was not a complaint. The Musgroves, in a manner that spoke of long-held indulgence of Mary, ignored her gripes and tried to include her in their pleasures. Caroline began to realize that Mary was not a person to be scorned, instead her feelings changed to pity.

Caroline could not quite understand why Mary was not happy, but she wanted to find some way to help. In Caroline's mind, the problem must root from being married but waiting for inheritance, that would be horrid to herself. Maybe if Mary was able to take on some of her role, she would be more contented? Caroline, seeing this problem, was at a loss of what could be done. Mary was older than herself and must be firmly set in her ways. However, if only for her own ease, Caroline was determined to attempt... something.

Caroline had one idea, which sprang suddenly to her mind. She took time at the end of the dinner to invite Mary, and Mary alone, to Kellynch the next Tuesday. She promised to send the best carriage for her comfort. Mary was gratified and Caroline schemed. If this worked, it would solve two pressing problems.

61
Tom Bertram

"She finds Miss Pope a treasure. 'Lady Catherine,' said she, 'you have given me a treasure.'" **Pride and Prejudice Ch 29**

Tom had ridden rather further while hunting than usual and accidentally crossed into the estate of the Maddoxes. The families were on friendly terms and he had no fear of offending anyone, but as he turned to go, the second young man of the house called out to him. Charles was out shooting and upon seeing Tom said, "Bertram! I heard you were back in the country. Is it true you mean to reside at Mansfield permanently?"

"Yes, that is my resolution," Tom said.

"You are greatly missed in London."

"I got married," Tom offered as explanation.

"An all too common affliction," Charles said in a conciliatory tone, "But not one that usually prevents a man from doing whatever he likes."

"No, not usually," Tom agreed, but said no more.

"Do you know, we have a mutual friend in town. A certain Mr. Charles Anderson, do you remember him?"

Tom answered mildly, though he was distressed to hear the name., "Yes, of course. Though I have not seen him these two years."

Charles looked at Tom meaningfully, "I have been trying to meet you, now that you are settled at Mansfield. According to my friend, you and I take great enjoyment in the same diversions."

Tom was momentarily taken aback; did he really mean what Tom hoped? He asked cautiously, "What, are you thinking of marrying yourself?"

"Not for the world!" Charles laughed, "I have never had the inclination. Never much seen a woman I like."

Tom was not sure if he had ever felt so absolutely excited in his life. There could be no greater luck than this! To have found a person like himself such an easy distance from home was more than he had imagined possible.

"Now that I am establishing my law practice," Charles said, "I have taken some offices and a few rooms in Northampton. You ought to come and see them sometime."

This invitation was readily accepted. Thus began their intimacy and thus Tom returned to his more usual happy self. Now his only problem was his miserable wife.

Tom knew there was no use in talking to Elizabeth so instead he thought back to everything he knew about her. When she was in Bath, she had always had that woman, Miss Steele around. Tom understood that his mother liked having Susan for a companion and Elizabeth had complained about being alone. He was absolutely certain of his genius and went to speak about it to his mother. He had a plan!

Lady Bertram had some idea of what to do when a lady's companion was wished for. She wrote to a woman of her acquaintance, whom she had not seen for some time. This lady, she was sure, knew exactly how to find a suitable young woman. In due time, Lady Bertram received a response with a very favourable offer.

"Her name is Lady Catherine de Bourgh," she said, while reclining on her couch, "It was she that helped me secure Miss Lee, our governess, for my own daughters. I have kept up correspondence with the lady, she is always recommending remedies for my indisposition. None of them have had any effect, but I trust her judgement completely."

Elizabeth, now an eager participant in the plan, while not entirely sure she trusted anyone who kept up correspondence with the dullest lady in the world, was eager to hear of the outcome, "And what has she said?"

"Lady Catherine has written that a young woman, Miss Pope, has recently completed a contract with a Lady Metcalf. Miss Pope is talked of as an absolute treasure. She is certain that this woman would be a delightful companion," Lady Bertram said, and then on making such a long speech, looked rather tired. Susan took up the letter.

"'I must mention that Miss Pope is rather plain and while I think her young, she is nearly seven-and-twenty.', that is the rest of the letter," Susan finished.

Elizabeth readily consented. Miss Pope sounded exactly like the proper woman. Letters were sent and everyone secretly agreed that if a companion would make Elizabeth even one quarter less disagreeable, she would be worth every penny of her salary.

62
Caroline

"These are the sights, Harriet, to do one good. How trifling they make every thing else appear!—I feel now as if I could think of nothing but these poor creatures all the rest of the day; and yet, who can say how soon it may all vanish from my mind?" **Emma Ch 10**

Caroline was not entirely sure of her plan. If it did not work, she felt that it would be almost cruel to subject Mary to Miss Gates, but if it was successful, Caroline would solve two problems of her own with very little difficulty. Caroline first hosted Mary for refreshments and indulgently listened to her complaints and imagined illnesses and slights. Then she presented her true plan.

"There is a mother and daughter in the village, the widow of the former rector?"

"Yes, the Gateses. I have seen them at church, back when I lived at home."

"When I visited last, Mrs. Gates expressed a dear wish to see you again. She had seen you frequently at one time, I understand."

"Mrs. Gates, when her husband was alive, visited us at Kellynch. I remember her fondly. We had not thought it proper to see her after they were reduced to such a state."

"I assure you, with your family connection to the Gateses, there is nothing anyone could say about the visit."

Mary regarded Caroline sceptically; undoubtedly assessing how much she should trust the new lady of Kellynch, whom she knew to be of lesser birth than herself. Caroline continued, "I have some vegetables from the home farm if you wish to bring them as well. I will accompany you, though I must visit a family in the village with a new baby. I think you are the only one that can make Mrs. Gates feel at ease, my visits have been insufficient."

Mary assented and Caroline was elated. She could only hope that the rest of the plan went off smoothly. The ladies were conveyed and Caroline left Mary at the doorstep of the Gates home. Everything else must unfold as it would, Caroline could not interfere, only wait.

Caroline, finishing her own visit, looked towards the Gates' house, which was in view of the house where she had been calling, and seeing no Mary, continued to the only shop in town to find some ribbon. She lingered as long as possible, and then when she still saw no Mary, she sat in her carriage and read a book. Eventually, the door opened and Mary emerged. Caroline could not discern her mood and went at once to meet her.

"It was very charming to visit the Gateses I must say," Mary began, with a look of gratification that Caroline had never seen before on her face, "They were so very complimentary about the basket, I hope you do not mind that I let them think it my own doing. And Miss Gates was ever so kind as to listen to my grievances. Her mother must have the same constitution as myself. Mrs. Gates was very pleased to see me, just as you said she would be, she gave me this handkerchief for little Mary, is it not lovely?"

Caroline gave it all the praise she could, "Do you wish to visit again? I would be happy to provide the carriage."

"Oh yes, I should like that above all things."

Caroline was gratified. She liked to think herself secure in her beauty, intelligence, and rank, but she appreciated the small reminder of her own importance that charity afforded. Mary never, if she could help it, associated with anyone below her and in Caroline's opinion, only compared herself to those even higher than herself. It must be good for Mary to visit the poor and be reminded of her own importance.

Upon hearing that the Gates were in very good health, Caroline reflected fondly on how very good of a patroness she must be to the poor people of Kellynch. How much they must appreciate her kind condescension! Perhaps her motives were not always entirely generous, she had a keen interest in being thought much more benevolent than Elizabeth had been and in recommending herself to the world as a benefactor of those in want. It is always possible, however, that one who plays a role will eventually become that which she seeks to emulate. To those under Caroline's protection however, all of this mattered very little, as long as they were fed and clothed, they cared very little for the motive behind it.

To complete her day, Caroline wrote a long letter to her friend Susan, who had been forever meaning to visit, but had begged forgiveness for her most recent delay. There was a very interesting man in town whom Susan was eager to know better. Susan was confident that Caroline would like him, once she was more certain of his intentions. No name was supplied, but Susan hinted at the letters H.C. Caroline missed her friend but she could not begrudge her a second chance at a happy marriage. She was sure whomever H.C. was, he must have shown marked interest to keep Susan in town.

63
Mrs. Martin

The housekeeper added, "I have never known a cross word from him in my life, and I have known him ever since he was four years old." **Pride and Prejudice Ch 43**

Mrs. Martin was walking away from her mistress's room, feeling quite pleased. For Lady Elliot to already suspect, with great evidence, a most desired condition, could only be a cause for celebration. Mrs. Martin had made known to her the best midwife in the county and she was now anticipating the happy day when the news could be announced. She would be delighted to see Kellynch full with children again; it had been much too long since the last Elliot baby was born. It was not for the family's sake that she was really happy, a housekeeper must always detest change in management and an heir would keep the house from falling into different hands on the sad day of Sir Walter's demise.

Additionally, Mrs. Martin had a very smart girl of fifteen of her own, she would be the exact right age to serve as a nursery-maid! What a good position for her girl. Much better to work in the nursery than the kitchen.

She noticed Aliénor heading towards her mistress's room, bearing a cup of tea. Lady Elliot had been suffering a headache, one of the consequences of her condition Mrs. Martin suspected. Lady Elliot had been fortunate thus far, the former mistress had always been extremely ill during her pregnancies. Or at least she had always said that she was.

As Mrs. Martin passed the butler's kitchen, where the tea for Lady Elliot had been prepared, she stopped. There was a strange smell, one she recognized, though she could not place it immediately. Suddenly the memory came flooding back, it had been nearly ten years! A scullery maid had become pregnant and she had taken that very thing, Mrs. Martin shuddered at the thought. The maid had nearly died, though she had achieved her goal. Since that day, she had always expressly forbidden it to the maids. Why would it be here? As far as she knew, none of the unwed servants were with child...

Mrs. Martin could not imagine that any of her maids would ever prepare it, but there was one female servant not under her control, and she was headed to the bedroom of Lady Elliot! Mrs. Martin broke into a run, her skirts billowing around her. It was not far, Aliénor was already within. Mrs. Martin threw open the door to see Lady Elliot holding the poison tea, her lady's maid waiting patiently beside her.

Mrs. Martin did not wait to catch her breath to speak, she saw that the cup was still full and she dashed it from her lady's hands in one rough motion. It smashed spectacularly on the floor, undoubtedly ruining the carpet.

"Mrs. Martin!" Lady Elliot cried. Aliénor fled the room. Mrs. Martin struggled to take a deep breath.

"John!" she roared. Lady Elliot shrank back in her bed, clearly frightened. Mrs. Martin breathed deeply again, "It was poison." she managed, before rushing out of the room. John, the footman who she knew to be nearest at hand, was running towards the chamber. Mrs. Martin rushed to meet him.

"Ma'am?"

"Aliénor, the lady's maid has fled, you must detain her."

"Ma'am?" John said again, but the severe look on Mrs. Martin's face sent him flying in the given direction. Several servants had heard the noise and were coming towards Mrs. Martin. She chose another footman.

"You must go to Aliénor's chamber, lock the door and do not admit a soul."

Mrs. Martin was breathing quickly still, but the effort of the running had passed. She was horrified at what had nearly happened; she turned back inside her mistress's room. Lady Elliot was standing now, looking at Mrs. Martin with unrestrained fear and wonder.

"Ma'am, I cannot begin to explain the motive, but your woman, she had brought you a tea-"

"Yes, for my headache."

"No, I have seen it before among the maids. It is meant to end a child, my lady."

Mrs. Martin watched Lady Elliot's growing horror as she realized what had been meant, "Aliénor? But she has been with me these last five years..." Lady Elliot began to weep. Mrs. Martin, breaking decorum, held her.

"I have sent a man to guard her room, we will find her out," she said to the inconsolable lady. To one of the gathered maids she whispered, "Find Sir Walter at once."

64
Sir Walter

"Is there no one to help me?" were the first words which burst from Captain Wentworth, in a tone of despair, and as if all his own strength were gone. **Persuasion Ch 12**

Sir Walter was in the breakfast parlour when he heard bellowing from within his manor. It seemed rather strange; he thought he had very proper servants. Caroline had assured him that the house was in excellent order. He could hardly imagine what had been the cause of such uncouthly raised voices. Setting down his cutlery, he started towards the source of the commotion. A maid nearly ran into him as he left the room.

"Your wife-" was all she said and Sir Walter was running towards her chamber. She was only in bed with a headache, he had thought. The scene he beheld as the servants parted was alarming, there was a deep brown liquid spilled on the bed and floor, a smashed fine china cup in the midst of it. Caroline, not yet dressed, was sobbing loudly in the arms of his housekeeper. This had never happened before. He stood there dumbly.

Mrs. Martin motioned for him to come closer and she deftly transferred his weeping wife from herself to him. She was soon directing the servants, Sir Walter moved Caroline further from the mess on the floor as two maids began to clean it. One had a basket where they carefully placed the cloths, carpet, and cup. Sir Walter watched in some confusion, the smell coming from the liquid was not one he recognized.

"Your wife is with child," Mrs. Martin said. Sir Walter could not connect those words with the current circumstances, but he felt his heart leap with exultation. So soon! Her next words were nearly lost in his rapid happy thinking, "I have seen this tea used before, for women who find themselves *in a way*. Her maid brought it to her. I have no doubt she knew what it was."

"Aliénor?" Sir Walter demanded; Mrs. Martin nodded.

"She brought it," Caroline managed, in a low strained voice, "after I spoke to Mrs. Martin about my condition. She said it was for my headache," Caroline took in a ragged breath, "If it had not been for you-" she looked at Mrs. Martin, and sobs took her once more.

Sir Walter was having difficulty understanding what was being said. His wife was pregnant, that was excellent news! Everything else was not penetrating his mind. Aliénor was a very elegant lady, how could someone so refined be evil? This did not seem entirely possible. Who would want to harm Caroline?

"Where is she?" Sir Walter demanded.

"I sent John after her, he has not yet returned."

Sir Walter was torn between the crying woman in his arms and the fleeing one, who might have been a murderess but for the actions of Mrs. Martin. He was trying to remember what Lady Russell had taught him to do with weeping women, but he was certain running after the culprit was not part of that lesson. Caroline broke out of his grasp and looked at him with a mixture of sorrow and fury.

"You must find her," she demanded.

Sir Walter addressed Mrs. Martin, "Alert the steward, he needs to send for the constable and notify the magistrate." She nodded and called one of the footmen to carry out the task. Sir Walter had meant to set out directly, but his boots were entirely unfit for chasing an attempted murderess and he was delayed for a full quarter of an hour selecting the right pair. He then assembled the remaining servants and formed them into parties, sending the women to each area of the house and half the men to the shrubberies and gardens. The rest followed him to the stable to search the woods. He would find Aliénor; he would discover why she had tried to ruin his happiness.

65
Caroline/Lady Russell

She continued by the side of her sister, with little intermission the whole afternoon, calming every fear, satisfying every inquiry of her enfeebled spirits, supplying every succour, and watching almost every look and every breath. **Sense and Sensibility Ch 43**

Caroline was still wearing her nightgown, wrapped in a warm shawl, when Lady Russell was admitted into her chambers. Mrs. Martin had stayed with her, standing like a guard beside her chair, and giving orders to rushing servants. When Lady Russell arrived, the housekeeper finally took her leave, bearing the box with the poisoned tea. Caroline appeared calmer, but she was deeply shaken.

"Dear Caroline, are you well?" Lady Russell began, sitting beside her and taking her hand.

"I do not know what to think," Caroline replied, "I do not understand what happened."

Lady Russell did not have any explanation to give, but she offered her presence as comfort. Caroline had no more tears, she felt numb.

"They will find her and find out her motive. Every man is searching the grounds. She could not have gone far," Lady Russell offered. She knew anything she could say was insufficient. It was too great a betrayal, too horrifying a prospect if it had succeeded.

"I do not know what to do," Caroline whispered.

Lady Russell had some answer for that, "You ought to dress soon. Sir Walter has called the constable. He will want to hear what has happened, if you can bear to speak of it, I can assist you."

Caroline nodded and together they selected a simple morning dress with dark fabric. Lady Russell helped Caroline into it and had enough skill to capture her hair with a turban. Caroline was grateful; she could not have done anything by herself: her hands were still trembling. She looked at the floor where the cup had smashed and shuddered. In a few moments, it would have been too late. She was lost in thought, Lady Russell stayed quiet beside her; her hand comfortingly resting on Caroline's arm.

A knock at the door announced Mrs. Martin's return. She was holding several letters in her hands, "We discovered these in her room," said she, as she handed them to Caroline.

Caroline took the letters and read the direction on the first. It was made out to her maid; though it was directed to their quarters in Bath. She opened it and looked at once at the signature, Mr. W. Elliot. She gasped and looked up at Mrs. Martin.

"We have not located her yet, ma'am, but the letters were well hidden and they have revealed all we needed to know. Mr. Elliot promised her something if she prevented his disinheritance."

Lady Russell took the rest of the letters from Caroline, who was shaking as she held the first. She was trying to read the neat handwriting but she could not make a word out. She remembered when he had attacked her in Bath, the fear she had felt when he held her. He had not been seen in London or Bath since that day, she had thought him gone, defeated. Her own maid…

"She was prudent enough not to burn these," Lady Russell observed, "Each one demands that she does. What could he have promised her? To marry? You cannot hold a man to an agreement such as this before the law. She can only condemn them both!"

"She asked me for a day's holiday, quite suddenly, in Bath, to meet with childhood friend. It was two days after I saw Mr. Elliot," Caroline said. The request had been unusual, but she had agreed readily. She had liked Aliénor.

Lady Russell took Caroline's hands and looked at her steadily, "At least we understand, that must be a small comfort. They will find her; they will find Mr. Elliot. Sir Walter will see them brought to justice. Given what I know of Mr. Elliot's character, I am no longer surprised by any of this."

"What do you know of him?"

"I do not think Sir Walter believed the whole of it, but I did. Mr Elliot is a man without heart or conscience; a designing, wary, cold-blooded being, who thinks only of himself; whom for his own interest or ease, would be guilty of any cruelty, or any treachery, that could be perpetrated without risk of his general character. This, I suspect is why he acted through such means! He has no feeling for others. He is totally beyond the reach of any sentiment of justice or compassion. He is black at heart, hollow and black."

Caroline could not help but be terrified by such a description and cried out, "All of this!"

"Try to remember that you have friends here, I will not leave you today, and Mrs. Martin has done you a great service."

Caroline nodded. She was deeply frightened, if her own maid could be turned against her, how could she trust anyone else. Aliénor had been with her such a long time; Caroline had always been kind to her. She had given her an extra half day holiday each month! Had Mr. Elliot turned anyone else? Caroline tried to recall- Sir Walter had once said Mr. Elliot had never been to Kellynch, but he had been away himself for nearly three years.

Caroline's only comfort was that Lady Russell remained until nightfall when Sir Walter returned.

66
Sir Walter

The two elegant ladies who waited on his [Bingley's] sisters. **Pride and Prejudice Ch 9**

Sir Walter's day had not been a prosperous one, Aliénor had not been found and more than that, he had ruined his boots and torn his sleeve in the fruitless pursuit. He had been among the search party until the arrival of the constable. When he arrived, Sir Walter became acquainted with the evidence thus far, the letters found between the maid and Mr. Elliot, the poisoned tea, and the apparent motives of the pair. He had also reported a stolen horse, the maid must have it. Mr. Elliot had not been seen since his attempt to assault Caroline in Bath. Sir Walter had no notion of how to find him.

There was far too much to do for Sir Walter's liking; he mostly wished to see Caroline again and see that she was in good health. This was of utmost importance, what if her shock had diminished her beauty! Mrs. Martin was found and it was she who gave Caroline's account. She had wisely retained both the cup, the liquid, and the original pot, still full with the poisoned tea which she quickly surrendered to the authorities. It was a clear case. Mr. Elliot had instructed Aliénor to observe Caroline carefully for signs of pregnancy, and when it was discovered, he had given her directions on the preparation of the poison. She had acted on his instructions.

Most worrying, Mr. Elliot's information must have been from an unreliable source. The poison he had chosen was not often used for this particular purpose and even if it had been, the dose he had recommended was too high. The constable concluded, after feeding the tea to some unfortunate small animals, that the concoction would have killed Lady Elliot. It was a horrible prospect to consider.

It was already growing dark by the time Sir Walter was free to seek out his wife. He found her in her room, sitting solemnly with Lady Russell. His old friend said some kind words of consolation. He hardly heard them and she took her leave. Sir Walter went to Caroline and helped her to her feet. She looked dazed. He carefully helped remove her dress; reminding himself to ask Mrs. Martin if someone from among the servants could serve for this purpose and then helped her into her nightgown. He took off his own coat and waistcoat.

He led her to her bed and laid down beside her, holding her in his arms. Sir Walter still felt like he did not know what to do with a distressed woman, but Caroline seemed to be more relaxed. He stroked her hair and, remembering Lady Russell's advice, waited for her to speak. At length she did, though she did not turn towards him.

"If Mrs. Martin had not known, I might have been sick and lost the child. It would have seemed natural."

Sir Walter agreed, "He was very clever. If your maid had been more careful, we never would have discovered the truth."

Caroline turned towards him, "You would have hated me."

"Hated you?" Sir Walter repeated, he had not expected her to say such a thing, "How could I hate anyone so beautiful?"

"Any man of sense marries to get a child, how many disappointments would it have taken?"

Sir Walter laid a hand on her smooth cheek, "It is true that I sought a wife to get a child and to speed my return to Kellynch, but I had not expected to find a woman such as you. I will always love you, Caroline. Even if the son does not come; I will love you still." He did not add, in all his magnanimous declarations of affection, that his regard was rather more dependant on her visage than anything else.

Caroline moved closer towards him, "Do not leave me tonight," she pleaded.

"I will stay," he said and he kissed her hair. He stayed awake, watching over her until she fell asleep. He wished to do more: if he could find his cousin, he would have killed him. But there was nothing to be done, Mr. Elliot was beyond his reach and the responsibility of the law. He felt helpless, but his wife had given him a task, so he stayed and eventually fell asleep.

67
Caroline

"but if Anne will stay, no one so proper, so capable as Anne."
Persuasion Ch 12

    Caroline woke the next morning and saw that Sir Walter remained. She felt better, confident in his regard. The events of the previous day still weighed upon her but when she reached unconsciously for the bell to call her maid. Sarah, one of the upper maids, arrived instead and offered her services until Caroline could find a suitable replacement. Caroline agreed with some apprehension. She felt a strong need to make her own tea; when Sarah offered to bring her a meal, she refused and instead made her way to the breakfast parlour. Sir Walter remained asleep.

    It felt silly to be so affected by the previous day's events when nothing had actually happened. Yet, to be betrayed so intimately by a woman she trusted was terrifying. Until Mr. Elliot was caught and they knew the full extent of his plot she would not feel easy. A servant walked close behind her and she was ashamed that she started. She did not wish to appear afraid.

    She wanted her brother and sister, or anyone whom she had known for more than a few months, but it would take them days to come visit her if it was within their power at all. Lady Russell had shown her great kindness, she was grateful, but their friendship was still new. Caroline realized she no longer felt at home, the feeling of comfort had been robbed from her. She had no notion of how to remedy that. Wandering from the breakfast room, she tried to find a room in the house where she felt secure, but nothing felt right. Caroline went outside.

    The day was fair, for late September, and she wandered the gardens and shrubbery. Caroline started to feel calmer, she sat on a bench and watched a fountain and heard the sound of the water. It was peaceful. She ought to write to her brother, but she also knew the news would reach him eventually. Such a ghastly event was sure to hit the London papers; not her preferred entrance into higher society. She ought to write to them and make sure they had the story straight.

Caroline did not know how long she remained but she was roused by the sound of soft footsteps. She looked up and saw Anne, Sir Walter's daughter, quite alone and looking rather concerned. Caroline was surprised that after so short an acquaintance she was extremely pleased to see her.

"My father sent an express, I left as soon as I could," she said, "You must be terrified." Caroline only nodded. "I have long known my cousin to be cruel, deceitful, and covetous, but I could not have imagined this," Anne continued.

"Thank you," Caroline said, standing to properly greet Anne.

"Come and take a turn around the garden with me," said Anne, "I assure you it is very refreshing after sitting so long in one attitude."

Caroline agreed and Anne talked to her of the gardens, her favourite places and walks. She, having sought silence, found the conversation inviting. Anne did not require a response; she was merely providing distraction. Before they returned to the house, Caroline was feeling somewhat better.

Anne brought Caroline within with the kind authority of a sister and made it clear that she and her husband, who was a former Captain in the navy, were intending to stay at Kellynch until Mr. Elliot was discovered. "I thought you might be uneasy, and enjoy the sense of my husband's protection, in addition to my father. Especially if Sir Walter is to be called away by the search."

Caroline was extremely grateful, but Anne gently rebuffed her thanks as family duty. Caroline felt Anne's presence relieving a small part of the fear, the drawing room was again something of home. When Caroline, after a few days of Anne's gentle presence, wondered at her being so helpful, Anne merely replied, "My husband always said I was good in a crisis."

Captain Wentworth, who happened to be present, added, "You must tell her someday what happened at Lyme." Anne blushed, but Caroline was only interested to hear more. Mary's version of the story had not really included Anne. The real tale was told and Caroline was astonished by Anne's presence of mind and humility. If Caroline had been involved in saving a young woman's life, she would have told everyone without hesitation! She must count

Anne's friendship as one of the advantageous things she had gained by marrying Sir Walter.

68
Charles Bingley

She was wild to be at home—to hear, to see, to be upon the spot to share with Jane in the cares that must now fall wholly upon her, in a family so deranged **Pride and Prejudice Ch 46**

The Darcy and Bingley families were again visiting when the morning post arrived. Charles opened the letter from his sister and spent so much time reading and re-reading it that eventually the entire party was waiting for him to speak with great anticipation.

Charles, finally looked up and exclaimed, "Caroline's maid almost murdered her!"

This was met with great cries of disbelief and horror. Charles knew that only about half of the people present really liked his sister, but it must be a shock to everyone in the room. The letter, which Caroline had explicitly allowed to be shared before the news was in the papers, was passed round the table.

"You should not say the maid, Charles," Elizabeth corrected, "It appears she was under duress. Mr. Elliot, the cousin you told me about, seems to be the true villain."

"This is very shocking!" Jane said, as she read with Elizabeth, "I cannot believe that there could be so much evil in the world! I want to believe that there has been some mistake. And to all be the work of Sir Walter's own family. Shocking indeed!"

Darcy held his judgement until the women had finished and then slowly read the letter himself. He said gravely, "This is why one should never speak a cross word to a housekeeper."

Elizabeth turned to Charles, "I would never wish such distress on anybody, I hope your sister will recover from this fright."

Jane looked at her husband, "We should go to see her at once; do you not think she will be wanting us there? I am anxious to see her."

Charles, taking possession of the letter again, looked at the farewell lines, "She does not request it, I will write directly and offer myself. If the house is in great disorder; I would not want to impose myself upon it."

"We were invited a few weeks ago," Elizabeth added, "Let us know what Caroline desires, for we might all travel together."

"An excellent idea," Charles agreed and he went immediately to write his letter. The next few days would reveal the whole of the affair, by both a second letter from Caroline and several reports in the newspapers. Charles's application was received and cordially answered, she requested that they all come in a few weeks, now that everything seemed resolved. The Bingleys and Darcys therefore planned to come down together and stay for a month.

69
Caroline

When the plan was made known to Mary, however, there was an end of all peace in it. She was so wretched and so vehement, complained so much of injustice in being expected to go away instead of Anne; Anne, who was nothing to Louisa, while she was her sister, and had the best right to stay in Henrietta's stead!
Persuasion Ch 12

An anxious week passed with no word of Mr. Elliot or Aliénor. Caroline had been seen by the midwife and her condition had been confirmed. She was considered fortunate to be so well after such a severe shock. Captain Wentworth and Anne remained, neither leaving the estate. Their presence had the exact effect that Anne had hoped for, both Caroline and her father were comforted. Anne and Caroline had taken to walking in the garden which had a beneficial effect on Caroline's poor nerves.

The party was about to sit for dinner when a woman was announced to the entire party's utter amazement: it was Mrs. Clay. Captain Wentworth stood and Caroline realized he had a pistol with him. Mrs. Clay was admitted and she entered with her father, Mr. Shepherd.

"You may call the constable, but I had no part in this affair. If you hear me out, I will tell you where Mr. Elliot is hiding. Well, for a price, of course."

"How are you privy to this knowledge?" Anne said in a low but commanding voice.

"I have been staying with Mr. Elliot for these last two years. I know where he took quarters after hearing that Sir Walter was engaged." Mrs. Clay replied, "You will not find him without my help. He is well hidden."

"Would he not relocate the moment you left?" Captain Wentworth demanded.

"I think not," Mrs. Clay said, "I told him a lie, which you might wonder if he believed, but he knows I will return. I left our daughter behind."

"If you can locate him, then we can discuss your reward," Anne said.

"We will discuss my reward first," Mrs. Clay said, "and then I will wait at my father's house for your return. I have every confidence that you will recover Mr. Elliot and that poor girl."

"Poor girl?" Caroline said, finally finding her voice.

"Aliénor? She has not ceased weeping since she arrived. I do not know what Mr. Elliot is holding over her, but I have never seen a woman so miserable."

Caroline felt a rush of relief, he had blackmailed her maid! Aliénor was miserable! She had not been deceived in her character after all. Though what Mr. Elliot could be holding over Aliénor, she could not conceive.

Mrs. Clay was still speaking, "I was happy to stay with Mr. Elliot, in a less than ideal situation, if I was one day to inhabit Kellynch Hall. But when she arrived and I discovered he had gone so far as to try and poison the new Lady Elliot, I could not abide it. He has become obsessed with the baronetcy; he had regular information of Sir Walter's doings in Bath."

"What is it you want?" Sir Walter asked.

"Only an annuity of four hundred pounds, to keep myself and my children," said Mrs. Clay mildly.

"Certainly not!" said Caroline, thinking to herself that people always lived forever when there was any annuity to be paid them. She would be reminded of the horrid events in perpetuity, "It will be settled now and you will quit Somersetshire forever when we have found him."

Mr. Shepherd was entirely silent, he could not imagine joining in an argument between his daughter and his long-time employer. If he had been forced to speak, he would have taken Sir Walter's side, but only in the interest of self-preservation.

"I would be a fool if I took a farthing less than ten thousand pounds," Mrs. Clay said. Now the discussion of terms began in earnest. Mrs. Clay of course wanted more than she could get; but at length was reduced to be reasonable. Everything being settled between them; the constable was called and Mrs. Clay gave exact directions to the apartment in Bath where Mr. Elliot was hiding. She requested only that her daughter be returned to her. She would stay under the protection of her father until Mr. Elliot was found.

Anne remained with Caroline at Kellynch and Captain Wentworth and Sir Walter rode off to confront Mr. Elliot. Caroline might have felt somewhat less secure, with the men out of the house, but no sooner had they departed that Mary and Charles Musgrove arrived.

Mary was angry already, "Anne! You have treated me wretchedly! It is injustice of the acutest kind for you to come hither and not call for me. I have as much claim to be here as you, as much right to be present. Why am I not to be as useful as you? It has been very unkind of you, Anne, not to call for me as well."

Caroline would have been unkind herself if she was not determined to stay silent, but Anne patiently apologized to her wretched sister and assured her that now was the time of greatest use, for the men had just departed and Caroline would be wanting more companions. Mary was at length satisfied and they were invited inside to the drawing room. Caroline called for cold meat and bread and Anne sat down at the pianoforte to play. By the end of an hour, Caroline was much improved. She ought to have told Mary that it was on her account, if only because she loved having someone to feel superior to. With Mary, Caroline was comfortably ahead in beauty, rank, and intelligence, and that was always consolation in a time of distress.

70
Narrator

"Remember the country and the age in which we live. Remember that we are English, that we are Christians. Consult your own understanding, your own sense of the probable, your own observation of what is passing around you. Does our education prepare us for such atrocities? Do our laws connive at them? Could they be perpetrated without being known, in a country like this, where social and literary intercourse is on such a footing, where every man is surrounded by a neighbourhood of voluntary spies, and where roads and newspapers lay everything open?"
Northanger Abbey Ch 24

Sir Walter had never spoken to Mr. Henry Tilney, but his assessment proved only too true. England is a country of laws. There would be no duel at dawn and no clandestine escape for a man that had attempted to poison the pregnant wife of a baronet. He had acted out of jealousy, hatred, and greed and his punishment was swift.

Let other pens dwell on guilt and misery. I quit such odious subjects as soon as I can, impatient to restore everybody, not greatly in fault themselves, to tolerable comfort, and to have done with all the rest. I will therefore describe the essentials. When the law arrived at the home of Mr. Elliot, he knew that he was ruined. He had been assured of his failure since almost the moment Aliénor had arrived. Mr. Elliot surrendered, admitted his crime, and begged for Sir Walter's pity. He was to hang, but mercy, if it could bear that name, was granted in the form of passage to the penal colony of Australia. His wealth was forfeit, and when the crown and law had taken its due, a large share went to Kellynch; as Mr. Elliot had no legitimate heirs of his own. The resulting fortune, in excess of forty thousand pounds, was surely enough to keep even the extravagant Sir Walter out of debt forever or at least for the rest of his life.

Aliénor's story was told and there was much to be pitied. She had been assured that the tea would only end the pregnancy, she meant no harm to Caroline. But how had she been persuaded? Aliénor had been the servant of a wealthy lady before her current mistress, who was often with child but had yet to deliver any living baby. When the man of the house took interest in Aliénor, she found herself pregnant at the same time as her employer. When the legitimate child was again lost, they planned in secret for her baby to take its place. Aliénor delivered and left a healthy baby boy to a comfortable home. She had procured as part of the deal a very excellent reference and an annuity paid to her ailing mother. Only about a month later, she was employed by Caroline.

Mr. Elliot had been watching when Aliénor took a day's holiday in Bath, for she had visited with the lady and child, now five years old, and he had guessed the connection. The resemblance between the child and his true mother was obvious when they were seen together. Aliénor was trapped: she could not betray her own son to poverty. The secret had to remain. Not understanding the full intent of his plans, Aliénor agreed to correspond with Mr. Elliot.

Caroline, when she was told everything, agreed to keep her former maid's confidence, and swore all those involved to silence. She was sympathetic, within reason, and Sir Walter sought Aliénor's pardon. It was granted but the problem of where she might go remained. Mrs. Clay, however, was still to be paid, and Aliénor left the county with her, a promise secured from each to never return to Somersetshire.

Most of this was resolved quite quickly, though lawyers remained to quibble and bargain. Sir Walter returned home within the week and was pleased to assure his new wife that all perceivable danger had passed.

71
Susan Price

"Certainly, my home at my uncle's brought me acquainted with a circle of admirals. Of Rears and Vices I saw enough. Now do not be suspecting me of a pun, I entreat." **Mansfield Park Ch 6**

"Susan, I have noticed something strange?" said Lady Bertram one day.

"What is that?"

"Well, my new daughter, Elizabeth, does not spend very much time with Tom at all. She seems to spend almost every moment with Miss Pope! Or in her garden."

"I spend most of my day with you, Aunt Bertram."

"Yes, that is true I suppose. But do you not notice as well, that Tom is always with his friend, Mr. Maddox. They see each other nearly every day!"

"They must be very good friends, but then, is it not normal for men to go hunting and riding together? That is what Tom has always done."

"Yes, I suppose you are right. He must have become a very bad shot though, because even though it is hunting season he hardly brings back a single bird. I do not think the groundskeeper is neglectful. The stocks must be as numerous as ever."

"Yes, the birds are numerous, I am sure," Susan agreed mildly.

"Well, maybe Mr. Maddox keeps them. He does after all live alone. Though I should ask Tom next time to bring a few home; I do enjoy partridge."

Sir Thomas happened to walk by.

"Sir Thomas, do you not think it is strange how much time Elizabeth and Tom spend apart?" Lady Bertram asked in her mild tone.

"No, we do not spend the whole of the day together either, my dear."

"There is something about their manner when I see them, that suggests to me that there is a lacking- I cannot quite put it into words."

"I am sure that nothing is amiss," Sir Thomas replied, "but even if they are not strongly attached- his feelings, probably, are not acute, I have never supposed them to be so; but their comforts might not be less on that account. A well-disposed young man, who did not marry for love, is in general but the more attached to his own family. Tom has, in his time with me, shown a great deal of diligence towards his duties."

Lady Bertram, of course, could not long oppose such logical statements, and she only added, "Well I suppose when the first child comes, we will know that everything is right."

Susan, who had made her own observations of the couple, only smiled. With her head bent over her work, she was sure it was an unnoticed expression. She had, quite by chance, observed her cousin Tom with his "friend" and she would not be at all surprised if a baby did *not* in fact come along in due time. She would not speak of it for the world, however, and she let her aunt and uncle continue in their misplaced hopes. She was not one to judge; her cousin had never been happier. With all that Susan knew of the navy, she felt some pity that Tom had not been a younger son. He might have done very well *there*.

Susan could not understand why he had ever married that hateful woman Elizabeth anyway. She could not help but think that it might be very just desserts if Elizabeth did not become Lady Bertram after all. She must hope for her uncle and aunt to live very happy, very *long* lives.

72
Mrs. Nancy Tilney

For Lucy it seems borrowed all her money before she went off to be married, on purpose we suppose to make a show with, and poor Nancy had not seven shillings in the world **Sense and Sensibility Ch 49**

The entrance of the newly married Tilneys to Northanger Abbey had gone much better than Nancy or her husband had expected. General Tilney, desperate to keep his son's disgraceful wife away from society, had consented to their staying in Northanger Cottage, away from all of his carefully collected acquaintances. This was acceptable to Nancy and she was also pleased to spend the first few weeks at the Abbey while their house was prepared.

Nancy walked around the abbey in wonder for the first few days. She was well aware that she was now richer than her sister, richer than even the senior Mrs. Ferrars! Nancy had spent a good deal of her life comparing the wealth and clothing of other people; she knew exactly how lucky she was. Her only problem was General Tilney, he seemed to despise her even more than her brother-in-law. Yet, she refused to be driven off this time, not when everything she had wished for was finally within her possession. His rants and orders had little effect on her happy disposition, something that made him all the angrier.

Luckily for her, General Tilney had been so agitated by Nancy's uncouth manners and disappointing fortune that he took a wrong turn and tumbled down a very handsome, recently-improved staircase. The consequent broken leg and three months convalescence with Nancy and a very smug Frederick made up the General's mind. He took a house in town the moment he recovered and escaped to London, where he could pretend that his new daughter-in-law did not exist and regret the day that he had freed Frederick from his control.

Established in the Abbey, Nancy took the opportunity to invite Mr. and Mrs. Ferrars to her new home. To see her sister turn nearly green with envy was almost enough to set Nancy up forever, but her first words would supply infinite joy upon reflection.

"I should have been quite disappointed if *you* had not been so well provided for," Lucy said, with a strong emphasis on the word, "I always thought *you* deserved it. I am so very pleased with *your* good fortune. It would have been a great pity if *you* remained in Bath as you were. I am amazingly glad to discover you *so* well settled."

Nancy's delight was not finished, for Lucy was also to meet her husband, who she knew to be prodigiously handsome, and when the men stood beside each other, Nancy was sure that Lucy was almost melting in jealousy at the comparison. Robert, for all his fine clothes, (the jacket itself must have cost at least five pounds with all the embroidery!), was of person and face, of strong, natural, sterling insignificance. Her dear Frederick was most often the handsomest man in any room.

When they were alone, Lucy demanded to know, "How did any of this happen?"

Nancy smiled, "Well, I did tell you in the letter, but you know, these things can happen and this is how it did: I was staying with Miss Elliot, now Mrs. Bertram, in Bath and I told her we were cousins- before I was staying with her, of course. And she liked me intensely so I remained with her for a long time. She arranged for me to dance with Frederick and you know, that dancing is the first step to falling in love. But I must first tell you more about Mrs. Bertram, for I have told you of her before, but there is so much against her that I feel I may now say. Do you know that she dyes her hair? It is entirely grey, every lock! And she would send me to the chemist because she feared everyone knowing it. A level of vanity that I have never had, no not in the least."

"A level of vanity that would be foolish on your part," Lucy said dryly. Nancy could tell that Lucy was already inattentive to the story, but Nancy also knew that Lucy would sit to listen, she loved being in the places of the wealthy. Smiling inside, Nancy realized that she would be able to talk as long as she wanted to anyone, for the rest of her life; unless they were titled or in some other way higher or richer than herself. She took a deep breath and continued.

73
Sir Walter

But they must long feel that to flatter and follow others, without being flattered and followed in turn, is but a state of half enjoyment. **Persuasion Ch 24**

Sir Walter was very pleased to hear that the Darcys would be visiting. He and Mr. Darcy had met before, though only briefly several times in London and always in large parties. Sir Walter was excited to renew the acquaintance. The nephew of an earl would always be acceptable to him; but the knowledge that he was handsome and wealthy made him a valuable connection. Sir Walter anticipated a great friendship between himself and Darcy. It was only natural for an intimacy to develop between two men so well-balanced, for while he had the advantage of rank, he yielded that Darcy was the superior in fortune.

When the carriages arrived, Sir Walter was at the door, in his best, newest coat, ready to make a meaningful impression on Mr. Darcy. He eyed him in the daylight and eyed him well. He was very much struck by Darcy's personal claims and the cut and make of his fine green coat. Mrs. Darcy, on the arm of her husband, was perhaps not his full equal in appearance but she had a rather bright pair of dark eyes and Sir Walter saw nothing to disappoint in her visage. Her gown was fashionable and perfectly suited to a woman of her stature.

Sir Walter welcomed Charles graciously but was then wholly absorbed in examining his wife. He was quick to distinguish that Caroline had a different sort of beauty, with her auburn hair and light eyes, but Mrs. Bingley was extremely handsome. Light hair, long eye-lashes, glowing skin, and full lips. Her pelisse was very well-made and he almost envied the embroidery. Sir Walter was very much in love with his wife, but he could admire a woman such as Mrs. Bingley as one might admire a painting or a prospect. She must make every social event she attended brighter by her very presence. He was very pleased that his wife had such a beautiful sister.

They all looked so well that Sir Walter quite forgot himself and offered them a tour of the grounds before remembering that they would want to dress before dinner. Caroline courteously took everyone to their rooms instead. Sir Walter had ensured that the Darcys would be in the best guest chambers, the Bingleys a close second. While he wished to pay proper attentions to the brother of his wife, he was acutely conscious that the Darcys, by their merits, deserved more.

Sir Walter could do nothing until dinner. He was already dressed to receive his guests, so he went to the library. Caroline had mentioned that Mr. Darcy and his wife were prodigious readers. Sir Walter hoped that the library, which he rarely contributed to, would be acceptable. He had unfortunately burned the baronetage, in a fit of pique, since it still contained the crossed-out name of his despicable cousin. He rarely read anything else. He looked at the various bookshelves, trying to determine which volumes might be best to display on the table. Naturally, he selected the few books he had read, one a history of Kellynch, one a tour book for the surrounding area, and the third a biography of Sir Walter Raleigh, which he had purchased because he shared a Christian name with that particular historical figure. Sir Walter could only wish that the new copy of the baronetage had come, it was a sorry loss to his library.

He met his wife and they entered for dinner. Charles began exactly as Sir Walter liked, with praise of Kellynch.

"It is a beautiful dining parlour, Caroline, the style is so very like Pemberley," he observed, Caroline thanked him.

This was acceptable to Sir Walter, for though Mr. Darcy was not a baronet, Caroline had been sure to impress the prominence of Pemberley in guidebooks of Derbyshire. He was pleased to boast, "Lady Elliot had been busily employed in the decoration of the rooms since her arrival."

"Caroline's sense of style is impeccable," said Mrs. Darcy, "I have long known her preferences when it comes to homes."

"You are too kind," Caroline said, though Sir Walter thought she might be displeased. He could not imagine why. To him, this seemed like a great compliment.

Sir Walter happily spoke with Mrs. Darcy for the chief of the meal, then when the women departed, turned nearly all his attention to Mr. Darcy. In speaking of his house, his horses, and his title, he felt that he had indeed impressed the proud Mr. Darcy and when the gaiety of the evening was over, congratulated himself on having formed such a mutually beneficial acquaintance.

74
Mrs. Elizabeth Darcy
She had a lively, playful disposition, which delighted in anything ridiculous. **Pride and Prejudice Ch 3**

Elizabeth Darcy had greatly enjoyed her increased opportunity, since her marriage, to observe the follies and foibles of a much greater selection of humanity, but to meet the man who had willingly married Caroline Bingley was an unequalled pleasure. It was not a great surprise that Caroline had married, or indeed that she had married well, for there are always men who will accept fortune and beauty no matter the character of the woman, but the speed with which the match had been formed, the violence of Sir Walter's affections, and his rank had raised Elizabeth's curiosity. She felt, in that moment, much like her father anticipating the arrival of Mr. Collins. Sir Walter did not disappoint.

Elizabeth seated herself beside Sir Walter at dinner so that she might share in conversation and she delighted in every minute of it.

"Mrs. Darcy," said he, "I hope that the dinner is to your taste?"

"It is delicious," said she, "Though I must admit I prefer the curry to the ragout."

"Do you not eat ragout at Pemberley? I have been told many times by Lady Elliot about the finesse of your French cooks."

Elizabeth smiled, "I would not dare speak a word against the cook of Pemberley or Kellynch, it is only a personal preference."

"I must think that when you dine at the house of the Earl of —, that the table is much finer than what we have here."

"Oh no!" Elizabeth cried, "I have never seen such a handsomely set table or such fine furnishings, not even at the home of my honoured uncle."

This increased Sir Walter's good humour and he humbly replied, "Why, as I inherited such rooms, it would be very simple not to make use of them; but, upon my honour, I believe there might be more comfort in rooms of only half their size. The Earl of —'s house, I am sure, must be exactly of the true size for rational happiness."

Elizabeth hid another smile and having made a nearly complete calculation of his character, replied, "Those who have any doubt as to the noble tastes of baronets have not yet viewed Kellynch Hall. It is a sterling imitation of aristocracy."

As Elizabeth expected, Sir Walter entirely mistook her meaning, "If *you* think Kellynch has every mark of nobility, *I* cannot disagree."

Elizabeth's expectations were fully answered. Sir Walter was as absurd as she had hoped, and she listened to him with the keenest enjoyment, maintaining at the same time the most resolute composure of countenance, and, except in an occasional glance at her husband, required no partner in her pleasure. Her assessment of Caroline must come next and when the women removed to the drawing room, she took a seat beside the new Lady Elliot.

"I am very sorry to hear about the dreadful events," Elizabeth said kindly and honestly.

"I appreciate your consolation," Caroline said, "And I must thank you for coming with my brother. It is so good to be in company that I am familiar with after such an occurrence. I am only sorry that Georgiana could not accompany you."

"She did very much wish to come," Elizabeth answered, "However, as my sister had several engagements in Derbyshire, she was forced to remain under the care of her aunt. I have brought a letter for you; I am sure it covers five pages."

"That is very kind of her," Caroline answered, "What do you think of Kellynch?"

Elizabeth smiled, "You were wrong, Caroline, back at Netherfield when you spoke of impossibilities, you can get Pemberley by both purchase *and* imitation."

Elizabeth could see by Caroline's face that she felt the full meaning, but she immediately added, "You must take me on a walk of the grounds tomorrow, I hear they are quite lovely."

The conversation carried on without any lingering animosity. Elizabeth had placed her barb but she did not feel any lingering hostility towards Caroline *now*. No, Elizabeth was determined, she would think only of the past as its remembrance gave her pleasure. Jane was more than safe from Caroline's fickle friendship and with such a distance between their houses, Elizabeth would only be in

Sir Walter and Lady Elliot's company long enough to have her fill of their delightful eccentricities before retreating back to the more rational company of Derbyshire.

Elizabeth waited until she and her husband were alone that night to learn his opinion. She knew that both Charles and Jane would only be too delighted to see their sister happy and would not dare criticize her choice.

"You must tell me what you think of Sir Walter, I am certain you can guess my opinion," Elizabeth began.

"I know you are diverted," Darcy replied, "but I cannot say that Sir Walter of any interest to me. He is only an extreme of a wearisome kind; I have met a hundred Sir Walter's in my life. Vain, illiterate, and careless, educated enough to pass as intelligent for ten minutes of conversation and hopelessly lost after the regular civilities are completed. But I will try to be kind; Caroline does seem very happy."

"Of course she's happy! She has everything she could have ever wanted: a title, a grand estate, and a husband whom she can control. Now that I have seen what she really likes, I only wonder that she tried so determinedly for you!"

Darcy gave his wife a sardonic glare, "Any woman between fifteen and thirty, with any claim to beauty, wealth, or rank wanted to marry me. Except yourself."

"Well you wounded my vanity. Luckily, I am not Sir Walter or the wound might have been fatal."

"I doubt anyone could puncture that man's inflated self-image. You would need much more than a single insult heard over the din of a ball."

"It was a very cutting remark, it's a wonder I survived. However, I must ask, do you not feel just at home?" Elizabeth smiled.

"There is more to home than decoration."

"I could not be more diverted by it! She has copied Pemberley as exactly as possible. The next time we visit I will not be surprised if there is a lake!"

"I cannot blame anyone for aspiring to imitate my estate. After all, you could not help but accept me after you saw Pemberley, if I am not mistaken."

"Yes, the moment I saw those well-appointed halls and charming prospects I became entirely enthralled and there was nothing that could have prevented me from marrying you. No woman can resist the charms of elegance without pretension."

"If only I could have made more clear the vastness of my estate when I proposed to you in Hunsford," Darcy mourned, "Perhaps I ought to have brought Caroline's paintings."

"Caroline has purchased herself elegance *with* pretension. Who can say which woman got the better bargain?" Elizabeth laughed.

"One day her temper may be soured, by finding, that like many other members of her sex, that through some unaccountable bias in favour of prestige, that she is the wife of a very silly man- but I know this is the kind of blunder that is all too common for any woman to have lasting hurt by it," he observed.

"I doubt it will harm her at all, I believe very few married women are half as much mistress of their husband's house than Caroline seems to be. I think Caroline is truly beloved and important; always first and always right in her husband's eyes."

"Do I sense a hint of jealousy?" her husband said with a smile.

Elizabeth winked, "Not in the least! I would be horrid by the end of the first month. No, both Caroline and I have the husband who will exactly suit us. I am determined that we must visit in the future. And you must introduce them to your uncle, I am already wishing to see Sir Walter in the presence of his superiors."

"I cannot inflict such a punishment on my honoured uncle," Darcy smiled, "But we must introduce him to Lady Catherine." Elizabeth was highly diverted by this suggestion and this line of conversation was continued until fatigue overcame them.

75
Caroline

To convince him, therefore, that he had deceived himself, was no very difficult point. **Pride and Prejudice Ch 35**

Caroline was sitting, composing another letter to Susan, who was again delayed because of this mysterious H.C., when Sir Walter came in from shooting. Caroline saw instantly that he had some sort of wild idea, which meant that she would need to convince him otherwise. She smiled warmly.

"I have a notion that this winter we should take a house on Wimpole Street, for your first season as Lady Elliot nothing else will do," he declared.

Caroline was flattered, and she also knew that with the extra income they had acquired, it was possible, but it was not something they ought to do, "That is a very pretty notion, but do you not recall? I may miss the season for confinement. It would be so difficult for me to close such a handsome house early. What a loss to the society of London!"

"A loss indeed, what a pity that your confinement will coincide with the height of the season."

Caroline nodded gravely, "Yes, I am quite put out. I am fairly distressed about winter travel in my condition. I suppose it would be better to stay here, or to go for a shorter time if we must."

Caroline could see Sir Walter's mind working, he would now suggest something more reasonable, or Caroline would resort to baser methods, "A few weeks enjoyment then, around Easter?"

"Of course! That will suit us both exactly. I am in raptures thinking of the friends we shall meet, the shopping to be done; a delightful time I am sure."

"We shall need a new carriage of course, for the occasion."

Caroline calculated the expense in her head quickly, "Yes my love, that will be required. May we have a blue on with silver spots?"

"Anything you desire for the carriage; I know you have very refined tastes. I have a mind to acquire new horses as well, I feel like chestnuts do not suit the colour scheme this season, we ought to have bays or dapple grey."

Caroline internally rolled her eyes; the grooms did not want to have to deal with that! "You cannot sell the chestnuts! I would be in agonies; I have a particular liking for at least three of them! Besides, I have it on good authority that Lady Lancelle rides a chestnut horse."

"Well then we must keep the chestnuts," Sir Walter conceded, "she is very fashionable."

Caroline nodded, "I hope we do meet her in London, my sister can claim her acquaintance. It will be very diverting I am sure, especially in our new carriage."

"You know Lady Lancelle? That is good to hear, we must strengthen that acquaintance," Sir Walter sounded excited and Caroline had every hope that he would be sufficiently distracted by the prospect of high connections to drop his ridiculous notions.

"Yes, I am exactly of your mind, it is a connection I wish to encourage as well."

"Then we ought to get new table settings for London, how long do you think it would take to have them imported?"

"The set we have is magnificent! I do not think for a single month in town we need to incur such an expense. No one would judge such fine settings as we already possess!"

"Ah, my love, you may not be entirely understanding the duty of a baronet's wife to set the fashion."

Caroline, seeing that she might fail and wondering if Sir Walter would ever be sufficiently distracted by mere words, stood up and approached him. She had more effective means of persuasion now. "I am feeling so heated, do you think you can come to my chamber and help me out of this dress?"

"Why can your maid not assist you?"

Caroline smiled suggestively. Sir Walter realized what she meant and before long, she was both satisfied and triumphant. The dinner settings were entirely forgotten.

76
Letter

He is the most horrible flirt that can be imagined. If your Miss Bertrams do not like to have their hearts broke, let them avoid Henry **Mansfield Park Ch 4**

Dearest Caroline,

   I am coming as soon as I can, my business is town has finally reached a conclusion; though not the one I had hoped for. Seeing you happily married and queen of your domain is everything I need to restore me to spirits! Your descriptions of your husband, house, and neighbourhood are all so favourable that I almost envy you. I extend my most sincere congratulations on your condition and I am glad that you are still in good health.
   As for me, I am not overly distressed and my sorrow will not be lasting. It is clear now that Mr. Henry Crawford has no thoughts of matrimony at present and I was entirely mistaken in his intentions. Do not despair for me, dearest friend, I have not been harmed by the flirtation; I do not believe that my heart was plunged too deep. There may, however, be a small, lasting hole. One must take pleasure with disappointment; I do not think you will mistake my meaning when I hint that whatever woman does finally lure Henry to the altar will be very fortunate indeed! Especially after dark.

   Yours ever etc. Susan Taylor

77
Caroline

Mrs. Weston's friends were all made happy by her safety **Emma Ch 35**

Caroline had imagined that she was prepared, that it would not be that hard, that she could, as a well-educated and healthy woman, glide through childbirth: she was wrong. This was the longest, worst, and most painful thing she had ever done. She was no longer convinced that marriage and intercourse were worth it; she ought to go back to being Caroline Bingley. Caroline Bingley never faced an exertion beyond a long carriage ride or a bracing walk in the country. If it had been an option, she would have in that moment traded her title for the baby to be born. Why would it not come?

The first signs of labour had come at breakfast, it was now late into the night. The pain was excruciating, the constancy of it was worse. As each wave ended, she knew that only moments later it would begin again. She did everything that Louisa, Anne, and the midwife suggested but nothing was helping. After a long day of labour, the time had come to push. She had been pushing for nearly three hours. The baby was not coming.

"You must push again my lady, the first child is always the hardest one" the midwife said, encouragingly. Caroline looked at her in utter exhaustion. She knew she must push, her body demanded it, but she did not wish to.

"How many more?" she demanded, only to hear the response she expected.

"A few more," the midwife said, in the same happy tone. It had been a few more for at least an hour.

"Then you must not actually know how many more!" Caroline snapped.

"It will be over soon," Anne said. She was at Caroline's side, one of the two women that Caroline had requested. Caroline saw the full value of Anne Wentworth; she wanted no one else in a crisis. No matter that childbirth was a common thing, it was still dangerous. "You must find the strength to go on."

"Why will the baby not come!" Caroline cried.

"The babe was not in the proper position," the midwife explained again, "You have turned it over, now you must push."

"Stupid child," Caroline thought angrily. The wave began and she held the hand of her step-daughter and sister and pushed with all the determination she had. The pain changed. She looked up at the midwife.

"I can see the head," the midwife said happily. Caroline gasped for breath; this was the end. She waited for the next wave. "One last push, my lady," the midwife encouraged.

Caroline did as she was told, seconds later she heard the first tiny screams of a new-born child. To her surprise, when she later reflected on this moment, she did not think of the gender of the child, she only wanted to hold her baby. The midwife was doing her work, washing the baby and wrapping it in a blanket. Caroline reached out her arms and took a perfect child into them. An angry, screaming, perfect child.

"It is a boy!" Louisa said, having watched the midwife clean him.

Caroline heard, but she was consumed by the tiny face. He had ceased to cry and closed his tiny eyes. One hand wriggled free of the blanket and rested beside his face. Caroline had never seen such a handsome baby. He had fine almost white hair, she stroked it. He gurgled; it was a beautiful sound.

"Shall I tell my father?" Anne asked.

Caroline broke away her gaze and fixed on Anne, "Yes, Sir Walter will want to know. Thank you."

Anne left and Louisa, on Caroline's other side, spoke, "He looks to be a healthy baby."

"He is perfect," Caroline sighed, "Look at his little hands!"

Caroline did not see Louisa roll her eyes, "I suppose you will no longer be affronted by my attentions to little John?"

Caroline chose not to hear, "Would you like to hold him?"

"Sir Walter will want to, I suspect, I will wait. You will be glad for me to take him in time."

Caroline thought for a moment of her confinement, she would be primarily in this very room for the better part of six weeks, with Anne and Louisa for company. Other visitors would come, but it would be limited until the danger of fever had passed. The prospect had seemed horrid to Caroline weeks ago, now she wondered if she could ever leave this dear child.

The midwife and Louisa quickly helped Caroline out of her soiled clothes and changed the linens on the bed. By the time they finished, Sir Walter was waiting to enter.

"Caroline, are you well?" he asked, Caroline smiled, his first thought was for her.

"As well as any woman in my position can be," she replied, "This is your son."

Sir Walter took the tiny boy, "Young Master Walter Elliot. He is so very handsome!" This was exactly what Caroline had imagined that Sir Walter would say, for the baby was very well formed. How could anyone think anything else?

Caroline noticed now that Sir Walter had brought with him a heavy book, now laid on her bed. She picked it up, "The baronetage?"

"Yes, I have gotten my new copy," Sir Walter said proudly, "And now I have made my additions," he held up the book.

Walter Elliot, born March 1, 1760, married, July 15, 1784, Elizabeth, daughter of James Stevenson, Esq. of South Park, in the county of Gloucester, by which lady (who died November 5, 1800) he has issue: Elizabeth, born June 1, 1785 – married July 15, 1817 Thomas Bertram, son and heir of Sir Thomas Bertram 8th baronet of Mansfield Park in the country of Northampton (see page 125); Anne, born August 9, 1787 - married, June 7, 1815, Captain Frederick Wentworth; a still-born son, November 5, 1789; Mary, born November 20, 1791 - Married, December 16, 1810, Charles, son and heir of Charles Musgrove, Esq. of Uppercross, in the county of Somerset.

Married, July 30, 1817, Caroline, daughter of Charles Bingley of Newcastle, by which lady he has issue Walter Elliot, born April 31, 1817, *heir apparent.*

Caroline read the page with as much delight as her husband must have had when he made so many small additions, with his own hand, to the text the printer had provided. The mention of Mr. Elliot, was now truly gone. Caroline was proud to grace the page of such a noble family and heritage.

As she finished reading, she was given back young Walter Elliot, who must be getting hungry, and Sir Walter, after kissing both and reminding them of his love, left the room with his beloved text, restored to its full glory in his heart. Caroline accepted the help of the midwife to feed her new child. She watched him eat with wonder and when he was done, she watched him sleep. It was time for her to rest as well, but Caroline only wanted to hold little Walter. Anne took him eventually and laid him in his cradle. Caroline had not imagined she would fall in love twice in the span of a single year.

78
Sir Walter
The value of an Anne Elliot **Persuasion Ch 13**

Sir Walter left the chamber with a multitude of feelings, the exhilaration of success, the relief of finding his wife and son healthy, the assurance that labour had not diminished his wife's good looks, the pride of finally getting an heir, and the pleasure of being once again able to display his favourite book prominently in his home. He went directly to the large drawing room and displayed the book, open to the most important page, on the table. The book that had caused him consternation only a short year ago was restored to his admiration. It might again be his consolation in times of trouble, should they arise.

He was regretful that he had not thought to marry before. He had spent so many years in an imperfect happiness, blinded by his imagined duty to Elizabeth, when he ought to have been encouraging her to move on as well. He could have settled the inheritance of Kellynch years ago. Sir Walter caught himself, he would not have met Caroline ten years ago. Maybe, everything had worked out for the best. He had found the perfect companion for his future life and she had made him the happiest of men and of fathers.

Thinking suddenly of the birth of Elizabeth, his eldest daughter, Sir Walter thought that maybe soon they ought to visit Mansfield Park and see how Elizabeth was getting along. She had written many letters and it did not seem she was entirely happily settled. Sir Walter found this odd, for his daughter was one of the most beautiful women in the world, who could fail to appreciate her talents? It was certainly mysterious.

This train of thought naturally, but surprisingly, led to his daughter Anne. Sir Walter, whose character started and ended in vanity, had finally seen Anne's value. The loyal attention that Anne had shown to both himself and Caroline had produced an effect on Sir Walter's heart. He might not perfectly understand her or value her soft beauty as much as he should, but he saw her as the caring and useful woman that so many others had relied upon for years.

He was suddenly glad she had settled nearby, that she was attending Caroline for her confinement. There was no one so proper, so capable as Anne.

Sir Walter was distracted from his more noble line of thinking to noticing that the table in the drawing room was somewhat shabby. They needed a new one to properly display the baronetage! How long had it been since Caroline had done up the drawing room? Six months at least! He wondered if he ought to go back to her room and suggest something be done about it. He was halfway out the door before he remembered that she was not to be disturbed. He sighed and wondered if he should make a note. No, he would remember, it was plain as day that the table was unfit to be seen! He sat down to read his favourite page of the baronetage again.

This time, the table survived his scrutiny.

79
Mrs. Elizabeth Bertram

but Anne, with an elegance of mind and sweetness of character, which must have placed her high with any people of real understanding, was nobody with either father or sister; her word had no weight, her convenience was always to give way--she was only Anne. **Persuasion Ch 1**

Due to the inclinations of both, and a tendency on the part of Elizabeth to quite forget her age, the marriage of Elizabeth and Tom remained sterile and without intimacy. It was nearly ten years before Elizabeth realized that perhaps they ought to try for an heir: it proved to be too late. Tom's health had never fully recovered from his unfortunate illness and a bout of consumption left the Bertram family bereft. Elizabeth was shocked, she had always been quite certain in becoming the mistress of Mansfield Park. It was not to be.

There were two choices before her, both mortifying. She was either to return to her father's house as a childless widow or remain in one of Sir Thomas's houses in the village. She realized that she could not bear the humiliation of removing to Kellynch, where her father remained devoted to the dreadful new Lady Elliot, especially without the distinction of a child or title. She would remain at Mansfield.

A few months later she was settled in the White house, enjoying all the affection that the Bertram family had shown to one of its previous tenants (that is to say, almost none). The second bedroom was occupied by Miss Pope's successor, as the "treasure" Miss Pope had in fact been more of a collector of treasures and had eloped with a footman after being accused of theft. Elizabeth had managed to hire a most acceptable companion next, a Miss Collins, sister to a rector in Kent who she was told, in nearly every respect was a near twin of her brother. While everything else remained a degradation, Miss Collins's company was exactly what Elizabeth liked.

Unwelcome in the great house and forgotten by its residents, Elizabeth worked in her flower garden at the park and raised pheasants on her small property. When Sir Thomas died, she tried to forget that the despised Fanny Price would become Lady Bertram. She attempted not to notice when Susan Price, helped by her sister, married a minor lord. She focused on her flowers and her birds and pretended that the world around her did not exist. This continued to the point that when one of Lady Bertram's daughters, who was taking a turn about the shrubbery with a friend, was asked whom the lady was tending to flowers, she said:

"Oh, she's nobody, only Aunt Eliza."

80
Narrator

And setting aside the jealousies and ill-will continually subsisting between Fanny and Lucy, in which their husbands of course took a part, as well as the frequent domestic disagreements between Robert and Lucy themselves, nothing could exceed the harmony in which they all lived together. **Sense and Sensibility Ch 50**

One might imagine that entering into a marriage for the sole purpose of offending your father, no matter how cruel and evil he might be, is not a very solid foundation for lasting felicity. Fortunately for Frederick and Nancy, while they began with feelings of greed, deception, and lust, they soon found themselves growing in each other's true affections. Frederick, who continually existed in the space between laughing *with* and *at* his wife, did not grow tired or cross with her. Nancy, who had never been as greedy or grasping as her sister, had everything she could have ever hoped for and held her husband in the highest esteem for granting her every possible comfort. As long as her muslins were at least eight shillings a yard and her elegant maid trimmed her bonnets, nothing could disturb her.

Nancy was clever enough to ingratiate herself with the rest of the family by doting on their children and complimenting their appearances. While she would almost never understand Henry when he spoke, she was an accepted and loved member of the family. They always gave her credit for chasing off their father, which had greatly increased their mutual felicity. When Nancy's own children began to arrive, one can imagine a constant intercourse between Woodston and Northanger and cheerful cousins playing happily together.

As the mistress of a house greater than she had ever stayed in, Nancy's happiness was the sort that could not be touched by her husband occasionally being gone to enjoy himself in London or Bath. Her home, her gowns, her children, and all their dependent concerns never lost their charms. Her husband did always return and eventually the trips were few and far between. He came to appreciate that it had been his father, rather than his distaste for the country itself, that had always kept him in town.

Frederick and Nancy (though I give her all the credit) proved the General wrong by producing a very handsome brood of eight healthy children. Anyone would call them a handsome family, had they legs and arms enough between them, but they were beautiful in fact as well. She would have spoiled them all if she had not limited herself to only doting on them as infants. She then had them all educated by a highly recommended governess followed by the very best schools. She did not dare to educate her boys privately, but instead sent them to Eton where he might not fall into the clutches of any scheming young women.

Between their children, their family, and their wealth, the Tilneys lived in almost perfect happiness, troubled only by the occasional visits from Lucy, who always seemed right on the edge of stealing the silverware. Nancy's elevation only increased Lucy's dissatisfaction with every aspect of her own home and establishment, which was a constant source of gratification to Nancy. After all, there is nothing so glorious in great achievement as being able to gloat.

81
Sir Walter
His superiority of appearance **Persuasion Ch 24**

Sir Walter, entirely led by vanity, had indeed chosen his perfect wife (of this he was confident). He had now lived many years more and enjoyed remarkable health and good looks. If he was asked, however, he would maintain a very proper level of false modesty. His hair, much to his delight, stayed full even while it required dye. His visage and figure were exceptional for someone at his advanced stage of life. He was fairly certain of this; his many mirrors could not lie.

He was able to watch his sons grow, his wife remain beautiful, and his income increase. He was never very attentive to his daughters or benevolent to the poor, but he did show every arrear of civility to Captain and Mrs. Wentworth after their service to him, and by his wife's insistence, he granted both of his younger daughters an equal share to Elizabeth's fortune and paid it before his demise. It was an act that was not unfelt by either woman.

Walter, Charles, and Philip were the constant delight of his twilight years. He had judged that each of them had superior personal merits, in addition to intelligence and good nature, and he was sure that each of them would do very well. He remained extremely pleased with himself, whenever he was in the presence of his favourite son Walter, for deciding to remarry.

82
Lady Elliot or Caroline

"I am afraid you do not like your pen. Let me mend it for you. I mend pens remarkably well." **Pride and Prejudice Ch 10**

Caroline set down her expertly mended pen and proudly regarded the completed manuscript. It was a true account of everything that had happened since that fateful day when she had accepted Susan's invitation to Bath. It had been the work of many years, countless careful interviews, and a few stolen diaries. She hesitated for a moment, then drew out a clean sheet of paper and wrote her final goodbye:

*Dear reader, let me explain what I have learned, after many years of marriage. What I felt all those years ago in Bath should have been described as **lust** not **love**. Ah, what a difference a few letters can make! It is a common mistake, I believe. Yet, I have been fortunate; I have always been perfectly happy. I am Lady Elliot, I have three healthy boys, and a very devoted husband. I could not ask for more! I believe that Sir Walter has always been fervently in love with me, and to tell you the truth, to be an object or adoration for another person is delightful. I cannot think of a better situation for a woman of my stature.*

(Please don't tell my husband how ridiculous he looks with his dyed hair. It has been long enough; he should let it go grey. Luckily, he still always wears a hat!)

Sir Walter and I have not gone back into residence in Bath, I never would have allowed it! We are quite well thought of now, in the neighbourhood and beyond. I have even made a more rational companion out of Mary Musgrove, if you can believe it. Though I would much rather spend time with Anne or my dear sisters Jane and Louisa. We frequently see them in town. After that first year we took a house in London, it was the rational thing to do.

Yes, town has been delightful. I cannot count how many members of the nobility we are now intimate with. I would not be bragging, but merely recording an accepted truth, to say that I have been a leader in fashion among my peers. To be so admired and followed is sometimes tiresome, I must admit, but that is the price of genius. I am already preparing my plans for next year; I am quite in raptures over some designs for long sleeves.

    Walter, Charles, and Philip are all at school now. I do miss them when they are away, but I am sure it is best for them to have a good education. Still, I have little Caroline to dote on. She is only a year old now and is the most lovely child I have ever beheld. She will be entirely spoilt by the time she's ready for a governess, but I cannot help it. She is so beautiful.

    I must go now; I have a visit with Lady Russell. We have a steady friendship; I believe she loves me even better now. We are not so very much the same, she is so like Anne, but we have always gotten along famously.

    I cannot imagine now, when I look back on the choices and follies of the past, anything that could be quite as perfect as what I have today.

Extras

The Miss Bingleys

This is a re-writing of Chapters 8 and 10 of Pride and Prejudice. Credit to the original author, Jane Austen, and to John Thorpe for his creative insults (Northanger Abbey).

What if both of the Bingley sisters were still single at the beginning of Pride & Prejudice:

"Do you prefer reading to cards?" said Miss Louisa Bingley; "that is rather singular."

"Miss Eliza Bennet," said Miss Caroline Bingley, "despises cards. She is a great reader, and has no pleasure in anything else."

"I deserve neither such praise nor such censure," cried Elizabeth; "I am *not* a great reader, and I have pleasure in many things."

"I have pleasure in the company this evening," said Louisa said pointedly, with a glance towards Darcy.

"In nursing your sister I am sure you have pleasure," said Bingley; "and I hope it will soon be increased by seeing her quite well."

Elizabeth thanked him from her heart, and then walked towards a table where a few books were lying. He immediately offered to fetch her others; all that his library afforded.

"And I wish my collection were larger for your benefit and my own credit; but I am an idle fellow, and though I have not many, I have more than I ever looked into."

Elizabeth assured him that she could suit herself perfectly with those in the room.

"I am astonished," said Caroline, "that my father should have left so small a collection of books. What a delightful library you have at Pemberley, Mr. Darcy!"

"It ought to be good," he replied, "it has been the work of many generations."

"Many diligent generations with such noble taste," Louisa added.

"And then you have added so much to it yourself, you are always buying books," said Caroline.

"I cannot comprehend the neglect of a family library in such days as these."

"Neglect! I am sure you neglect nothing that can add to the beauties of that noble place. Charles, when you build *your* house, I wish it may be half as delightful as Pemberley."

"You are foolish sister, to suggest it," Louisa interjected, "No house may rival Pemberley."

"I wish it may be near as delightful," said Charles.

"But I would really advise you to make your purchase in that neighbourhood, and take Pemberley for a kind of model. There is not a finer county in England than Derbyshire," said Caroline.

"Yes," burst Louisa, "Did I not remark the last time we visited that my health was much improved by the air in Derbyshire. So superior to London, or any other place."

"With all my heart; I will buy Pemberley itself if Darcy will sell it."

"I am talking of possibilities, Charles."

"Upon my word, I should think it more possible to get Pemberley by purchase than by imitation."

"I would never desire for Mr. Darcy to lose Pemberley, even to you, my dear brother," said Louisa.

Elizabeth was so much caught by what passed, as to leave her very little attention for her book; and soon laying it wholly aside, she drew near the card-table, and stationed herself between Mr. Bingley and his eldest sister, to observe the game.

"Is Miss Darcy much grown since the spring?" said Caroline; "will she be as tall as I am?"

"Or as tall as myself?" Louisa added hastily, straightening in her chair.

"I think she will. She is now about Miss Elizabeth Bennet's height, or rather taller."

"How I long to see her again! I never met with anybody who delighted me so much. Such a countenance, such manners!—and so extremely accomplished for her age! Her performance on the pianoforte is exquisite."

Louisa, disappointed that Caroline had covered almost all of Georgiana Darcy's good qualities, added, "And she is so very forward for her age!" and then felt rather silly for the observation.

"It is amazing to me," said Bingley, "how young ladies can have patience to be so very accomplished as they all are."

"All young ladies accomplished! My dear Charles, what do you mean?" said Caroline.

"Yes, all of them, I think. They all paint tables, cover screens, and net purses. I scarcely know any one who cannot do all this, and I am sure I never heard a young lady spoken of for the first time, without being informed that she was very accomplished."

"Your list of the common extent of accomplishments," said Darcy, "has too much truth. The word is applied to many a woman who deserves it no otherwise than by netting a purse or covering a screen. But I am very far from agreeing with you in your estimation of ladies in general. I cannot boast of knowing more than half a dozen, in the whole range of my acquaintance, that are really accomplished."

"Nor I, I am sure," said Miss Bingley.

"I must count my dear sister among that number," Louisa said, hoping that the compliment would be returned, but Caroline was in no humour to comply.

"Then," observed Elizabeth, "you must comprehend a great deal in your idea of an accomplished woman."

"Yes; I do comprehend a great deal in it."

"Oh! Certainly," cried his Caroline, his faithful assistant, "no one can be really esteemed accomplished who does not greatly surpass what is usually met with. A woman must have a thorough knowledge of music, singing, drawing, dancing, and the modern languages, to deserve the word; and besides all this, she must possess a certain something in her air and manner of walking, the tone of her voice, her address and expressions, or the word will be but half deserved."

Louisa, feeling that she was not getting the better of this conversation, added, "And she must be able to ride and arrange flowers. Those you have forgotten!" These were two accomplishments that she prided in herself and she looked meaningfully at the vase that displayed her work on a side table.

"All this she must possess," added Darcy, "and to all this she must yet add something more substantial, in the improvement of her mind by extensive reading."

Louisa had never regretted playing cards more in her life.

"I am no longer surprised at your knowing *only* six accomplished women. I rather wonder now at your knowing *any*."

"Are you so severe upon your own sex as to doubt the possibility of all this?"

"*I* never saw such a woman. *I* never saw such capacity, and taste, and application, and elegance, as you describe, united."

"No no! You have only not been enough out of your own neighbourhood to have met them!" cried Caroline.

"I am sure that I have met with many, especially among *my* peers at school!" Louisa cried.

"Yes," Caroline continued, "In *our* acquaintance there are many such women."

"It is a great injustice to our sex!" Louisa continued.

Bingley called them to order, with bitter complaints of their inattention to what was going forward in the card game. As all conversation was thereby at an end, Elizabeth soon afterwards left the room.

"Eliza Bennet," said Caroline, when the door was closed on her, "is one of those young ladies who seek to recommend themselves to the other sex by undervaluing their own; and with many men, I dare say, it succeeds. But, in my opinion, it is a paltry device, a very mean art."

"Undoubtedly," replied Darcy, to whom this remark was chiefly addressed, "there is meanness in *all* the arts which ladies sometimes condescend to employ for captivation. Whatever bears affinity to cunning is despicable."

Miss Bingley was not so entirely satisfied with this reply as to continue the subject. However, Louisa continued to press her point, "I am quite convinced that she was only embarrassed to posses so very few of the merits of a truly accomplished woman. It is unfortunate that her upbringing has left her with so little to recommend her, beyond *fine eyes*."

Darcy said nothing and Louisa, with unreasonable confidence, continued on in that vein until Elizabeth returned.

The day passed much as the day before had done. Louisa and Caroline had spent some hours of the morning with the invalid, who continued, though slowly, to mend; and in the evening Elizabeth joined their party in the drawing-room. The loo table, however, did not appear. Mr. Darcy was writing, and both Miss Bingleys, seated near him, were watching the progress of his letter, and repeatedly calling off his attention by messages to his sister. Bingley was reading the paper.

Elizabeth took up some needlework, and was sufficiently amused in attending to what passed between Darcy and his companions. The perpetual commendations of each lady either on his handwriting, or on the evenness of his lines, or on the length of his letter, with the perfect unconcern with which their praises were received, formed a curious dialogue, and was exactly in unison with her opinion of all.

"How delighted Miss Darcy will be to receive such a letter!" said Caroline.

"I am sure she will treasure it dearly," added Louisa.

He made no answer.

"You write uncommonly fast," said Caroline.

"Very fast indeed!" Louisa agreed.

"You are both mistaken. I write rather slowly."

"How many letters you must have occasion to write in the course of a year! Letters of business, too! How odious I should think them!" said Caroline.

"I do not think them odious, what strange ideas you have Caroline!" Louisa protested.

"It is fortunate, then, that they fall to my lot instead of to yours."

"I believe it very important to write letters of business," Louisa continued, "and I commend the person who takes it upon themselves to write letters with such devotion."

"I take joy in all my correspondence," Caroline scoffed. She glared at Louisa.

"Perhaps then you should not neglect your friend," Louisa hinted.

"Pray tell your sister that I long to see her," said Caroline.

"I have already told her so once of your longing, by your desire."

"I wrote her myself yesterday," Louisa bragged, "I covered a whole four pages and the envelope."

"Then I shall write her tomorrow!"

"I am sure you will forget."

Turning back to Darcy, Caroline said, "I am afraid you do not like your pen. Let me mend it for you. I mend pens remarkably well."

"No, no, my knife is sharper and I shall do it better!" Louisa cried.

"Thank you—but I always mend my own."

"How can you contrive to write so even?" asked Caroline.

"I have never seen such straight lines!" declared Louisa.

He was silent.

"Tell your sister I am delighted to hear of her improvement on the harp, and pray let her know that I am quite in raptures with her beautiful little design for a table, and I think it infinitely superior to Miss Grantley's," said Caroline.

"And tell her that we long to hear her sing again, she has the voice of a nightingale," added Louisa.

"Will you give me leave to defer your raptures till I write again? At present I have not room to do them justice."

"Oh! it is of no consequence. I shall see her in January. But do you always write such charming long letters to her, Mr. Darcy?"

"How lucky Miss Darcy is to have such an attentive brother!"

"They are generally long; but whether always charming, it is not for me to determine. As for her luck, I cannot judge."

"It is a rule with me, that a person who can write a long letter with ease, cannot write ill."

"Certainly not! It is impossible that your letters are not charming, Mr. Darcy."

He made no reply.

"Allow me to call for more paper," Caroline entreated.

"Do you require more ink?" Louisa added, "I really must insist on mending your pen, it looks so worn."

"Yes, Louisa," Caroline said, "you really ought to fetch more ink."

Unwilling to leave Darcy's side, Louisa replied, "No, it would be better for you to fetch it, you would not want a gown as fine as *mine* marred if a drop was to spill."

"I cannot speak to *your* gown, but mine was made up in the best shop in town, but then, I could order several more if anything was to happen to it."

Louisa sneered, "If only your taste was equal to your fortune!"

Darcy, now free from their questions, continued to write and ignored them.

"My taste has been praised by the Dowager Vicountess, Lady Dalrymple!" Caroline declared.

"Lady Dalrymple is nearly blind and half-deaf, but Lady Metcalf, who is a widely regarded expert, said I had a quiz of a hat."

"That was no compliment," Caroline laughed, "I heard her say that hat made you look like an old witch!"

"You *are* an old witch," Louisa mumbled, unable to think of a good retort.

"I was complimented by three peers the last time I wore this gown," Caroline bragged.

"I am intimate friends with Lady Lascelle!" Louisa declared.

"I was once told I, 'should have been born a duchess.'" Caroline countered, "By a very sensible young clergyman."

"I have..." Louisa tried to think of anything that put her ahead of her sister, "a prettier horse!"

"You have a similar look to your horse," Caroline sneered.

"Caroline!" cried Bingley.

"Miss Bennet," Darcy said, as he finished folding his letter, "Would you like to take a turn in the garden?"

"I shall come as well," Louisa said, jumping to her feet.

"I need only a moment to get my bonnet," added Caroline.

"No, I cannot allow you," Darcy said gravely, "for it is very dirty and you may stain your dresses. Miss Bennet is clearly the only one fit to accompany me."

Thwarted and angry, the sisters sat back down and glared at each other as Miss Bennet, who triumphed over them without a single strike of her own, could not help but smile at their folly.

Essay
Why Caroline Bingley?

You've just read a novel with the heroine as Caroline Bingley, and I gave her a happy ending! You might ask, why? Why would I give such a horrid woman a whole novel and a happy ending? Does she deserve it? Isn't she a false friend and a shameless social climber? Wasn't she mean to Elizabeth Bennet, our favourite heroine?!?

This essay is a defence of Caroline Bingley. I will not argue that she is a paragon of virtue (keep in mind, Elizabeth isn't either), but that she is a very real person with understandable flaws and reasonable motives. I will also argue that she did at least one noble thing in Pride and Prejudice, maybe two. I will show why the way she acted is very understandable, given her circumstances. When it comes to Jane Austen, I firmly believe that she does not write psychopathic or one-note characters. There are always touches of true humanity in all of her characters.

I am going to clarify something first, when I quote or refer to Caroline's opinions, often Mrs. Hurst is included or saying the same thing. The book makes it very clear that the two sisters think together, so while I will be quoting Caroline, it will often say "they" or "the sisters". When the story begins, Caroline is trying to attract Mr. Darcy. He doesn't seem interested, but she keeps trying. Why?

Modern readers may not understand fully (and this is from a lot of reading myself), but Mr. Darcy is one of the most eligible bachelors in England. If there was a Regency People magazine, he'd be on the cover every year. He's not a peer (duke etc.), but he is the nephew of an Earl, that places him near the top of the gentry class in status. He is fabulously wealthy. Don't trust those currency convertors, they don't work well over two hundred years. If we rank Darcy against everyone else, he's in the top 1%. The average income of a titled man at this time is 8,000 pounds, he has 10,000. As a point of interest, the average for a member of the gentry is 1,500 (that's Darcy's own class). Also, he is only 28 years old and already in control of his fortune. A lot of young men at this age are still waiting to inherit. His mother is deceased, so no annoying dowager hanging around.

He has one more interesting feature that today we might not appreciate, he only has one sibling. Because the first son usually inherited almost everything, he would also have a duty to provide for his younger brothers and sisters. If Darcy was the first of a large brood, he'd be buying younger brothers commissions into the military, livings as a clergy, and every time a sister married fortunes would be leaving the family. Darcy has one sister and because his family is so wealthy in general (the Earl and Lady Catherine seem fine), he also gets to keep almost everything for himself. To sum up, he's handsome, tall, in control of his fortune, high status, filthy stinking rich, and no one is grubbing for his money. Can we blame Caroline for trying so hard? He's basically fallen into her lap by staying with their family.

Here is the first description of Caroline, which is narration: *"They were in fact very fine ladies; not deficient in good humour when they were pleased, nor in the power of being agreeable where they chose it; but proud and conceited. They were rather handsome, had been educated in one of the first private seminaries in town, had a fortune of twenty thousand pounds, were in the habit of spending more than they ought, and of associating with people of rank; and were therefore in every respect entitled to think well of themselves, and meanly of others. They were of a respectable family in the north of England; a circumstance more deeply impressed on their memories than that their brother's fortune and their own had been acquired by trade."* So yes, Caroline is snobby and selfish. Caroline is also very wealthy, so like Mr. Darcy, she has some claim on being proud. She also knows that to make her family entirely respectable, her brother needs to buy an estate and she needs to marry into the gentry.

When it comes to Jane, Caroline seems to actually like her or at least think she's the best person to befriend in Hertfordshire. Here is Caroline's first impression of Jane Bennet: *"but still they admired her and liked her, and pronounced her to be a sweet girl, and one whom they should not object to know more of."* and the second impression, *"though the mother was found to be intolerable, and* the younger sisters not worth speaking to, a wish of being better acquainted with them was expressed towards the two eldest."* Notice that? Caroline likes both Jane and Elizabeth enough to want to know them better. Also notice that Caroline's assessment of the family is the same as the one formed by Darcy and Elizabeth herself. Jane and Elizabeth are the only two members of the family that conduct themselves in society properly. Caroline sees that Jane is sweet and well-mannered and she decides that forming a friendship would be acceptable. Elizabeth is also judged to be fine. What happens? Well that very chapter, this happens:

"Your conjecture is totally wrong, I assure you. My mind was more agreeably engaged. I have been meditating on the very great pleasure which a pair of fine eyes in the face of a pretty woman can bestow."

Miss Bingley immediately fixed her eyes on his face, and desired he would tell her what lady had the credit of inspiring such reflections. Mr. Darcy replied with great intrepidity,
"Miss Elizabeth Bennet."

Darcy tells Caroline, point blank, that he is interested in Elizabeth. Of course Caroline gets jealous! But why did Darcy do this anyway? It doesn't seem like he told anyone else, not even his male friend Bingley. He either did it to give Caroline a hint that she would not succeed or (my favourite) he did it because he disregards other people's feelings. We know that at this point he makes jokes at expense of the Bennet family (*"She a beauty!—I should as soon call her mother a wit"*) and we know that he considers himself far above them in rank (*he really believed, that were it not for the inferiority of her connections, he should be in some danger*). After this evening, Caroline no longer likes Elizabeth Bennet. They have been set up as rivals by Mr. Darcy himself. When Caroline wants a friend, she sends for Jane alone.

Next, her treatment of Jane when she gets sick at Netherfield. We hear from Elizabeth's perspective, *"The sisters, on hearing this, repeated three or four times how much they were grieved, how shocking it was to have a bad cold, and how excessively they disliked being ill themselves; and then thought no more of the matter: and their indifference towards Jane when not immediately before them, restored Elizabeth to the enjoyment of all her original dislike."* Now at this point, Caroline has known Jane for a few weeks and Jane has a cold for a crazy reason: her mom sent her out on horseback in the rain. Also, the illness of Jane has brought Elizabeth right into the house, which obviously is making Caroline jealous. Since Elizabeth is doing most of the work anyway, I can forgive the Bingley sisters for not being attentive. If Elizabeth had not come, we can probably assume the sisters would have been more actively involved.

It's also not like Caroline completely ignored Jane, *"Miss Bingley had spent some hours of the morning with the invalid".* We also know that by the time the Bingleys leave, Jane and Caroline are intimate enough as friends that they use each other's first names.

Then we come to the letter of departure and the visit in London. A very important event happened before these two slights to Jane: the Netherfield Ball. We all know that at the Netherfield Ball, Mrs. Bennet, Mary, Lydia, and Kitty all made fools of themselves and importantly, Mrs. Bennet loudly talked about how rich Jane would be after marrying Bingley. We also have good information from Elizabeth, Charlotte, and Mr. Darcy that Jane did not look like she was in love. In fact, when Elizabeth reflects on it later, she admits that, *"Jane's feelings, though fervent, were little displayed, and that there was a constant complacency in her air and manner not often united with great sensibility."* So, knowing that Caroline helped separate Charles and Jane, how harshly should we judge her for it?

Caroline is Jane's friend, but her loyalty must be to her family first. If as Darcy suspected, Jane was only a fortune hunter, pushed into the relationship with Bingley by her mercenary mother, then as his sister, I cannot blame Caroline for helping to separate them. Both Darcy and Caroline have ulterior motives for not wanting Bingley to marry Jane (the same motive actually, they want Bingley to marry Georgiana), but that does not mean they don't also share concern for him. Who would want their brother married into such a vulgar family unless the woman really loved him? Caroline gives up her friendship with Jane, exemplified in the letter and the cold visit in London, to protect her brother. While Caroline doesn't apologize on page, it's easy to imagine that once the marriage actually occurs, she would try and repair her relationship with Jane. She does like Jane, I mean, who wouldn't?

Additionally, the letter can be seen as a kindness in itself. Caroline knows exactly what the family is expecting, she's telling Jane that it won't happen. Don't pin your hopes on marrying my brother! That gives Jane the time to move on, instead of staying in love with Bingley. Jane only has so much time to marry, Caroline is telling her not to waste it.

Caroline interfering with Jane and Bingley can be judged as good (service to her brother) or bad (attempt at social climbing), but there is one thing that Caroline does that I judge as wholly good and even self-sacrificial. **Caroline tries to warn Elizabeth away from Wickham**. Now this is what Elizabeth thinks about it, *"Insolent girl!" said Elizabeth to herself. "You are much mistaken if you expect to influence me by such a paltry attack as this. I see nothing in it but your own wilful ignorance and the malice of Mr. Darcy."* Now we know that Darcy did not truly act with malice towards Wickham, but Elizabeth also misses an obvious fact here, it would be much better for Caroline if Elizabeth did like Wickham.

Remember Caroline's motivations, she wants to marry Darcy. She knows that Darcy hates Wickham, so the best thing for her to do is actually encourage Elizabeth to go for Wickham, it solves all her problems! Now you may think that she just wants to make fun of Elizabeth, but there are far better ways to do that. Four good ways to make fun of Elizabeth are wandering around Netherfield as Caroline speaks. Also, Caroline is not usually rude in public. All of the fun she has mocking the Bennets happens behind closed doors and with people who are responding in kind. So why would she warn Elizabeth about Wickham? My explanation: Regency Girl Code.

Remember, in 1800s Regency England, marriage was forever and women are almost entirely subject to their husbands. If Elizabeth is deceived in Wickham's character, she could doom herself for the rest of her life. It is my opinion Caroline was so disturbed by Darcy's anger towards Wickham that she acted against her own interest and warned Elizabeth. There are two other explanations, she is trying to protect Darcy from slander (not a bad motive) or Caroline is an idiot, because making fun of Elizabeth once against her interests is just stupid. Yes, she warned Elizabeth with a sneer, but she did warn her correctly.

Caroline Bingley isn't a saint, but she's also not a devil or villain. Remember, the real villain of P&P is the guy who ran off with a teenager with no intention of marrying her. She is a normal person with rational motives. She probably does like Jane Bennet, even though she separated her from Bingley. She is jealous of Elizabeth, but she still warns her away from Wickham. She is snobby and selfish, but those are faults she shares with Darcy for about half of the book. I cannot hate her enough not to give her a happy ending. And for all those people who imagine her unmarried and a dependent on her family? You forget that she is stinking rich herself. Someone is going to marry that 20,000 pounds, no matter who is attached to it!

About the Author

Bethany Delleman was introduced to Jane Austen when she saw Pride & Prejudice 2005 in high school. The book was purchased soon after and a new Jane Austen fan was born. Bethany has been writing since she was fifteen and this is her first novel.

Bethany lives in Ontario, Canada with her husband and two sons, and a small menagerie of pets.

Printed in Dunstable, United Kingdom